FATAL
VERDICT

ALSO BY PETER O'MAHONEY

Dean Lincoln Series:

Reckoning Hour

The Joe Hennessy Series:

The Southern Lawyer

The Southern Criminal

The Southern Killer

The Southern Trial

The Southern Fraud

The Tex Hunter Series:

Power and Justice

Faith and Justice

Corrupt Justice

Deadly Justice

Saving Justice

Natural Justice

FATAL VERDICT

A DEAN LINCOLN LEGAL THRILLER

PETER O'MAHONEY

THOMAS & MERCER

Text copyright © 2025 by Peter O'Mahoney
All rights reserved.

Published by Thomas & Mercer, Seattle

www.apub.com

Amazon, the Amazon logo, and Thomas & Mercer are trademarks of Amazon.com, Inc., or its affiliates.

EU Product Safety contact:
Amazon Publishing, Amazon Media EU S.à r.l.
38, avenue John F. Kennedy, L-1855 Luxembourg
amazonpublishing-gpsr@amazon.com

ISBN-13: 9781662525391
eISBN: 9781662525407

Cover design by Dan Mogford
Cover image: © elwynn / Shutterstock; © Sean Pavone / Getty Images

Printed in the United States of America

FATAL VERDICT

CHAPTER 1

Rumors spread fast in Beaufort, South Carolina.

Everyone was connected, everyone knew each other's business, and everyone was interested in the latest gossip. Scandals spread like wildfire, controversies spread like a cold, and outrage was quick to take hold of the masses. I knew my latest case would gather the attention of the corrupt, I knew I was stepping into dangerous territory, but as a criminal defense attorney, I accepted it was part of my job.

Walking along the Henry C. Chambers Waterfront Park, I held a hot takeout coffee in one hand and my wife Emma's hand in the other. The morning sun shimmered off the slow-moving river, seagulls squawked overhead, and a fresh breeze blew through, carrying the briny tang of seawater. Children shouted and giggled on the play equipment nearby, their laughter ringing through the air, and the adults chatted, their low voices a hum beneath the lively ruckus.

"Look over there." Emma pointed toward the play equipment where young children were running around. "That could be us one day."

"In diapers?" I questioned. "I'm only in my late thirties. I hope it's a few more years until that happens."

"No." She slapped my arm. "I mean look at the parents pushing their toddler on the swing. That could be us."

"Much better." I smiled. "But I don't know how those parents have the energy to run after their kids all day."

"Feeling old?" She patted my flat stomach. "Maybe you should go on a diet?"

"Ouch," I said. "You should—"

"Before you finish that sentence, I should tell you something. I read an article yesterday that said women who carry a few extra pounds live, on average, twenty years longer than the men who comment on it."

"Forget I said anything." I laughed, trying to save myself from an early death. "I was going to say, you . . . would be an amazing mother."

"Nice save," she said. "And I hope we find out one day."

I could hear the pain in Emma's voice. It had been a sensitive subject for us. Over the past several years, we had hoped to have children, hoped to start a family, but we had lost two late-term pregnancies. Emma was starting to doubt her ability to have a family, and it broke my heart that I couldn't do anything about it.

Emma had always been the most incredible woman I'd ever met, and like all incredible people, she became more incredible the longer I knew her. The way she smiled, the way she cared for others, the way she had fun when life seemed overwhelming. Her easy grace, her charming elegance, and her understated intelligence were beyond anything I could ever be capable of.

As we strolled through the park, watching the families play joyfully, I noticed a man staring at us. He was on the far side of the park, away from the children, wearing a flannel shirt, dirty jeans, and worn-out sneakers. His eyes were concealed under an old trucker cap, he had the skin of a drug addict, and his face was twisted in an unfriendly snarl.

There were enough people in the area for it to feel lively, but not enough to make it feel crowded. It rarely felt crowded in Beaufort. There were tourists wandering around, families enjoying the early morning sun, and a horse-drawn cart trotting toward the parking lot. There were office workers taking the scenic route to work, dog walkers enjoying the fresh morning air, and groups of joggers huffing past. But my attention kept coming back to the skinny man on the other side of the park.

"How's the new client?" Emma grabbed my hand, snuggling into my tall frame, and pulled me toward the river. "Causing any big waves?"

"You better believe it," I said. "Haley Finch's story might rock the whole county."

"There are whispers," Emma said. "I've heard that her first husband ran off with someone else, so she had to find a new, rich boyfriend. And she finds Sammy Turner, twenty years older than her, and convinces him to update his will, murders him, and then takes all his money."

"Is that what I have to worry about?" I grinned. "It's bad enough that I have to deal with prosecutors and law enforcement, and now I have to worry about small-town rumors as well."

"Well, their age gap doesn't help. She's in her thirties and he was in his fifties. There's no way she would've dated him if he wasn't rich. He won the lottery, you know? That's how he got his money."

I looked over my shoulder. The man was still following us, keeping his distance, staying in the shadows. His jerky movements were making me uneasy.

"I had a friend who won the lottery." Emma smiled. "She had been unhappily married for five years to a nasty guy, and she came home and said to him, 'What would you do if I won the lotto?' And he replied, 'I'd divorce you, take half the money, and then marry someone younger and hotter.' 'Great,' she said. 'I won twenty dollars, here's half. Now get out.'"

I tried not to laugh, but my dimples gave my smile away. With smiles on our faces and love in our hearts, we continued walking past another tour group. Half the group were staring east with their mouths open, captivated by the beauty of the Beaufort River as it glistened in the golden sunlight. Some members of the tour group stood in the middle of the path, twisting and turning, trying to score the perfect photo on their cell phones. Emma and I paused our conversation as we stepped around the amateur photographers.

"I won't have a lot of time for jokes in the coming months," I said once we'd passed them. "This murder trial will be big news, and there'll be a lot of pressure coming from all angles."

"Do you think she might be innocent?"

"It's not my job to find her innocent." I looked over her shoulder at the man. He was closing the distance between us. "It's my job to defend her constitutional right to a fair trial."

Emma nodded, but I could sense the unease in her. "Did you talk to Rhys's friend about his case?"

"I did. I agreed to take it on," I responded. "Luke Sanford was charged with malicious damage to a property in the Ashdale neighborhood. Luke's a landscaper, and he redesigned someone's yard, but the client wouldn't pay. So, he took his compact excavator and dug up the driveway."

"Oh, wow." Emma smiled. "Whose driveway was it?"

I didn't answer, keeping my gaze forward.

"Dean." Her tone lowered. "Whose driveway did Luke Sanford dig up?"

"Stephen Freeman's."

Emma stopped in her tracks.

4

"We agreed you would stay away from him," she scolded. "That man is more trouble than he's worth. He has powerful connections everywhere."

"It's a favor for Rhys."

"And you know how much Rhys hates the Freeman family." Her voice was raised. "He has every right to be angry, but he can't keep going after them."

"Whatever trouble the Freeman family gets, they've had coming to them for a long time."

She shook her head and huffed. "We're only in Beaufort for a year, Dean. We just came back from Chicago to look after my mother while she goes through cancer treatment. We're not here to cause trouble, and we're not here to change things. And I know you're smart enough to figure out that the Freeman family is untouchable."

Over Emma's shoulder, I watched as the man came closer. Fifty yards away now. He was watching us, and he wasn't trying to hide it. Never one to back down, I stepped past Emma, and started to walk toward him. He held my gaze for a moment, and then turned around, walking quickly with his head down in the other direction.

"Hey," I called out, but he broke into a jog across the park. I ran after him. "Hey!"

He jogged around a corner of a nearby building. I ran over the grassy area of the park and around the corner, but by the time I arrived, he was gone. Nowhere to be seen. More than a tail, it was a message.

"What was that about?" Emma asked when she caught up to me.

I looked at Emma and offered her a half-smile. She glared at me, her arms folded across her chest and her jaw clenched shut. She knew what my reaction meant—there was trouble brewing.

And with the evidence I'd already seen on Haley Finch's case, with what I already knew about the people involved, I was sure there were months of danger ahead.

CHAPTER 2

The Lowcountry of South Carolina was an enchanting place.

There was a softness to the lands, a sensual feeling that felt like a calm embrace, drawing you in and convincing you that the stresses of modern life were a million miles away. People were unhurried here. Bird songs were softer. Life seemed easier. The thick, humid air, filled with the salty goodness of the Atlantic Ocean, provoked a feeling of lethargy, encouraging everyone to move gently, relax, and float their way through their daily tasks.

On the edge of downtown, a stone's throw from the tidal marsh, Haley Finch's home stood strong and proud. Located in Beaufort's historic district, the 1850s Greek Revival mansion had survived a lot of history—from the Civil War, to devastating hurricanes, to the rising tides that were threatening some low-lying parts of the city. The south-facing entrance, complete with fluted columns that stretched across the two levels, was positioned to catch the breeze from the river, and the high-pitched roof was designed to let the cool air flow through. It was a Southern mansion steeped in history and wealth. It was the type of home that most could only dream of.

Haley Finch met my colleague Bruce Hawthorn and me at the door. Haley had a classical beauty about her, with an easy smile that could melt the coldest of hearts. Her green eyes held a quiet glamour, and her skin had the healthy glow of someone who liked the outdoors. She was a brunette, tanned, with an athletic figure. As we shook hands, I noticed a faint hint of jasmine around her. Her touch was soft, and feminine. Although she was around the same height as Bruce, coming up to my shoulders, she was easily a hundred pounds lighter.

"Mrs. Finch," Bruce said in his deep Southern accent. "I'm glad to see you're doing okay."

Bruce Hawthorn was the owner of a local criminal law firm, a solid man with a cheeky grin. He had wide shoulders, little white hair left, and hands large enough to cradle a small baby. He was a Beaufort man through and through, and his family history was closely tied to the area over many generations. My grandfather, a former defense attorney, had given Bruce his first job, and Bruce was keen to return the family favor while I lived in town for a year.

"I'm so happy the judge gave me bail." Haley welcomed us into her home, moving with an easy grace that seemed to flow with the breeze. The interior of the home matched the exterior in its charm. It had a simple, refined touch. Pastel colors dominated—pinks, lilacs, soft greens—and mature houseplants were growing in every corner. There was a white candle burning on the kitchen bench, filling the space with the smell of vanilla. The lighting was dim, and the rooms were cool. "I couldn't imagine spending another day in prison. I'm obviously not cut out for that sort of life."

We walked through the house and past the tall glass doors that led to the equally impressive yard. A covered timber porch sat elevated a few steps above it, complete with a vintage wooden table and five chairs. The expansive yard was lined by thick bushes along the fence, flowers at the edges, and fruit trees through the middle. Many of the fruit trees were covered with netting, protecting them from the hungry birds, and the smells of the garden were abundant.

Haley looked up at me, smiled, and pointed for us to take a seat. "You're the city lawyer everyone's talking about?"

"I hope they're saying good things," I replied. The overhead fan was working hard to ward off the humidity. I looked up and spotted two cameras facing the yard. "You've got an elaborate security system here."

"The very best. Living by myself, I couldn't risk people breaking in when I'm home alone."

"Understandable. And how's the ankle monitor? Not giving you any trouble?"

"None at all. It's annoying having to wear a bag over my foot in the shower, but I can handle it." She lifted her flowing green dress to show her new accessory. "And it's a little hard being confined to my home, and only being allowed to leave between the hours of ten and two, but I'm coping."

"This is a lovely yard." Bruce sat down and placed his briefcase on the chair next to him. He tucked his chair forward, squashing his stomach against the wooden table, and adjusted his tie. "It looks like you've taken a lot of care here."

"Gardening is my passion. I've studied it a lot over the years and love a yard that produces results. I've got peaches, pears, and apples, and I've just planted some new plum trees." She pointed over her shoulder. "Would you like some sweet tea?"

Bruce and I nodded, and she went inside the house, returning a few moments later with a tray carrying a pitcher of sweet tea and three glasses filled with ice. She placed the tray on the table, poured the tea into our glasses, and then sat down.

"Thank you," Bruce said as he sipped his drink. "What are these trees here?" He pointed to the ones closest to us. In a yard full of growth, the two six-foot-tall trees nearest to the deck were perishing. "These trees don't seem to be thriving, or is it just the heat?"

"They're sugar maples, my favorite type of tree in the world. We used to have them in the yard where I grew up in Wisconsin, and my older brother would tap the sap. It's one of my greatest childhood memories. My father died when I was young, and I looked up to my older brother for guidance." She stared at the dying trees for a long moment. "But I couldn't stand the cold weather up north, so I got in a van and drove south. I met my husband, Prescott, here, but unfortunately, that relationship ended two years ago when he ran off with another woman. That's when I planted those sugar maples, but they've struggled to survive in the Lowcountry weather."

"Not tempted to dig them up and start again with something else?"

"I'm persistent. I would never dig them up," she said. "And they almost feel like a symbol of my feelings about him. I kind of like how they're withering."

Haley Finch was known throughout the small town of Beaufort. A social young woman, her first husband had run out on her, leaving his considerable wealth behind. She moved on, and found a new boyfriend named Sammy Turner, spending a year with him before he disappeared. When he was first reported missing, everyone pointed the finger at Haley. Rumors swept through the social elite of Beaufort, and Haley was the topic of every coffee shop, every knitting group, and every book club. When a fisherman found Sammy Turner's body in the tidal marsh, the police charged Haley within days. The local papers ran the facts of the case, but the rumors were so much more interesting. The gossip mill was in overdrive, and everybody seemed convinced of her guilt.

Our office had already received phone calls about the case. We'd also already received emails pleading for us not to defend her. And I was sure the physical threats were coming soon.

"Haley, as you can understand, the charges against you are very serious." I placed my briefcase on the table and opened it. I took out a file and placed it in front of me. "You've been charged with one count of murder under Section 16-3-10 of the South Carolina Code of Laws for the murder of your boyfriend, Samuel Turner. In—"

"Sammy," she interrupted, looking at her hands. "Everyone called him Sammy."

"Sammy," I repeated. "In South Carolina, there are no levels of murder. This state's homicide law defines murder as a killing with malice aforethought." I glanced over the first page in the file on the table. "Sammy went missing last month on the 5th of July, and you reported him missing the next day. His body was found five weeks later, washed up in the tidal marsh in the Harbor River, off St. Helena Island. You were the last person to see him alive, and they found your blood, along with his, under the private fishing dock at his home. They also found the murder weapon in the tidal marsh near the dock, and they matched the knife to a set in your house. Bruce and I can't lie for you in court so we're not going to ask you whether you had anything to do with Sammy's death. We—"

"I didn't kill him," she stated. She looked at me. Her eyes didn't flicker. "I could never hurt Sammy. He was such a sweet man."

"Then we better get to work building your defense," Bruce said. "Today, we're going to ask you some questions that will allow us to find a starting point. Over the coming weeks, we'll discuss the case with the prosecution, and they're likely to present several deals, depending on how the evidence looks. Part of our job is to get the best outcome for you, which may include a plea deal."

"No deals. I didn't do it, and I'm not going to prison for something I didn't do."

"Understood." Bruce looked at me, and then continued. "How long had you and Sammy been dating?"

"Just over a year. A lot of people have talked about the age gap, there was twenty years between us, but I didn't see that. I just saw a beautiful, kind, caring man. Dating him gave me a sense of security." She shook her head. "We even talked about getting married. I would have to finalize my divorce from my husband, Prescott, to make that happen, but I haven't seen Prescott in years. I hear from him occasionally, an email here and there, but I have no idea where he is. Somewhere in South America, I think." She looked at her hands again. "I feel so bad for the fisherman who found Sammy's body in the marsh. The man said that his body was all swollen from the water in the rivers." She shuddered at the thought. "I would've hated to see Sammy like that."

"Try not to think about it," Bruce said. "When was the last time you saw Sammy alive?"

"At his home on Dataw Island. It's a gated community, and it's in a beautiful part of the world. He owned a million-dollar property but didn't like living out there. He bought it after his lottery win. Sammy didn't quite fit in. He grew up poor and everyone seemed to be rich on the island. Nice people, friendly, but just not Sammy's type. He kept to himself and spent most of his time on his private fishing dock out the back of the property."

I drew a long breath and moved on to the hard-hitting questions. "You mentioned that Sammy won five million in the lottery. Sammy updated his will only five days before he died, and the new will leaves all his money to you. This motive forms the backbone of the prosecution's case."

She put her head in her hands. "I know how that looks, but it was a coincidence. I didn't need his money. This is the house I own with my husband, but the will was Sammy's way of showing that he loved me. He was so excited to update it."

I made a note on my legal pad. "The police say you were the last person to see him alive. They note that you entered the gated community at 3 p.m. on July 5th and left at 4:45 p.m. Nobody saw him alive after that."

"He was here with me in the morning, and then he left to go fishing. That's why he took the knife from here." She blinked back tears. "I went out fishing with him. I did that sometimes. He would sit on the dock and fish, and I would set out a camp chair and read a book. It's so beautiful out there, and the hours disappear quickly."

"The police found traces of Sammy's blood under the end of the dock, and traces of your blood near the start of the dock," Bruce stated. "Can you explain how your blood got on to the dock?"

"I cut myself while fishing there weeks before he went missing." She held up her hand, but the cut had long healed. "It was just my finger. I'm not the best fisherman, and I'm pretty clumsy. It wasn't unusual for me to cut myself."

I made another note on my legal pad, and then leaned forward. "I know this is hard to think about, but is there anyone who might've wanted to hurt Sammy? Perhaps someone after his money?"

"Yes." She drew a long breath and bit on her fingernails. "There were some drug dealers threatening him in the weeks before he went missing."

"Drugs?" I questioned. From what I had read about Sammy Turner, drugs seemed a long way from what I expected.

"Not for Sammy. He wouldn't touch the stuff, but he was pulled into the mess by his younger brother, Ken. Ken had a bad drug habit. He'd been in and out of rehab most of his life. It was fentanyl, mostly, but also a lot of meth. Both are terrible drugs, but fentanyl is really terrible. Sammy and Ken grew up poor and had nothing between them. They lived most of their lives week to week, you know? Two years ago, Sammy won the lotto and all of a sudden had five million dollars to his name. Ken took advantage of him, and while Sammy tried to help his younger brother, it was hard."

"Do you have a photo of Ken?"

She nodded and took out her cell phone. She scrolled through her photos and found a photo of Sammy and Ken from a year earlier. She zoomed in on Ken's face, and I recognized him. He was the man who had been following me at the park. "Do you think Ken is dangerous?"

"Ken has been in and out of prison most of his life, so yeah, he knows how to create trouble. He's only a small man, but yes, I'd say he's dangerous."

For the next hour and fifteen minutes, we sat in the humidity, sweating, drinking sweet tea, and talking about the brutal murder of Sammy Turner. It seemed strange to be talking about something so savage in such a serene setting. When we were sure she understood the process ahead, we thanked her for the sweet tea and packed up our files.

"When will this all be over?" she asked.

"This a marathon, not a sprint." I closed the file in front of me. "Murder trials can take many months, sometimes years. We've got a lot of evidence to dig through."

"Just . . . be careful where you dig." She looked at me. "Sammy knew some dangerous people, and they won't be afraid to protect themselves."

CHAPTER 3

A summer storm had arrived.

The rain threw itself against the land with aggression as the large and threatening clouds marched over the city. The winds did their best to knock down trees, pushing and pulling in strong gusts, and the rain pelted against our office window, drowning out any thoughts I had. Beaufort was receiving the edge of the tropical storm, still feeling the wrath of nature with a torrential downpour, with gusts strong enough to knock over people, but the heaviest winds were hitting farther south.

There was a raw intensity to the summer storms here, a pulsating electricity that buzzed through the air. The smells that accompanied the storms, the smells of the heat and humidity and saltiness, were some of my favorite smells in the world.

Sitting at the head of the boardroom table, Bruce tapped his hand on the edge of it, staring at the file in front of him. Kayla Smith, Bruce's assistant and office receptionist, sat to the right of the room, taking notes on her laptop.

The conference room was calm, a quiet refuge from the wild squall raging outside. A whiteboard stood at the side of the room, cluttered with notes, stickers, and scribbles about the case. Sammy Turner's name was in the middle of the whiteboard, circled in red, with lines stretching out to the other names, linking them in a web of details and connections.

"What are your initial thoughts?" Bruce asked.

"It's completely circumstantial," I responded as I turned away from the window. "They've got the murder weapon, but no direct evidence to link it to Haley. They've got a speck of her blood on the fishing dock, but that's not unusual. Haley was the last person to see him alive and was seen arguing with him days prior to when he went missing, but that doesn't convict her. They've got one angle and that's it."

"The motive," Kayla added. "That's why they arrested her."

Always well dressed, Kayla wore a sleeveless red dress, which showed off her toned biceps. Her skin looked radiant, her smile was easy, and her tone was warm. A social woman, she was married to a popular realtor, and was the mother of two high school boys, who as she put it, had "more energy than a group of Jack Russell terriers on speed."

"The motive is what the entire charge is based around," I agreed. "Once they found the body, the investigators established the motive, then found the evidence to fit that story. They've done this the wrong way around. They chose Haley as the suspect and then pulled together circumstantial evidence to prove their theory. They've worked this case backward, which means they've missed evidence. If we pull this case apart, we'll find the things they didn't take the time to review."

"Agreed," Bruce said. "The pressure was on the Sheriff's Office to arrest someone as soon as Sammy went missing, but they had no evidence of foul play. I would say they'd already convinced themselves that Haley did it before they even found the body. And once they found Sammy in the marsh, they focused on looking for a link to Haley. Her explanation of the blood on the dock is weak, and her presence at the scene of the crime is unfavorable, but none of that will convince a jury she did it."

"The murder weapon doesn't help." I reached forward and opened one of the files. "The knife is a perfect match for her unique set of boning knives and she told the investigators that it came from her home."

"Any prints on the weapon?" Kayla asked.

"None," Bruce replied. "The knife was exposed to the elements for five weeks, sitting in the marsh beside the dock where he was last seen alive. The weather conditions had washed most of the evidence from it, but it still had a small amount of blood on the blade, although they weren't able to extract any DNA from it."

"Was there anything illegal in the search of her home?"

"We'll challenge all the evidence," Bruce confirmed, "but it looks solid. When they found the body, they interviewed her under the guise that Sammy was still a missing person. They told her they had found a knife near the dock and questioned her about it. Haley admitted it was from her home, and that's when they told her they had found his body."

"Did they already know about the updated will?"

"They did," I confirmed. "They found that information when they were investigating the missing persons report."

"Their theory is that Sammy Turner was fishing on the private dock at his home in Dataw Island, and Haley showed up later in the afternoon." Bruce reached forward and opened another of the case files, running his eyes over the police report. "They got into an argument, and they scuffled. She cut herself at that time as well, and that's how her blood got on the dock. She then got the knife, and when Sammy turned around, she stabbed him from behind, in the base of the neck. She then retrieved his diving belt from his home, weighed him down, and pushed his lifeless body into the river. She wiped the knife down, and tossed it into the river as well, but it washed up in the marsh nearby. She then cleaned the dock with bleach, in an attempt to get rid of the bloodstains, but missed the parts underneath the dock where the blood had leaked. It's a solid theory, but we have a better one."

"Our early angle is that Sammy's drug-addicted brother, Ken Turner, was involved," I responded. "Ever since Sammy won the lottery two years ago, he was constantly bailing his brother out. Whether it was out of prison, or out of his drug debts, Sammy had his brother's back. But then Haley enters the picture a year ago and eventually puts an end to Sammy bailing his brother out. A possible theory is that Ken racked up drug debts, and knowing Ken couldn't pay, the dealers went to Sammy for the money. And when Sammy refused to pay, things got nasty."

"Any evidence to back that up?"

"Not yet, but it's early."

"Or . . . there's another option." Bruce leaned back in his chair and looked at the ceiling. "The will was updated only five days before his death, so maybe Ken didn't know about that. Ken could've killed his brother, thinking he would've received a fair lump of cash in estate. That's a clear motive."

"Ken Turner is our main focus," I agreed. "The Sheriff's Office report says they interviewed him over the phone the day after Sammy's body was found, but they ruled him out. He didn't give an alibi for the night Sammy went missing, but the deputies didn't ask him many questions."

"What about access to Dataw Island?" Kayla asked. "It's a gated community. We should have evidence on everyone who went in and out of the security checkpoint that day?"

"We don't have it yet," Bruce confirmed. "But we'll request it."

"And Haley's not interested in a plea deal?"

"Not at this point," Bruce replied. "Which means we need to prepare for a possible trial."

"Thoughts on the jury?"

"If the genders were reversed in this situation, the jury would vote guilty in a heartbeat." Bruce shrugged. "But Haley is pretty, small, and looks vulnerable. That works in our favor."

Bruce said what we all knew—pretty privilege was real. Conventionally attractive people received advantages in life, from social benefits, to job opportunities, to general life prospects. People were naturally biased toward more attractive people.

There was bias in the courts, as there was in all human behavior, and it was our job to leverage it. Research had shown that attractive people were more likely to be believed, more likely to be trusted, and if convicted by a court, they were more likely to receive lenient sentences.

"What about the first husband?" Kayla asked as she typed into her laptop. "Prescott Finch. Where is he in all this?"

"Left Beaufort two years ago." Bruce read the file in front of him. "Haley said he left with another woman, but they never divorced, even when she started dating Sammy."

"Why did she never lodge a divorce?"

"And split everything? That would be messy. Because they had joint bank accounts, nothing has changed in her finances."

A pause hung over the room as Kayla went to say something but stopped.

"What is it, Kayla?" Bruce leaned back in his chair and rubbed his forehead. "I know that look. You've got something to say, so spit it out."

Kayla leaned her elbows on the boardroom table. "Bruce, I've known you for so many years, and we work well together. And I know you have a soft spot for protecting pretty girls, like it's your masculine duty." She paused again, considering her words. "I'll tell you what I think—you're a red-blooded male who could be blinded by Haley's beauty."

"And I think you're jealous of her," Bruce retorted, shaking his head.

"Just an observation." Kayla raised her hands in surrender. "No need to fight over it."

"And this is the reaction we'll get on the jury," I noted. "Any jury will need to be carefully selected. Men will want to protect Haley, and women may be jealous of her beauty, money, and good fortune. If this makes it to trial, the outcome is going to be decided by the make-up of the jury."

Bruce stood and walked to the window, watching as the sheets of rain blew against it. "And this isn't about trusting Haley. It's about building the best possible defense for her. That's our job. We need to look at the evidence that the police missed and find another suspect."

"I'm just saying that you're stepping into hazardous territory," Kayla said. "Because in the South, where there's money, there's danger."

CHAPTER 4

I heard Luke Sanford before I saw him.

Not that he was physically hard to miss—at six foot two and 225 pounds, he was an imposing physical presence. Wide shoulders, big hands, square jaw. With skin weathered by the South Carolina sun and veins popping out of his forearms, it was clear he was a hard worker. The man even smelled like hard work—he had an aroma like freshly cut grass, body odor, and beer.

Despite the substantial presence, Luke Sandford had a jovial voice, which always seemed near to laughter. "Ah, the city lawyer." He greeted me with an outstretched hand and a smile as he walked into my office. "It's good to see you again. I had a great drive over here."

"Really?" I smiled. "Why is that?"

"I put a bumper sticker on my truck that says, 'Honk if you think I'm handsome.' And when I was on the main road, I slowed right down to walking pace so people in the cars behind me could take a good look at me in the rearview mirror. It turns out lots and lots of people think I'm handsome."

"I'm sure that's why they were honking." I laughed.

"You're a big guy, Dean. If this law gig doesn't work out for you, then you can come and work for me any day. I need strong guys out there."

"I'd much rather this air-conditioned office," I said. "But if I ever decide that I want to lose half my bodyweight in sweat every day, I'll give you a call."

Luke laughed, and as was the Southern way, he and I started our meeting with a discussion about our personal lives. He spoke about his family, his wife and two young children, and I spoke about Chicago, Emma, and returning to Beaufort.

"We should focus on the court case," I said after fifteen minutes of chatting. Luke nodded his approval. "You've been charged under Section 16-11-520 of the South Carolina Code of Laws: Malicious damage to a house, fence, or fixture. As the value of the property damaged is under ten thousand dollars, you've been charged under paragraph B, two. Paragraph two is still a felony offense and, if convicted, you'll be fined or imprisoned for not more than five years."

"They can't send me to prison for this." He shook his head. "The guy didn't pay for the work I did for him. I gave him every chance to pay, but he refused."

I sucked in a breath. "Of all the people in Beaufort to do it to, you chose one of the most politically influential families in the county. You dug up *Stephen Freeman's* driveway. And looking at the photos, you made a massive mess with the compact excavator."

"It'd been a year since I did the work, and I gave him every opportunity to pay. I'd even taken him to the Magistrate's Court that handles small claims, but they just kept pushing my case back. It's been a year and they still haven't heard my case. Nobody will help me, and nobody will force him to pay. What else was I supposed to do?"

"Not dig up his driveway."

"Oh, thanks, genius." He threw his hands up in the air and laughed. "Where were you a year ago? That's the type of solid advice

21

I could've used. I knew lawyers were great at giving advice, but that advice, well, I can see now why you guys earn the big bucks."

"Take me through what happened in more detail." I smiled, holding my pen ready for notes. "Anything you can tell me might help our defense."

"Right. Stephen Freeman contacted me because he wanted to redesign his front yard. He wanted me to do the landscaping work, adding several large stones, changing the plants, and updating the street appeal. I had some work lined up, but his job sounded like a good deal. It's always best to have work planned at least ten weeks ahead. So, I called around, but lots of people warned me not to work with him. He—"

"Why did people warn you not to work with him?"

"Stephen Freeman has a reputation for being a terrible client and has a history of not paying contractors."

I made a note on my legal pad. "Go on."

"Knowing that he didn't have a good reputation, I put together a watertight quote and asked for a deposit. He paid the deposit that day, and we started the job ten weeks later. We did a great job over the couple of weeks, and he was so friendly to me and the work crew. Always coming out for a chat and offering us a beer at the end of the week. A real smooth talker and a real charmer. On the Friday before we were due to finish, we were sharing a beer, looking at the yard, and he talked about how his driveway needs to be updated. With all the extra work he wanted to do, I told him we could do the job for five thousand. He agreed, and said he was out of town for the next week, and it was perfect timing. We agreed to the price and that was that."

"You didn't send a new quote, did you?"

"I didn't think I needed to. We had a verbal agreement to do the work. We shook hands."

"He charmed you, and you let your defenses down."

22

"I see that now." He groaned. "But I didn't think anyone could be that sly. A hard lesson to learn, but I won't be taken for a fool again."

"And once the work on the driveway was finished, what happened?"

"He disappeared. Wouldn't answer the front door, wouldn't take my calls. Told me to contact him through email and threatened to take out a restraining order on me." Luke shook his head. "And then his lawyer sends me an email saying that Stephen never gave us permission to do the driveway work, and that I was the one trying to rip him off. Can you believe that? He had the audacity to say that I was the one trying to rip him off by claiming extra work outside the original quote."

"He claims that you did it as a work scam," I said. "And there are precedents for this. Several contractors have been charged for doing this exact thing. They add extra work without the owner's knowledge and then try to bully them into paying for something they didn't agree to."

"How ridiculous." He threw his head back. "I'm not that type of guy."

"As your lawyer, I need to advise you on the next steps. We can fight this, but you need to consider what the fight is worth," I said. "If this goes public, then Stephen Freeman will drag your business reputation through the mud. He's destroyed people who have gone up against him in the past. You don't have to look far to see his trail of destruction. He's a specialist in smear campaigns."

"So be it. I'm going to fight it. I'm not going to let him win. For me, this isn't about the money—it's the principle of it. I won't stand by and be bullied just because he's rich. If he'd just paid me for the work, we wouldn't have a problem."

I nodded. "I'll meet with the prosecution next week and we'll discuss plea deals. We'll argue and go back and forth for a while, but hopefully, we can have this charge downgraded to a misdemeanor. We'll state that, as no money changed hands for the payment of the service, it was clearly valued by the owner as under two thousand dollars. If they agree to that, you'll be charged under paragraph three of the same law. The penalty under paragraph three will be under a thousand dollars, or thirty days' prison, depending on the judge's decision. That will be our angle for the case."

"I shouldn't be charged with anything at all," he protested. "Stephen Freeman is the one in the wrong. Why hasn't the prosecution gone after him?" He shook his head numerous times. "You don't have to answer that. I know why he hasn't been charged. He's more connected than Wi-Fi in a coffee shop."

"He knows how powerful he is," I agreed. "He's a former circuit solicitor, and he's now a political lobbyist. He's in everyone's ear. If something needs to be done around here, people go to him."

"I know he's untouchable, but I'm not going to be bullied by anyone, and especially not by that rich prick. I'm not going to let him win just because he has money."

"The justice system needs to be fair for everyone, regardless of money and connections," I said. "I can't make any promises, but our best option is to negotiate with the State and ask them to reduce the charges to a misdemeanor."

Luke nodded his approval. After a further fifteen minutes of case discussion, he left the office with a confident step. I had warned him about the potential fight ahead, but he still wanted to proceed.

He thought he could win, he thought fairness would prevail in the justice system, but against a man like Stephen Freeman, I didn't like his chances.

CHAPTER 5

The Young Buck Tavern was full. It always was.

A local favorite, the bar was more than a place to eat and drink; it was a place for community, a place where people mingled between tables, where old friends greeted each other with hugs and handshakes, and where outsiders were welcomed as family. Music played in the background of the dimly lit bar, but it was drowned out by the lively conversations. The smells of salt and steak and seafood filled the air. There was a room full of tables and a wood-fired pizza oven to the left, and a back patio for those that hadn't booked a table, but it was at the bar where the energy was surging. The noise rose and fell with a rhythm, laughter broke out every few minutes, and everyone was welcomed into every conversation. It was a place where stories grew legs, where tales became legends, and legends became stories that lasted generations.

Rhys Parker greeted a lot of people as he entered the bar. He was well known around town. A big man with a loud voice, his deep timbre seemed to reverberate around any room he entered. He wore his blue cap backward, I assumed to cover his growing bald spot, and a red checkered shirt. His black jeans were dirty, and his boots were caked in mud.

We greeted each other with a handshake and a solid pat on the back.

"Thanks for taking on Luke's case," Rhys said as he ordered a beer. "All the other lawyers in town wouldn't touch it. They said it was a political death sentence to take on a man like Stephen Freeman. The only ones who would consider it said they wanted Luke to take the plea deal."

"I don't like his chances, but Luke seems like a good guy."

"He is. One of the best. Solid. He'd bend over backward for anyone. He has helped everyone I know. He once ran into a house fire to save the neighbor's dog. That's the type of guy he is. And when he told me what he did to the driveway, I laughed so much. It was classic Luke behavior. But then he told me whose driveway it was, and I knew he needed your help." Rhys paused as he thanked the bartender for the beer. He sipped on his ale, smiled, and then continued. "Luke grew up as a small kid and was bullied a lot. When he hit his teenage years, he had a growth spurt that made him into the monster of a man he is now, and he made it his life's mission to beat down the bullies."

"I'll see what I can do, but there are no promises."

"I knew I could rely on big Dean Lincoln to sort it out." Rhys turned to me and rested a hand on my shoulder. "Because if you don't hurt that family, then I'm going to have to do it myself."

The conversation paused between us because we both knew the approaching date.

"It's Heather's birthday tomorrow." Rhys looked at his beer and whispered, "It's the worst day of the year."

I didn't answer. I kept my eyes straight ahead and held my beer out to the side. We clinked glasses in a silent acknowledgment of our grief.

Ten years ago, Rhys had married my older sister, Heather. They were great together. Rhys was a hard-working man, loud and energetic, the opposite of Heather. Heather was calm, had a great sense of her own self, and was full of love for the world. They had two children, Zoe, aged seven, and Ollie, five, and were the perfect family unit until her death.

The silence sat between Rhys and me for a while, until Rhys found the moment to continue.

"I take the kids out to her grave every year on her birthday. It'll be three birthdays now," Rhys said. "We'll say a prayer in the morning for her, and then I'll pick them up after school and head straight out there. It'll be a tough day for the kids. Last year, they talked to her just like she was there with us. Zoe talked the most. She misses her so much. And I've got a nice cake for the evening if you and Emma want to come over."

"We'll come over." I patted him on the back. "And I'll go out and visit her grave tomorrow morning."

For Heather, we still had so many lost hopes and lost dreams. There were moments that never were and memories that could never be. She was forever stuck at the same age, that smiling, happy, calm mother of two.

"I can't stop thinking about Paul Freeman." Rhys shook his head. "He's in my head. That smug little smile, walking out of prison a free man. That's not right, Dean. How can that be justice? He got drunk, decided to drive without a license, and then killed my wife in a car accident. He needs to be held responsible for killing her. How can they give him a ten-year sentence and then let him walk out so early?"

I let the silence sit between us. I had heard it all from Rhys before. I understood his pain. Paul Freeman, the twenty-one-year-old son of Stephen Freeman, served five months of a ten-year sentence, released early due to apparent overcrowding in the prison system. He killed our Heather, he took a mother from her children, and he was now walking the streets of Beaufort like nothing happened.

It wasn't right, and while I knew Stephen Freeman had pulled strings to get his son out of prison, I couldn't prove anything.

"How can rich people do that?" Rhys whispered, more to himself than me. "How can money overthrow justice?"

"The law needs to be a guard for the vulnerable, not a weapon for the rich," I said. "What happened isn't right. That's not what justice is for."

Rhys nodded a few times, keeping his eyes on his beer. "I followed him yesterday."

"What do you mean?"

"When I was coming home from work, I saw Paul Freeman's car driving out of the street he lives on. I don't know why, but I wasn't thinking. I turned my car around and drove after him."

"Rhys, you can't do that." I placed my beer down. "Do you think he saw you?"

"I know he did."

"How do you know?"

"Because after fifteen minutes, he turned around and drove back to the police station."

"Did you follow him to the police station?"

Rhys nodded.

"And?"

"And I wanted to get out and beat him to a pulp. I wanted to wipe that smug smile off his face and kick his little head in. I wanted to give him real justice with my boots." He gripped his beer tightly. "But I drove off when a police officer came out of the station with him."

"Rhys. You can't do things like that. Your kids need you more than you need revenge. You have to control yourself."

"That's why I need you to take them down, Dean. I need you to do whatever you can that is within the law to destroy the Freeman family." Rhys finished his beer and thumped his glass down on the bar. "Otherwise, I might do something stupid."

CHAPTER 6

I arrived at the Beaufort County Courthouse at 9 a.m., after spending an hour at my sister's grave.

I had talked to her as if she was there, and I told her about the city, about the storms, and how everyone was on edge about the upcoming hurricane season. I told her about Rhys, about her children, and about their lives. I told her about Emma. I told her about our father in Florida and how he was doing well. I told her about our grandparents, and how they never seemed to age. I spoke to her about the Haley Finch case, about the evidence, and about the courts. I told her there wasn't enough evidence against Haley, and how we were preparing for trial. I spoke to Heather for twenty-five minutes and never once did I feel alone.

Bruce was waiting for me in the foyer of the courthouse, studying the emails on his cell phone. We greeted each other, conferred on our tactics, then walked into the courthouse conference room, ready for battle.

The large conference room was cold, thanks to an overactive air conditioner, and the smell of pine cleaning products hung heavy in the air. There was a long wooden table in the middle of the room, and a raised flat-screen television to the left. A framed photo of Henry C. Chambers Waterfront Park at sunset hung on the right wall, and natural light flooded in the windows at the rear.

Assistant Solicitor Charlotte Sinclair sat at the head of the table. She had an effortless style. She wore a black skirt with a cream shirt, her brown hair was tied back, and her smile was welcoming. She had a firm handshake, and despite her friendly appearance, she had a reputation as a tough, relentless, and uncompromising lawyer.

To her right was Stephen Freeman, a former circuit solicitor and now a political lobbyist, and part-time volunteer consultant with the Solicitor's Office. He was a tall, slim man in his sixties with tanned skin and glowing white teeth, whose influence, and corruption, had stretched far and wide across the Lowcountry. His short-cropped brown hair had flecks of gray, his face seemed to have a permanent smug grin, and the smell of his woodsy cologne was potent.

After I shook hands with Sinclair, Freeman didn't move. He didn't stand, he didn't offer his hand to shake, and he didn't speak. He simply glared at me as I sat down.

"How's the driveway?" I asked him. "Bumpy?"

"I heard you were defending Luke Sanford against his charges of criminal damage." Freeman lifted his chin. "And trust me, my driveway will be sorted soon."

"I would never trust you."

"That's not very friendly."

"That's because you and I aren't friends."

"Now, Dean, I know you've been in Chicago for a decade, but I hope you haven't forgotten how things work here in the South," Freeman said. "We're all connected here. We all need each other. It's not like the big city, where people are faceless robots in the masses. Down here, we're a community. And we need to treat each other with respect."

Bruce offered his hand to Freeman, trying to ease the tension. Freeman held his glare on me for a long moment, then turned to Bruce. They shook solidly and Bruce sat down.

"Sure is hot out there," Bruce said, wiping his brow. "They say the humidity is going to reach 85 percent this afternoon. Not a lot going to get done when it gets that hot. Would hate to be out there trying to work."

"Which is why we stay inside and focus on this case," Sinclair stated. Her tone was assertive. She gripped her pen tightly. "Let's get back on track. We're here to talk about Mrs. Haley Finch. She's been charged with the murder of Mr. Sammy Turner, and we've considered the evidence against your client. Considering the amount of public interest in this case, we're willing to put an offer on the table."

"Go on," Bruce said.

"Twenty years for an early guilty plea."

"No chance," I said. "With that offer, she'd be better to take it to trial. All your evidence is circumstantial, and you're basing your entire case off a weak motive. Any jury will see the lack of evidence and find her not guilty."

"She was the last person to see him alive. She admitted she was at the fishing dock where he was murdered. A knife from her kitchen was used as the murder weapon. We have her blood at the dock. It's clear there was a struggle. She was at the scene of the crime when he went missing. And her motive is obvious to everyone—she wanted his money. What more do you want?"

"An eyewitness," Bruce said. His voice was calm, as was his demeanor. "This is ridiculous."

"The blood on the dock shows there was a struggle," Sinclair stated. "There was so much underneath the dock, it proves that he was murdered there. The blood on the top was cleaned off, but the killer didn't think about the blood sticking to the underside. When the forensic team went to the scene, they found bleach stains on top of the dock. It's obvious there was an attempt to clean up."

"That suggests there was a struggle, and an attempt to clean the crime scene, but it doesn't prove Haley was involved," I stated. "As defense lawyers, we usually walk into a room and expect something solid against our client. You've got nothing. You can't win this at trial."

"Let's discuss the murder weapon, then," Sinclair said. "The detectives will testify that they found the knife in the marshes near the dock, and when Mrs. Finch was questioned about it, she admitted it was from her unique set of knives at home. She even admitted that this knife had been missing for weeks."

"The deputies questioned her without a lawyer present," Bruce said.

"She didn't request one, and they hadn't arrested her yet," Freeman stated. "It was fair and reasonable to ask her questions, given the circumstances."

"She also told those same deputies that Sammy took the knife to go fishing." Bruce leaned back in the chair. "She says he took many knives from her house."

"Let her tell that to the jury." Freeman waved his hand in the air, dismissing Bruce's comment. "Public opinion is against her. Everyone knows she did it. The whole town is talking about her."

"Any suggestion that the public has a say in these charges is prejudicial," I stated. "If you're suggesting the jury is tainted by small-town rumors, we'll request a change of venue."

"Oh, come on," Sinclair groaned. Her hands rolled up into fists. "She killed him for his money. That's clear to everyone with half a brain. She convinced Sammy Turner to update his will, then killed him five days later. We all know what happened to her first husband, and now she's done it again."

Bruce sat up straighter, eyeing Sinclair. "Prescott Finch is in South America."

"Really? Is that what you think?" Freeman laughed, clapping his hands together. "You don't know about Prescott, do you? You haven't talked to her about it yet."

Bruce and I looked at each other. Neither of us had any idea what he was suggesting.

"Haley says her husband is in South America, but the reality is that nobody has heard from him since he left," Sinclair explained. "Haley says she has, but nobody else has heard a single word. Not Prescott's brother, not his daughter, not his ex-wife, not his cousins, not his friends. Nobody has heard from him except her."

"And"—Freeman leaned forward, resting his elbows on the table—"can you guess why she hasn't reported him as missing?"

I looked at Bruce, and he still looked as confused as me.

"No?" Freeman smiled broadly. He chuckled to himself for a moment and then continued. "I'll tell you why she hasn't reported him missing. It's because Prescott's will leaves all his wealth, including the house that Haley lives in, to his brother and ex-wife. Prescott made his money with a chain of pharmacies and was a wealthy man, but his will leaves nothing to Haley."

"And she can't divorce him because she signed a pre-nuptial agreement," Sinclair added. "Or did she forget to mention that as well? She'd be out of that house the second Prescott is declared deceased."

"They were married," I stated. "She'd be able to dispute the will through probate. Homestead protection and elective share rights protect the spousal property from being transferred. In South Carolina, the elective share rights override any will or testament that could exclude the surviving spouse."

"It seems you know your local laws, Mr. Lincoln." Sinclair nodded. "Homestead protection and elective share rights give her one-third of his wealth, but any will would be disputed, and any judge would consider the pre-nup as part of Prescott's estate intention. She knows he can't be declared deceased, or she loses two-thirds of his wealth."

Bruce was staring at the table in front of him, his mouth hanging open.

"You didn't know any of that, did you?" Freeman laughed. "Mrs. Finch didn't tell you the truth about Prescott. She conveniently left that information out of your discussions, didn't she? She didn't tell you that she's living off the joint bank accounts opened under Prescott's name, and she didn't tell you that she's draining his money. Rumor is it's just about to dry up."

Bruce and I didn't answer.

"As soon as Prescott is declared deceased, she loses everything," Freeman repeated. His smug grin widened. "She knew Prescott's family was coming for the money, and she couldn't hold off their claims forever. Common law says it's seven years until someone is declared deceased, but Prescott's family was pushing for his death to be declared sooner. She's telling people he's alive, but he's not."

"And that's why she had to find another rich boyfriend." Sinclair smiled. They were clearly enjoying the double-act and watching the surprise on Bruce's face. "And she found poor old Sammy Turner. A sweet man in his fifties who never had a serious girlfriend in his life. A nice man who grew up poor but won the lottery. A man who fell for Haley's charms and then ended up murdered in the tidal marsh near his home."

"That's outrageous." Bruce shook his head, but sounded uncertain. We'd been ambushed by their theory. Neither of us had seen it coming. "If you'd met Haley, you'd know that's outrageous. She's not a killer."

"I've met her, Bruce," Freeman said. "And I've known you for decades, and there's one consistent thing about you—you've always been blinded by beauty." Freeman leaned forward. "Haley Finch is a killer. Plain and simple. She deserves to be behind bars for killing

Sammy Turner, and when we find Prescott Finch's body, we'll put her away for that as well."

"Any suggestion that Prescott Finch is missing is prejudicial against the defendant," I stated. "There's no evidence that he's missing, and there's no chance you can present that in court. No judge will allow bogus theories with no basis in truth to be presented to the jury."

"We're not suggesting anything about Prescott will be presented in court," Sinclair said. "We've got enough evidence to convict Haley for the murder of Sammy Turner, and any jury will be convinced by Haley's very clear motive. Based on the motive alone, this case is a slam dunk."

"All you have is a flimsy motive. It's not enough."

"You can fight all you like, but she's going to prison." Sinclair closed her file and stood. "Twenty years for an early guilty plea. That's our best offer. If she's not going to accept it, then we'll see you at trial."

CHAPTER 7

The Law Office of Bruce Hawthorn, a two-level white colonial-styled building, stood proud on a corner block off the main thoroughfare of Carteret Street. Several mature live oaks provided shade over the building, a hip-high hedge acted as the fence, and groups of perennial flowers lined the area in front of the porch. As I rolled my SUV into the gravel parking lot, I pulled up next to two large pickup trucks. Bruce didn't have any meetings listed for the morning, and I wondered who the vehicles belonged to.

Stepping out of my car, I was met by humidity so thick it felt like a heavy blanket weighing me down. I wiped my brow and walked the few steps into our air-conditioned building.

Kayla wasn't at her desk as I entered, and I could hear voices coming from the boardroom. The door was open, but I didn't stop to look inside. I strode into Bruce's office and greeted him. The stress on his face was evident.

Bruce offered me a half-smile. "Sorry, Dean, whatever you had scheduled for this morning is going to have to wait. We have a meeting now."

"With whom?"

"Prescott Finch's family."

I raised my eyebrows. "You invited them into the office to meet?"

"I wanted to understand the whole picture of the situation before we went back to discuss the case with Haley." Bruce rubbed the back of his neck. "I wanted to see if there was any weight to the prosecution's theory that Prescott is deceased."

"Bruce, it's never a good idea to talk with the victim's family. If they think Prescott is missing, and possibly murdered by Haley, they're going to be angry. This isn't a meeting we need to go to."

"Maybe that sort of thinking applies in the big city, but down here, everyone knows everyone. I went to school with Prescott's ex-wife's father, and I've known Maria since she was knee-high to a grasshopper. I met Prescott, and I even visited his pharmacy on occasion." Bruce leaned against his desk and rubbed the back of his neck again. "I know this isn't the greatest idea, but when you're in a small town, you can't avoid other people. We're going to talk to the Finch family and we're going to do it politely."

"How many are there?"

"Five. We're meeting with his ex-wife Maria, his brother Bronson, and three cousins. I need to know what they think," Bruce said. "You know this is the angle the prosecution is going to play in court, and we need to be prepared for any of their tactics. We need to know the full story, and Bronson was very keen to tell his side of it. He was waiting for me at the office when I arrived here this morning."

I shook my head as Kayla stepped into the office. Her face betrayed reluctance. "The Finch family is waiting in the boardroom."

Bruce drew a long breath, exhaled heavily, and then led us on. Kayla followed, and I was a step behind her.

Maria Frazer sat at the front of the room and greeted Bruce with a hug and a kiss on the cheek. She shook Kayla's hand and then mine. She was well dressed in a flowing red and white dress, and her blonde hair was immaculate. Despite the subject matter, she greeted us with a polite smile.

The three cousins greeted us with polite nods as they were introduced.

Bronson Finch was less welcoming. He stood at the back of the room, arms folded across his chest. He was tall and skinny, and looked toned enough to be a middleweight boxer. He wore a black polo shirt with black jeans, and his jaw was clenched tight. He had several tattoos covering his right forearm, and he didn't move as we entered.

After the prosecution's revelation, I had spent the night researching the Finch family. Prescott and Bronson owned ten pharmacies together. Before Prescott went missing, they were expanding the business, looking to buy more pharmacies throughout the state, and create a brand that could last generations. When Prescott went missing, the business expansion stalled. From what I'd read, the brothers had borrowed heavily to expand, and Bronson was struggling to keep the business afloat without his brother.

As I sat down, Maria leaned forward, eager to talk. "Bruce, you knew my father for many years before he passed, and I appreciate the opportunity to talk with you."

"Of course," Bruce said. "It's always a pleasure to see you, Maria. You look well."

"Thank you, Bruce."

"How's your daughter?"

"Katie is doing well, even though her father has been missing for years." Maria smiled slightly. "She's ten years old now, and she's starting to ask questions about why he doesn't call. I don't know what to tell her, but I know the truth about what happened to him. We all do." She drew a deep breath, and Bruce allowed her all the time she needed to continue. "I wanted to ask you, from the bottom of our hearts, not to defend Haley. Maybe you can't see it yet, but you will in time. She's evil, Bruce. She killed Prescott, and she most likely killed her new boyfriend."

Bruce grimaced, like the statement was unexpected. "What makes you think Prescott is dead?"

"We haven't heard from him in two years. Even after Prescott and I divorced, we still used to talk every day. He was an amazing father, and he was so involved in Katie's life. After Prescott married Haley, Katie was still his number one priority. He was at every sports game, at every parent-teacher conference, and at every school gathering. He loved her so much, and he was so proud of her." She paused and shook her head. "And then suddenly he jumps on a plane to South America without telling anyone? Runs off with a mystery woman nobody in Beaufort has ever heard of? There's no way that happened. There's no way Prescott would do something like that. He was a family man, and there's no way he left his daughter behind without even calling her occasionally."

"Have you tried to contact him?" I asked.

Maria looked at me like I'd asked the dumbest question ever. "We've tried, but we've had no response. When he left, he didn't tell anyone, he didn't plan it, and he didn't say goodbye. We haven't had a phone call, a text message, or even a postcard since. He disappeared off the face of the planet without a trace. We've looked for him, looked for any sign that he might be alive, but there's nothing. He's completely vanished."

"What about his business? Has anyone heard from him?"

"He was a chemist, and we owned ten pharmacies together." Bronson's voice was deep and commanding. He kept his arms folded, and stayed at the rear of the room. "Our profits are down 85 percent since Prescott went missing. We were doing great, preparing for the future, but then he disappeared. Now I can't do anything without his signature. We've been in limbo for two years. There's no way he would've done that voluntarily."

"We don't know what happens behind closed doors." Bruce tried to reason with them. "Maybe Prescott was struggling mentally. Maybe his marriage with Haley was falling apart. Haley says that he ran off with another woman. That's not uncommon behavior for a man going through a mid-life crisis."

"As if he did that," Bronson scoffed. "This was no mid-life crisis. Prescott wouldn't do that to us. There's no way he would've left our business behind."

"Haley was always after Prescott's money," Maria added. "That's all she wanted from him, and she knows that if he is deceased, then she loses most of the wealth. Prescott's estate leaves nothing to Haley. Not a cent. We know about the spousal laws, and we know she'll dispute the will, but even after a legal fight, she'll lose two-thirds of her wealth. And she also can't divorce him, because she'll lose access to his wealth, due to the pre-nuptial agreement. It's in her best interest if Prescott is never found. She'll pretend that Prescott is alive for the next twenty-five years and drain his bank accounts until there's nothing left."

"And we all know that's why Haley went looking for another rich partner." Bronson unfolded his arms, clenched his fists, and stepped forward. "We were gaining traction with the police department to agree to declare Prescott deceased. Haley claims he went to South America, but we finally got the information from the Department of State that he never left our borders. There's not one record of his passport at the borders. He didn't leave the country, and he isn't in South America like that little witch claims."

"You're suggesting he's still in the country?" Bruce asked.

"Prescott was killed. We all know it." Bronson's tone was firm. "Haley killed him. We don't know what she did with the body, but it's time for the truth to come out. He's probably in the marsh like Sammy Turner."

"Bruce, we confronted Haley with the information that Prescott hadn't left the country, and we told her we had a judge who was going to consider a death certificate. She looked panicked, and only two weeks later, her new rich boyfriend went missing. That's not a coincidence."

"And it didn't surprise us that the witch made him update his will days before she killed him," Bronson grunted. "She wasn't going to make the same mistake twice."

"And I know she's violent, because I saw her slap Sammy Turner," Maria added. "I'm sure she used to do the same thing to Prescott, but I never saw it."

"When did you see Haley slap Sammy?" I questioned.

"When I went over to her place to grab some of Prescott's things earlier this year, Sammy Turner was there. Haley spoke to Sammy like he was a dog. I was only there a few minutes, and she slapped him twice."

"Are you going to testify about that?"

"I've already talked to the Circuit Solicitor's Office." Maria eyed Bruce. "And I'm going to testify if this makes it to court."

Silence descended on the room. I looked at Bruce, who was looking at his hands, and then to Kayla, who was staring at the notepad in front of her.

"Please." Maria changed tack, pleading with Bruce. "Please, don't defend Haley. Please don't help her. We know, deep in our hearts, that she killed our Prescott, and she's done it again. She's killed this poor innocent man. We know it in our hearts, but nobody will listen to us."

"I'm sorry, Maria, but this is my job. Dean and I have been employed to provide her the best possible defense against the murder charge. That's the role of a defense lawyer."

"What about my daughter, Bruce?" Maria pleaded, trying to catch Bruce's eye. He kept his gaze locked on the table. "She

41

deserves to know the truth. She deserves to know what really happened to her father."

"There is no evidence that any of this is true," I stated, trying to save Bruce from the increasing pressure. "Haley has had emails and phone calls from Prescott over the past two years. There's no evidence to say he is dead."

"Of course he's dead." Bronson pointed his finger at me. "Listen to me. Haley killed our brother, and we deserve justice. Nobody would listen to us, but now she's done it again. We won't let her get away with it twice. We deserve justice."

I stood up, facing up to Bronson.

"Dean." Bruce stopped me from arguing any further. "Not here."

"Bruce, we're not asking you to do anything illegal." Maria lowered her tone. "We're just asking that you ensure justice is done here. That's all we want. Maybe Haley killed Sammy Turner, maybe she didn't, but we know, *we know*, she killed Prescott."

Bruce sighed and stood. "That's a different case, Maria. My job is to defend her against the charges of murdering Sammy Turner. If you have evidence that she killed Prescott, you need to take it to the police."

"We have evidence," Maria pleaded. "But nobody will listen to us."

Bruce offered her a half-smile, then held his hand toward the door.

The Finch family left without another word, but the tension remained long afterward.

CHAPTER 8

"It's not a good look," private investigator Sean Benning said. He was sitting in the hull of his houseboat, leaning back on a wooden chair, looking out at the tidal marsh. "It's not a good look at all."

Sean Benning was a lean man with muscular forearms that were etched with veins that snaked beneath the skin. His brown hair, brittle and dry, spoke of years spent living on the water, and his skin, deeply tanned and scarred, showed the marks of a life lived exposed to the elements. His eyes, narrow and blue, were constantly darting around, scanning his surroundings with a keen and assessing gaze.

Benning's houseboat was docked next to a long wooden pier, tucked into the edge of the marsh, on the Paige Point boat landing, next to Huspah Creek. The houseboat had seen better days. More than thirty-five years old, it had been weathered by salt and time, with the streaks of blue paint faded by the hot Southern sun.

"You're telling me there could be truth to the story?" Bruce wiped the sweat from his brow. "That Prescott Finch is dead?"

"I'm saying that in the twenty-four hours since you called me, I've been digging around, and nobody, and I mean nobody, has heard from Prescott since he 'left.' That's two years. He was a man with deep ties to the community, a regular at his church, and a devoted father. That's too much of a coincidence."

"Maybe he left, and then something happened to him?" Bruce seemed to be trying to convince himself more than us. He had taken off his tie, leaving his white-collared shirt undone to the middle of his chest. "Maybe he got in a car crash in Georgia, or he was mugged and killed in Florida. Maybe he's a John Doe sitting in a morgue somewhere."

"Not likely. His DNA is uploaded to genealogy sites. The family would've been notified," Benning noted. "And he was a dedicated businessman. It's very unlikely that he walked away from that without even telling his brother."

The tide pressed against the boat, rocking us slightly, and the bugs hummed around us. The melodic drone of the insects was a constant to life around the marsh.

Looking out at the tranquil flow of the creek, I watched as it glistened in the sunshine. A heron flew past, gliding through the blue sky with ease, before landing in the marsh.

The waterways in Beaufort County were hypnotic.

They weren't places of impressive grandeur, they weren't places of awe-inspiring greatness, but rather, they were places filled with a raw beauty that reflected a tremendous simplicity. It was easy to feel the heartbeat of something greater than yourself when spending time around the tidal marshes.

"What do you know about the business?" I asked.

"A chain of ten pharmacies." Benning stood and walked into the hull of the boat. He returned a moment later with five pieces of paper. He handed them to me and continued. "This is what I could gather on them in the last day. Three years ago, Prescott and Bronson borrowed heavily, with the intention to expand to fifteen pharmacies. That was the tipping point for them. With that many pharmacies, they'd have more buying power, and they could acquire stock cheaper. They'd expanded to ten before Prescott went missing, but now the business is losing money. It was a big risk, but the brothers would've been in front if they had kept going."

"Which is why Bronson wants Prescott declared deceased," I added. "Prescott's will was written ten years ago, long before he married Haley, and leaves all his wealth to his ex-wife and brother. Haley would likely dispute the will, but she signed a pre-nup, so it'd be a long, and expensive, legal battle. Homestead protection laws mean she would still have the spousal home, but it would be a fight."

"True, but the day Prescott is declared deceased, Bronson takes full ownership of the business and he's able to continue the expansion plans," Benning added. "The word is that the pharmacies are about to go under. He either needs to keep expanding or sell up, and he can't do either without Prescott. The brothers set up the bank accounts with joint signatures, and he can't do anything without Prescott's signature."

Silence lingered between us while we contemplated the new information.

A snowy egret circled the boat before settling on the nearby marsh. It was a graceful bird, with all-white plumage and long, dark-colored legs. It stepped through the shallow part of the marsh, probing, searching, and hunting for its prey. I turned to the hazy horizon and watched as it took off, cutting through the air with such ease. Being in the marsh, surrounded by wildlife going about its day as it had for centuries, was a soothing experience.

"If Prescott is never declared deceased, then his will is never actioned," Bruce said. "Common law states that a person is declared deceased after seven years without evidence that they are alive, but it's a legal gray area. The family has reported him missing several times over the two years, but Haley claims he isn't. She updated the police five months ago that he was still alive. Prescott's family made a request to record him as deceased so they could go through the will, but Haley stated she still had contact with him. Every time Maria reports him missing, the police talk to Prescott's wife, and she reports that she's had recent contact with him. She shows the police some emails from him, and then they close the case."

"And Haley is the only person who's heard from him," Benning added. "The longer this goes on, the less good that looks for her."

"Haley, Haley, Haley." Bruce sighed. "What a mess she's in."

"From what I can gather"—Benning picked up another piece of paper, and handed it to me—"Haley was in her mid-twenties and met Prescott at a function. His divorce to Maria was finalized only days earlier. They hit it off, despite the twenty-five-year age gap. Five months later, they were married."

"And a few months after they married, Prescott went missing." Bruce groaned. "That doesn't look good."

"Initially, everyone seemed to buy Haley's theory that he'd gone to South America with a mystery woman. But when nobody else heard from him over the coming months, they started to get suspicious," Benning noted. "It's in the family's best interest for him to be declared deceased, and it's in Haley's best interest for him to still be alive."

"Bronson is the most sinister-looking chemist I've ever seen." Bruce flapped his shirt, trying to get some cool air in. "You don't see many chemists with sleeve tattoos."

Benning nodded. "Interesting that you say that, because the rumor is that his business is not all above board."

"Meaning?"

"Meaning the business was going under without Prescott's signature, so he turned to other ways to make his money and keep the business going."

"You're saying Bronson was selling drugs on the side?"

"Rumor is that he was dealing large amounts of fentanyl to local dealers."

"Wow." Bruce groaned again. "Alright, alright. This is a deep rabbit hole, but it's a side issue. We're defending Haley against the charge of murder for Sammy Turner. Prescott Finch has nothing to do with it. It's just a rumor." I could hear the frustration in his voice. "We need to focus on Sammy Turner."

Benning nodded and went back into the hull of his boat.

It was intriguing to follow the trail into Prescott's apparent disappearance, but all we needed was enough information to prevent it from being mentioned in court. It was clear that it would form part of the prosecution's trial strategy, and we needed to ensure that his name was not even mentioned. The unfounded rumors would be extremely prejudicial against Haley.

"Interesting fellow, this Sammy Turner," Benning called out from inside. He returned a moment later with another file. "I've spent the past few days digging around and found out a lot about him. Everyone that knew him spoke highly of him. Never in any trouble, always helping others, kind to everyone. Grew up dirt poor and worked hard in several low-paying jobs. Was a dedicated worker and was loyal to his friends. Then two years ago, the lucky guy wins five million dollars on the lottery. He didn't go crazy with the money, though. He gave about a million away to family, friends, and charity, and bought a nice house on Dataw Island. Drove an average car, nothing flashy, and bought some new clothes."

"Enemies?" Bruce asked.

"For Sammy, none."

"But?"

"But there's Ken Turner," Benning said. "Ken Turner had a very different experience of life than Sammy. Same mother, different fathers, and I'd say that Ken must've received more than his share of his father's DNA, because those brothers were like night and day."

"Ken's our early target," I stated. "What do you know about him?"

"Ken Turner spent a lot of time in prison for drug possession charges, small-time theft, a few charges of dealing, and some violence." Benning passed a file to Bruce. "In and out of rehab for a long time. Again, grew up dirt poor and never really had any work. Sammy was bailing him out long before he was rich. Ken dropped out of junior high, but it still looked like he peaked in high school."

"And after Sammy won the lottery?"

"Sammy paid for Ken to attend rehab five times in the last two years, but none of it worked. He bought Ken a nice house in Port Royal, and a nice new car, which he crashed within a few days." Benning squinted as he looked toward the sun. "But here's the interesting part—Ken used Sammy's money to start dealing drugs. But the rumor is he found himself getting high on his own supply and ended up hundreds of thousands of dollars in debt to local dealers."

I looked at Bruce, and he looked at me. The case was heading into dangerous territory and we both knew it.

"Got any names we can talk to?" I asked.

"I suggest you start with Ryder Westinghouse." Benning drew a breath and slid a piece of paper across the table. "This guy was Sammy's old next-door neighbor. He'll talk to you, and he'll answer every question you have, but he wants no involvement in the case. He'll lead you in the right direction, but I need to warn you—that direction might get dangerous."

CHAPTER 9

I followed the address Benning supplied to a small house on St. Helena Island.

The blue clapboard house had two bedrooms, one bathroom, and a kitchen that was big enough for a small dining table. The dining table edged over the carpet into the living room, which was just big enough to fit a frayed two-seater sofa. The house smelled like five-day-old pizza, and the trash can was overflowing.

I had been inside the house for ten minutes, and still the owner of the house hadn't talked to me. Ryder Westinghouse was busy in the kitchen, a notepad in hand, talking to himself, taking the occasional break to write something down.

A small man with a long face, Ryder walked with jerky movements, and he seemed to have a constant supply of coffee pumping into his body. Every thirty seconds or so, he would stop what he was doing, sip his mug of coffee, pause, and then continue.

Eccentric characters were often found in small towns throughout South Carolina. Their quirks and unconventional ways were part of the rich tapestry of the towns they inhabited, integral to the cultural landscape, reflecting the creativity and resilience needed for life in the South.

When I knocked on the front door, he had opened and waved me inside, pointing to the couch. I sat and waited for him to interact with me. After ten minutes, when I was sure he'd forgotten I was there, I coughed loud enough to catch his attention. He turned and looked at me with surprise.

I stood. "Mr. Westinghouse, thank you for talking with me."

He smiled, placed his notepad down, and walked the few feet from the kitchen into the living area. I held out my hand to shake, but he ignored it and hugged me instead.

"We're all family, bro," he said as he drew back from the hug. "We're all humans. Me, you, my brothers from Europe, my cousins from Africa, my uncles from Asia, we're all family."

I couldn't help but smile. The man radiated warmth. Then I noticed the drug paraphernalia on the coffee table. I pointed to the homemade bong. "Big morning?"

"Always, man." He laughed. "Just a little bit to take the edge off. Got to live life."

"It seems like you're living well."

"I'm happy, brother. That's what life is about." He patted me on the shoulder and then gripped it. "You're a big dude. You work out?"

"I like to exercise. It keeps me sane."

"I microdose on magic mushrooms. That keeps me sane."

If this was Ryder Westinghouse sane, I would hate to see the crazy version. I moved an empty Coke bottle and sat back down on the worn couch. This time, I almost fell through it. I had to lean forward to make sure the couch didn't collapse under my weight.

"I'd like to ask you some questions about Sammy and Ken Turner," I said as Westinghouse pulled a dining room chair into the living room. "Were you friends with them?"

"Oh, yeah." He turned the chair around and sat down, spreading his legs wide and leaning his chest forward on the backrest. "But before we talk, you have to laugh at one of my jokes."

"Is that the price of a discussion?"

50

"You bet it is. The world can always do with more laughter."

"Go on."

"I spotted an albino Dalmatian yesterday." He grinned. "I thought it was a nice thing to do."

I didn't react. I couldn't laugh at the first joke. It would've looked disingenuous. I shook my head. "I need better than that."

"Okay, okay. I can see you're a tough nut to crack." He drummed his hands on the chair's backrest. "Well, I saw two guys in the locker room at the gym with glitter on their private parts. Yep, they were pretty nuts."

I smirked. I had to admit it, he got me.

He laughed and clapped his hands. "See? Even a serious guy like you can have a laugh."

"It was a good delivery."

"It's one of my classics." He waved his finger in the air. "But I can see you're a man of business. Someone who likes to get down to the nitty-gritty right away."

"I am."

"Then ask away."

"Were you friends with Sammy and Ken Turner?"

"I sure was. Sammy was such a sweet soul. He used to live next door. I moved in here at twenty-one, and I've lived here almost ten years now. He'd been my neighbor most of that time, right up until two years ago. He won the lotto and bought a bigger house over on Dataw Island." He leaned back and smiled. "Sammy offered to give me some cash after his lottery win, but I wouldn't take it. I don't need money, man. I'm high on life. And he deserved it way more than me. He was such a sweet, sweet man."

"Did you ever meet Haley Finch?"

"I sure did. She's a pretty girl." He shrugged. "The thing is, for his whole life, Sammy had been single. Never had any luck with the ladies. He was overweight, soft, and introverted. He was the

51

guy that women wanted to be friends with, and nothing more. He wasn't a handsome man, either, but my oh my, he was a real gem. As good as gold with a kind soul."

"And after he won the lottery?"

"He didn't change. The first thing he did was look after other people. He helped his family out, and helped everyone he knew. After he did that, he went off and got his teeth fixed and a whole set of new clothes. With straight white teeth, nice clothes, and a lot of money, women started falling at his feet. He could've chosen anyone, and he chose Haley."

"And Ken?"

"Little bro Ken." He grimaced. "I try my hardest to love everyone, but I never liked him."

"Why not?"

"Why does anyone not like anyone? Because they highlight the worst in ourselves. The world is just a reflection of our own perception." He looked at the ceiling. "Ken was addicted to drugs and would do anything for his next hit. He gives us good drug users a bad name." His statement was said with no hint of sarcasm. "Ken was selfish, mean, and took advantage of everyone. You could never leave the guy alone with your stuff. He'd steal it right away." Ryder snapped his fingers. "Ken got into dealing drugs and racked up a lot of drug debts as well. Nasty guy. Sammy loved Ken, but Ken loved drugs."

"Drugs make people do nasty things."

"Not my drugs." He waved his open hand at me. "I know some of the dealers Ken scored his drugs from, and they knew to never ask Ken for cash. They knew he never had the money. Even before the lotto win, the dealers would go to Sammy because they knew Sammy would always bail his brother out. And after the lotto win, well, the dealers wanted a piece of that money themselves. Ken had the big idea of using Sammy's money to start dealing drugs, but he would use too much of his own stuff. That man could never run a successful deal."

"Do you know any of the names of Ken's suppliers?"

He frowned and shook his head. "That's dangerous stuff, man. Don't go down that road."

"I need to go down that road."

"Okay, I'll give you a name, but you didn't hear it from me." He lowered his voice. "There's a chemist dealing fentanyl out of his pharmacy and making a nice little profit on the side."

"Name?"

"Goes by Bronson."

I leaned back on the couch as the realization hit. "What would happen if Sammy refused to pay Ken's drug debts?"

"Sammy would never have been that stupid."

"But if he was?"

Ryder bit his bottom lip. "If Sammy didn't pay, then Sammy wouldn't have lasted long."

CHAPTER 10

I stood in the boardroom, leaning against the wall near the window, arms folded, staring at the whiteboard.

The boardroom table was covered with files. On one side were the witness statements, the police reports, and the early forensic analysis. On the other side were two files detailing the information we had on the main people involved in the case—Haley Finch and Sammy Turner. The whiteboard was filled with scribbles, names, ideas, and notes. I added a name to the bottom and then circled it.

"Bronson Finch?" Kayla stared at the circled name. "How's he connected to this?"

"Ryder Westinghouse, bless his heart, is one strange cat," I said. "He's smart, but spends most of his time high on weed and mushrooms. He had several interesting things to say, but the most important is that we found a link between Bronson and Sammy."

"Bronson and Sammy?" Bruce whistled, his eyes widening in surprise. "This is becoming a real mess."

"After Prescott went missing, Bronson struggled to keep the pharmacies afloat. According to Ryder, Bronson Finch started dealing fentanyl, moving big amounts of it to several small-time local dealers, who then sold the drug to other users."

"How does that relate to Sammy?"

"One of the local dealers was Ken Turner."

"Ah." Bruce shook his head. He ran his hand over his head several times as he thought about the connection. "Bronson Finch was dealing drugs to Ken Turner?"

"That's right. When Ken racked up the debts, Sammy would pay them off," I added. "Sammy would do anything to help his brother."

"Wait." Kayla worked out the connection. "If Ken didn't know the will had been updated, he would've expected the money to come straight to him once Sammy died. He would've thought he was about to receive millions."

"We've got two leads, and they both relate to drugs," Bruce said. "So, what do we do? Third-party culpability?"

"If we go down that path, we have to choose between Bronson and Ken," I said, and turned to Kayla. "How did you do with the entrance logs on Dataw Island? Did Bronson or Ken go to Dataw Island on the 5th or 6th of July?"

"Given the information you've just found out, you'll like this." Kayla typed into her laptop and then turned it to face me. "The prosecution has given us the details on every car coming and going past the security checkpoint at Dataw Island for the month of July. I spent hours searching through the logs last night, matching the license plate numbers to the known plates that we have on file."

"This sounds promising." I could sense the excitement in her voice.

"It's this license plate here." Kayla pointed to the screen. "On July 5th, Ken Turner entered Dataw Island at 5 p.m. and left at 5:15 p.m. He didn't spend long there at all."

"Haley left at 4:45. So Ken was there after Haley?"

"That's right." Kayla nodded. "It looks like the investigators missed a lot of information about this murder."

"Too much. They had it in for Haley from the start." Bruce looked at the whiteboard and then at me. "Why was Ken there for such a short period?"

"They interviewed Ken when Sammy first went missing." I reached forward to the pile of folders and pulled one out. I flicked through several pages. "Ken said that he went to Dataw Island to talk to Sammy about midday, but Sammy wasn't home. That's why he went in, and fifteen minutes later, he went out. According to his statement, he left at 12:15 p.m."

"But that's not even close to right. The investigators didn't even check his story," Bruce said. "So where do we focus?"

"Ken needs to be our focus right now," I noted. "If we're going for third-party culpability, he's the perfect guy. He's violent, has drug debts, and now we also know that he was at the crime scene before Sammy went missing and after Haley left. The question is—how do we get him on the stand? The prosecution isn't going to use him as a witness, because they know it weakens their case. We could issue him a subpoena, but he'll see through our plan. He'll retreat into his shell and not give us anything. We need to approach this tactfully and choose the right time to talk to him."

"He'll be defensive no matter when we talk to him."

"Agreed. That's why we need to build a full picture of the events of July 5th beforehand." I turned to Bruce. "Do you know of anywhere Ken Turner might've sold his drugs?"

"That's a dangerous path to follow." Bruce frowned. "The people Ken Turner floated around are not friendly people who like to speak with outsiders."

"We need to talk to them. It's the smallest piece of evidence that might change this case. The police have looked at the big picture, but we need to find a clue in the details. We need to talk to the dealers to get the full picture."

Bruce looked at me and then back at the whiteboard. "I know some people, but I don't suggest you go looking for them."

"I need names, Bruce."

Bruce sighed and conceded. "There's one guy I know that's caught up in the fentanyl trade—Jasper Rawlings. They call him the 'Slipper,' because he slips in and out of places without being seen. He hangs out at a dive bar near Walterboro, but I need to warn you. Everyone at that bar is a felon."

"Will he talk to us?"

"I defended him once, so he might talk to me."

"When can we go to the bar and talk to him?"

"It's Friday." Bruce looked at his watch. "My guess is he'll be there this afternoon."

CHAPTER 11

I loved driving through South Carolina.

The wide-open roads, the dense greenery, the sense of calm on the highway. I tapped my thumb on the steering wheel as we drove an hour north of Beaufort, past the town of Walterboro, and on to the Augusta Highway. I was playing the classics over the speakers, singing badly to my favorite parts, and humming the parts I couldn't remember.

Bruce was less keen for the drive. He had spent some time at Paint's Biker Bar and knew what we were in for. "It closed down years ago," he said. Back then, he explained, the bar was run by an amazing woman named Jane, and then her daughter Suzy, both friendly kind-hearted people who welcomed everyone. Since they had left, there was no official establishment, but rather, a gathering of hardened locals behind closed doors. Bruce explained that paramedics made monthly visits after bouts of violence, but law enforcement never made any arrests.

When I pulled into the gravel lot, Bruce was sweating. The one-street town off the edge of the highway had seen better days, and those days were most likely many decades ago. The bar was inside a flat roof red-brick building with cages over the small windows, and graffiti covering the sides. The large sign advertising a national beer brand had faded long ago. At the front of the building, what looked to have once been a patio was now covered by a concrete slab. Trash was blowing around the parking lot.

There were five Harley-Davidsons parked near the back of the property, and one old white pickup next to the front door.

"What did you defend this guy for?" I asked.

"Drug possession charges. He got caught with a large dose of fentanyl." Bruce shook his head. "I got the charges thrown out as the police couldn't prove due cause in the search of his house. Rawlings said he owed me a favor after that, but I've never cashed it in."

"Why not?"

"Because he wasn't the sort of guy that you call up for a little chat. Every interaction I had with him left me with an uneasy feeling. He's got the cold, hard look of a man who's hurt a lot of people."

I reached across to the glove box and removed my Glock. "Will I need this?"

"Maybe." Bruce nodded. "If I place my hand on your shoulder, that's our signal to leave. Understood?"

"Understood."

Bruce sucked in a deep breath and then stepped out of the SUV. I tucked the Glock into my belt and exited. We were hit by a wall of thick humid air, laced with the smell of cheap cigarettes.

"Y'all cops?" a voice called out. There was an older man sitting on a wooden chair in the shade next to the entrance of the bar, beer in one hand, smoke in the other. He looked to be missing most of his teeth. "If y'all are cops, then this ain't no place for you. Get back in your car and drive away."

"We're not cops," I called back. "We're just looking for a friend."

"Ain't no friends here, pal." The man spat on to the ground next to him. "Only trouble around here."

I nodded and led Bruce into the bar. The heavy door creaked open, and I was hit by a strong musty smell.

It took a moment for my eyes to adjust to the darkness. This was a place where people came to escape the world, to disappear in a smoky haze of cheap cigarettes and even cheaper booze. The floor was sticky, all the chairs were mismatched, and the main light in the bar was flickering. There were two men hunched over their drinks at the bar, and the female bartender, covered in tattoos, was staring at her phone. There were several empty booths to the right of the room, and a pool table at the back.

With a subtle nod of his head, Bruce indicated a lanky presence behind the table, pool cue in hand. Jasper Rawlings stood around five foot ten, and his slender build made his arms appear too long for his body. The trucker cap sat low on his brow, hiding most of his brown hair, and he was wearing a black T-shirt and black jeans, almost blending into the shadows of the room. His eyes, sharp and unsettling, were staring at me as I approached.

"Mr. Rawlings," I said.

He glared at me for a few long moments, then placed the pool cue down. "Nobody calls me that unless they're looking for a fight."

"Not looking for a fight." I raised my hands and my jacket raised at the same time, exposing the handgun in my belt. "We're looking to talk."

Bruce stepped forward.

A look of recognition flashed across Rawlings's face. "You guys lawyers, huh?"

"Hello, Jasper," Bruce said. "Is there somewhere we can discuss our question privately?"

Rawlings stared at Bruce and then at me. He turned back to the man he was playing pool with and nodded. He then turned back to us and pointed to an empty booth.

The vinyl seats of the booth were stained, torn, and had little padding left. The table was tacky, and there was an empty beer glass on the back corner. It looked like it'd been there for days.

"I don't know this guy." Rawlings pointed at me. "Is he a cop?"

"He's a lawyer." Bruce used a calm tone. "He works with me. I can vouch for him."

Rawlings nodded and sniffed. "What do you want?"

"Information," I said.

"On?"

"How much money did Ken Turner owe Bronson Finch?"

He stared at me and then looked to the bartender. "Who are you a lawyer for?"

"Haley Finch."

He expressed his surprise again, and then chuckled to himself. "You want to know if Bronson had something to do with what happened to old Sammy-boy?"

"You know Bronson Finch?"

"We have . . . business dealings."

"And did he have anything to do with Sammy Turner's death?"

"That's not the right question to ask."

"Why not?"

"Because I don't like people looking into our business."

Rawlings waved over his two friends from the pool table. Both men were big, muscular, and had scars on their faces. I had pushed too hard too early, and that made Rawlings angry. And he didn't look like a man who took his time sorting out a problem.

Bruce placed his hand on my shoulder. It was good advice.

Bruce stood, keeping his distance from the two men, and stepped toward the door. I slid out of the booth, and one of the men stepped forward. We came eye to eye. I could see he was itching to fight. Talkers talk, and they love to tell you how much they can fight, but fighters fight, and they're always looking for the next opportunity to use their skills. This man wasn't interested in talking.

We stared at each other for a moment before his right hand came toward my throat. He gripped my collar, and I reacted instinctively.

I swung hard. A clean left hook. My fist connected with his jaw, rendering him a heap on the floor.

Another fist came over the top of the first guy, connecting with my left eye socket, wobbling me a little. I turned to see another fist coming, but leaned back out of range, before landing a clean straight right fist on to the second man's cheekbone. The second man stumbled but remained on his feet.

I shuffled back, creating distance between us. My hand went to my Glock, and the second man didn't come any closer.

As I waited for their next move, Bruce tapped me on the shoulder from behind. I edged backward from the bar. Rawlings stared at us, ready for the slightest mistake.

We edged out of the bar and back into the sunlight. Bruce and I didn't talk until we were back in the car and out on the open road.

As we drove away from the bar, one thing was clear—the deeper we dug, the more threatening the case became.

CHAPTER 12

In the two days since we confronted Jasper Rawlings, I noticed an old white pickup truck following me whenever I left the office. I tried to confront its driver, but he drove off every time I got out of my car. I didn't chase them any farther. I didn't have time to play games.

In the parking lot of the Beaufort County Courthouse, I watched an F-35 fighter jet fly overhead, returning to the base at the Marine Corps Air Station, around ten miles west of Beaufort. The roar of the engine was deafening, drowning out any other noise and rattling loose windows. The F-35s flew over the city several times a day, and no matter how many times I saw them, I still stood in awe of their power.

As I watched the beautiful beast disappear into the hazy horizon, I caught a glimpse of the driver in a black Mercedes nearby. The driver had her head in her hands. I recognized the black sedan and walked over to it. Haley Finch spotted me as I approached. She offered me a small smile, then checked her appearance in the rearview mirror. She dabbed at her eyes with a tissue and then stepped out.

She had dressed well for her court appearance. She was wearing a gray pant suit that hugged her feminine curves, and her brunette hair was tied back tightly.

"Are you okay?" I asked.

"I was just thinking about my Sammy. All this makes it so real that he's gone." She blinked back the tears. "It's overwhelming to deal with grief and all this at the same time."

"You don't have to be present for this hearing. This can be a long and overwhelming process, and it can become quite emotional, especially when we start talking about what happened to your boyfriend."

"I want to be in there. I want to see all of it. It's my future on the line, and I want to know what's happening." She dabbed her eyes again. "What are we doing today?"

"Today is an evidentiary hearing before the trial judge," I explained as we began the walk toward the courthouse. "We've lodged several pre-trial motions which will be discussed, but the most important motion is to suppress evidence about your husband, Prescott. The prosecution will try to use Prescott's absence against you. They're going to suggest that Prescott has disappeared and that you're responsible for his disappearance. They'll argue it shows a pattern of behavior, but they don't have any evidence that Prescott is missing. We're applying to the court to have any reference to him, or his absence, excluded from the trial. If we win the motion, the prosecution's case becomes weaker. They've based their entire trial strategy around the motive, and anything we can do to make it weaker is a plus."

"Will you win the motion?"

"It's possible," I replied. "But this early hearing also gives us the chance to show the prosecution that this case will be a fight for every inch. We're showing them that they'll have to be prepared if they take this case to trial if they want a resolution. Disputing the motion encourages them to present a better deal."

"No deals," she said. "I'm not going to admit to something I didn't do."

"Understood."

We walked toward the courthouse, and I looked up for a moment to take it all in. The Beaufort County Courthouse was built in 1990 and significantly redesigned in 2012. The east-facing red-brick edifice stood strong and stoic, with a projecting center section, three large windows behind the imposing columns, and a hipped roof. Redesigned by an architect from Charleston, and built by a contractor from Bluffton, the courthouse was an impressive symbol of justice for the county.

I led Haley through security, the courthouse foyer, up the narrow stairs and into courtroom number five. Bruce was waiting for us, sitting behind the defense table, reviewing documents and files. Bruce and I shook hands and guided Haley to a seat.

It was smaller than the courtrooms I was used to in Chicago, but it was no less important. The courtroom walls, ceiling, and carpet were cream-colored, in contrast with the brown shade of everything else. Cool air pumped through the overhead vents, taking the edge off the humidity. For that, I was thankful.

At 9:55 a.m., Assistant Solicitor Charlotte Sinclair, flanked by two junior assistants, entered the room. They greeted us in a polite tone, sat down, and focused on their documents. Fifteen minutes later, the clerk at the front of the room read the case number and asked the room to rise for Judge David Dalton.

Judge Dalton was a proud Black man in his sixties. He had a voice deep enough to sing bass in a choir, and his quick wit was renowned throughout the county. He had lost his hair decades before, but he still had a shortly cropped gray beard. He wore glasses occasionally and had a reputation for being objective and fair.

Once Judge Dalton had sat down and made himself comfortable, he greeted the court and then confirmed our names. He turned to Haley, explained that she wasn't required to be there, and when he was sure she understood, he began.

"I see we have a few motions today," he said. "Mr. Hawthorn and Mr. Lincoln, can you please begin with your first motion?"

"Thank you, Your Honor." Bruce stood behind the defense table. "The first motion we would like to present is to compel discovery from the prosecution. While we have been made aware that there have been administrative issues, we believe that we should've received the full file for discovery by now. We've made several written requests to the Solicitor's Office, and they've done nothing but stall."

"And what's missing from the discovery file?"

"We've been made aware that there have been several witness statements made but not provided to us, we haven't received the police photos of the scene that formed part of the initial investigation, and we haven't received all their forensic analysis. These items are essential to the prosecution's case, and we believe the defendant is being severely disadvantaged by not having access to them."

Sinclair stood. "Your Honor, we sincerely apologize to the court for the delay in some of the discovery information. There have been several administrative issues within the department, and that has caused the delay; however, we make a commitment to the court that we will provide this evidence to the defense by the end of the week."

"Your Honor, we would like it noted that it's simply not good enough to blame administrative issues for the delay in discovery. We believe that it's prejudicial to the defense."

"Your feelings are noted, Mr. Hawthorn; however, I consider the matter closed, if the information is provided by Friday." Judge Dalton looked over his glasses at Sinclair. "And we had better not be in here in a few weeks, wasting the court's time because there have been further administrative issues."

"Yes, Your Honor." Sinclair nodded.

"Next." Judge Dalton paused and looked at the file on his desk. "We have a motion for the jury to be selected from another county, pursuant to the Section 17-21-85. Please elaborate, Mr. Hawthorn."

Bruce adjusted his tie. "Your Honor, it's our belief that the jury pool in this county has been tainted by the consistent and untruthful rumors that have been spreading throughout the good people of this area. We believe the rumors will make any jury selected in this county prejudiced against the defendant."

"The State objects, Your Honor." Sinclair stood. "We're strongly opposed to selecting the jury from another county. The reason we have *voir dire* is to prevent any such prejudice from existing."

"Any reason why *voir dire* wouldn't suffice in this case, Mr. Hawthorn?"

"Your Honor, we believe the jury pool within Beaufort County is extensively tainted by the rumors, and we will not be able to find people within this county who are not influenced by them."

"I'm afraid rumors aren't enough to change counties for the jury pool selection, Mr. Hawthorn, and I'm confident in this county's jury pool selection process." Judge Dalton rocked on his chair as he spoke. "The motion for jury selection to be conducted from another county is denied, pursuant to Section 17-21-85 of the South Carolina Code of Laws." Judge Dalton typed several lines on his laptop and then looked back at Bruce. "Next is the motion in limine, containing numerous items, submitted by the defense."

A motion in limine was an appeal for the court to reject evidence that was unrelated, irrelevant, or prejudicial. Over the next hour, we debated that including Mrs. Finch's financial records was irrelevant, statements from her past boyfriends were prejudicial, and evidence about her spending habits was unrelated. We argued that including her employment history was immaterial, we argued that statements from her neighbors were unrelated, and including her minor driving offenses was prejudicial. We won on several fronts, and Judge Dalton dismissed a lot of minor evidence from the court case. They were small wins, and we would take all we could.

"Anything further?"

"Yes, Your Honor." I stood and took the lead on the next motion. "The defense requests that any reference to Mrs. Finch's husband, Mr. Prescott Finch, be excluded from trial."

"And why is that?"

"This goes to the rumors that we mentioned earlier, Your Honor. Mr. Finch left Beaufort County two years ago and has not returned. Mrs. Finch has been in contact with her husband during that time, although they're separated. We believe it's the prosecution's intention to exploit the fact that Mr. Finch has chosen not to contact his other family members, and we believe that they'll suggest that Mr. Finch is missing."

"Missing?" Judge Dalton considered the idea for a few moments. "And there's evidence that he's not missing?"

"Mrs. Finch received an email from him earlier this year," I replied. "There is precedent for this, Your Honor. In the State v. Jackson, 2005, the court ruled that making any admission to the defendant's missing wife should be excused from the trial. In that case, the wife was even listed as a missing person; however, the presiding judge ruled that any reference to her could be considered prejudicial."

"Mrs. Sinclair, do you have a response?"

"Despite what Mrs. Finch has told the police, we believe that Mr. Finch is a missing person. His family, including his brother and ex-wife, have lodged several missing persons reports with the Beaufort Police Department. We have the reports here, Your Honor." She handed a piece of paper to the bailiff, who then passed it to Judge Dalton. "Despite numerous attempts to connect with

Mr. Finch, the family has received no response. Mr. Finch was a dedicated family man, a father to a young daughter, a business owner with his brother, Bronson Finch, and had many ties to the community. We don't believe that Mr. Finch left all these people behind and hasn't contacted them in two years."

"And what was the result of the missing persons report by the Beaufort Police Department? Is it still an open case?"

"The Beaufort Police Department closed the case, Your Honor," I replied. "As you can see in the report, Mr. Finch's wife stated that she's heard from him several times over the past two years. She submitted an email she received from him on the 10th of February this year as part of the evidence that he's not missing. As you can see, the IP address of the email shows it originated from Brazil. The defendant responded to the email, and even asked Mr. Finch why he hadn't contacted his family, but she didn't receive a response."

"Apart from Mrs. Finch, nobody has talked to or seen Mr. Finch in two years," Sinclair argued. "The email could've been generated by anyone. The email address that the email was sent from was not Mr. Finch's regular email address. In fact, there's no other evidence to say it was from Mr. Finch, apart from the name at the bottom."

"Are you suggesting that Mrs. Finch is lying to the police?" Judge Dalton questioned. "Because I would caution you from making that accusation, unless, of course, you have evidence to the contrary."

"His family hasn't heard from him in two years, Your Honor."

"Rumors should not override the defendant's constitutional rights," I argued. "There's no evidence that anything has happened to Mr. Finch, and the police have closed the missing persons case. We cannot allow unsubstantiated rumors to be submitted to the court as evidence. If the court allows these rumors to be presented, it's a clear violation of the defendant's constitutional rights."

"I agree, Mr. Lincoln," Judge Dalton stated. "The police investigated Mr. Finch as a missing person earlier this year, and I trust the police department have made the right decision. If there is evidence to say something happened to Mr. Finch, then I will reconsider; however, at this time, any reference to Mr. Finch as 'missing' may unduly influence the jury. As such, the motion is approved, and while reference may be made to Mr. Finch in the trial, there's to be no reference to the rumors that he's a missing person. Referencing Mr. Finch as a missing person may be prejudicial against the defendant and may be cause for a mistrial."

"Thank you, Your Honor," I said.

Sinclair muttered her response before we moved on to the next item. For the next hour, Bruce and I argued for further evidence to be thrown out in the trial, and while we had some further small wins, most of the remaining motions were rejected. It didn't matter. We'd won the major motion of the day, and as we left court, I could see that Sinclair was still simmering about the loss. Now that referencing Prescott as missing could lead to a mistrial, she would need to change her entire strategy.

I tried to talk to Sinclair as we exited the courthouse, but she stormed out of the building, only giving me a glare over her shoulder. Her silent response made one thing clear—this fight was on.

CHAPTER 13

Despite pressure from the prosecution, the media, and the extended Finch family, our defense case continued to build.

I spotted the pickup truck several times while I was driving, but nobody confronted me. They were trying to intimidate me. Trying to scare me. Trying to stop me from digging into their business. But it was going to take a lot more than a trailing pickup truck to stop me.

I juggled my other cases as best I could. I had the two felony cases to defend but also two DUI cases and misdemeanor possession of marijuana for a seventy-five-year-old man. I met with the seventy-five-year-old at his home. He had had a recent hip replacement, and, as he explained, the marijuana cookies were the best way to dull his pain. "I would've run from the cops, if I could've," he joked. He had spent most of his working years as a firefighter, running into burning buildings and serving the community, but it had taken its toll on his body. An overzealous deputy sheriff, who had recently lost the final of a darts tournament to the firefighter's son, arrested him at his home. I told the client that we could dispute the reason the deputy sheriff had given for entry into his home, but marijuana was still illegal in South Carolina. He told me he'd hide it better next time, and I told him I would pretend I hadn't heard that.

Most of my time was spent on the felony cases for Haley Finch and Luke Sanford, examining the police files for the smallest of mistakes. Both defendants were likable, both defendants were challenging their charges, and both defendants had the possibility of winning.

Sunday was my escape from the office. Emma dragged me to church in the morning, and we invited several cousins and friends to our place for Sunday lunch, although they all referred to it as Sunday dinner. After a light lunch, the back porch was full of adults talking and the yard was full of kids running around. There was a great sense of community here. We spent an hour talking, laughing, and running after the children, before the house was empty again.

I felt at home here. Despite having lived in Chicago for the last ten years, I was still deeply connected to this place. I knew the streets, I knew the trees, and I knew the rhythmic cycle of the weather patterns. I understood where the clouds were blowing in from, and what it meant for the coming days of weather. I could sense the storms long before they threatened the horizon. I felt the smells of the pluff mud deep in my soul. I knew the patterns of the tides. I loved the gentle smells of the wisteria, and I loved the shade of the live oaks. As much as I tried to run from it, as much as I tried to ignore it, the Lowcountry had my heart.

After I had cleaned up Sunday lunch, as the day turned into afternoon, I walked across to my grandparents' house, ten minutes away.

"Pass the hammer," Granddad Lincoln instructed me as I walked through the gate. He stood at the top of his ladder, leaning against the roof, fixing the gutter above the front door.

Granddad Lincoln was well into his eighties but was still nimble and full of life. A short man with a thick barrel chest, he'd had a varied career, from Air Force veteran to criminal defense lawyer, and that had left him with more than enough stories to fill the time.

"Come on, Dean," he hurried me. "I ain't got all day."

I jogged across the yard, went to the toolbox, and then passed the hammer up to him.

"Argh," he complained as he tried to reach across the guttering. "It's in an awkward position."

"Then let me do it," I said.

I could see the thought process in his head. He didn't want to let me do it. He didn't want to admit that he couldn't stretch across the small tree and reach the guttering that needed to be fixed. He was reluctant to pass over the reins, but he did, slowly coming down the ladder.

"You've got longer arms than I do," he said as he passed the hammer. "That's all it is."

"Sure thing, old man."

"Hey, I'm still nimble enough to clip you around the ears." He smiled and held the bottom of the ladder as I climbed up. "You watch your mouth, young man."

"Oh, hello, Dean. I thought I heard your voice." Grandma Lincoln came out of the house with a smile on her face and love in her heart. She was a cheeky woman, always ready for a joke and a laugh. "I've been telling him to fix the gutter for months," she called up to me. "And I've learned that the best way to get a man to do something is to suggest he's too old to do it."

"Hey," Granddad Lincoln replied. "I heard that, and I'm not old."

Grandma Lincoln looked at me with a mischievous grin, winked, and then walked back inside.

I hammered the gutter into place, bending a piece of the metal to where it should've been, and came down the ladder. "Is that all you needed to do?"

"It is." Granddad Lincoln grinned and pointed to the ladder. "And I've got a joke for you while you put that thing away."

I looked at the ladder and smiled. I picked it up, folded it down, and then began to carry it to the garage. "Go on then."

Granddad Lincoln followed a step behind. "So, I volunteer at a local charity, and the organizer realized our local politician, a wealthy investment banker, wasn't making any donations. The organizer went to see the politician at his massive office. She entered and said, 'We know you make over a million dollars a year from your investments, but you don't give anything to charity. Why is that?' The politician got angry and defensive. He said, 'Did you know my father is dying and has enormous medical bills? Did you know that my brother is a veteran and requires enormous amounts of money to pay for treatment for his PTSD? And did you know that my cousin was in a dreadful accident and can't support his children by himself?' Embarrassed, our organizer apologized. She said, 'No, sir. I'm very sorry, I didn't know any of that. Please accept my apology.' 'So,' the politician continued, 'if I didn't give them a cent of my money, why do you think I'd give money to you?'"

I laughed, more than the joke deserved.

Granddad Lincoln was an expressive man. He'd grown up in a time of storytellers, when jokes and long fables and folklore filled the evenings. Over the years, he had polished his skills, working on his delivery, and he'd become quite the impressive orator.

After I put the ladder away inside the well-organized garage, Granddad Lincoln reached inside the cooler and handed me an afternoon beer. We took a camping chair each and set them up on the front lawn, watching as the sun set over the tall live oaks.

"How's the murder case coming along?"

As a former criminal defense lawyer, Granddad Lincoln kept his interest in the law. When I lived in Chicago, he would call me and want to know every detail of the big city cases I was working on. He'd offer advice where he thought it was appropriate, but he'd never overstep.

"There's not a lot of evidence against the defendant, and we've got a good angle for the trial," I explained. "The prosecution's case is centered around the motive, and if we can show that it's not grounded in fact, we'll be able to win the jury over."

"Everyone thinks she's guilty, you know."

"Public opinion is against her, but that doesn't mean she did it. I'm confident we can win it at trial."

"With a trial by jury, nothing is certain," Granddad Lincoln said. "Except the defense lawyer's bill."

I laughed and we spent the next hour chatting. We talked legal tactics and precedents and previous local cases that were similar. He suggested that the Sheriff's Office jumped the gun and arrested Haley before they had all the evidence. He said the motive wasn't enough to convict her, but the make-up of the jury was key. I agreed. We needed traditional men who would feel like it was their duty to protect someone like Haley.

Over another beer, Granddad Lincoln talked about local issues, including how too many real estate developments were being approved without proper review. He talked about the lack of flood planning, about the lack of storm protection, and how the new developments were putting long-time locals at risk. I told him that times change, population growth is inevitable, and we had enough land to expand the city. He disagreed. We talked about the rivers, how they were becoming polluted, and how to fix it. He talked about learning how bad single-use plastics were for the planet. Every little bit helped our planet, and we needed to care for it, he said. As the afternoon drifted on, I thanked him for the beers, went inside and gave my grandmother a kiss on the cheek, and then walked back home to see Emma.

When I walked into our house, I was met by the wonderful smells of fried chicken and hush puppies. There was a vanilla candle burning in the kitchen, and I almost went over to put it out. I would much rather the smells of homemade fried chicken.

After greeting Emma with a kiss, I noticed an unopened bottle of wine on the table, with one glass next to it.

Emma popped the top, poured me a glass, and handed it to me. I sipped on the Merlot from Luca's Vineyard in Upstate South Carolina. It was one of the best Merlots I'd ever had, full of punchy flavor.

"Award-winning," Emma said, smelling the red and twirling it like she was a judge at a wine show. She didn't drink it. "And it's from South Carolina. There must be some real passion in this drop."

"You're not joining me?" I questioned.

"Not yet," she said. "Maybe later."

I sat at the kitchen bench and watched Emma in the kitchen. I tried to help but she shooed me away. As she cooked, she talked about her mother, Jane, and how her chemotherapy treatment was going. Jane was full of positive energy and was sure she was going to beat the disease. Emma talked about how it had been the right decision to come back from Chicago, and how her mother needed the support. Her older brother lived in California and was trying to make it back as much as possible, but Jane needed day-to-day help, and Emma was happy to be there for her.

In her spare time, Emma was also volunteering at the library, and she talked about how the place was filled with wonderful people and amazing books. She had been a high-flying human resources manager in Chicago, but I could tell her heart was never in it. She wanted to help people, to help them succeed, and the fact that her job had also included firing people broke her tender heart. Emma looked at home in Beaufort, like it was where she was born to be.

I loved seeing her smile, and I would do anything to support her, but I missed the buzz of the city. I missed our life there.

Emma asked me about Chicago, and I was honest. I told her I missed my career. I missed being on the cutting edge of innovation, of thriving in a world full of successful people, of pushing myself to be better than I was yesterday. Emma acknowledged how I felt and suggested we could move somewhere in between as a compromise. We checked the maps and halfway between Chicago and Beaufort was a small town near the Kentucky border. We both declined that option.

Our future was up in the air, and life was coming at us fast. Our plan had been to come back to Beaufort so Emma could support her mother while she went through cancer treatment. After a year here, we had planned to return to the bright lights of Chicago. Could I take Emma back there? After seeing the smile on her face here, after seeing how comfortable she looked with her mother, her cousins, her lifelong friends, I didn't think I could do that to her. Which left the question—what would we do at the end of our year in the Lowcountry?

When evening dinner was ready, Emma served it up. Again, she wouldn't let me help. We stayed at the kitchen bench to eat, trying to make as little mess as possible.

"That smells amazing." I leaned across and gave Emma a kiss. "You know this is one of my favorites."

She smiled and handed me another glass of Merlot. "Well, it's a night to celebrate."

"What for?"

"This." She placed a hand on her stomach. "And hopefully, in nine and a half months' time, we can really celebrate together."

The breath caught in my throat. "You're pregnant?"

"We are." She beamed.

I embraced her in a tight hug, and she cried tears of happiness on my shoulder. Blinking back my tears, I held on to her tightly. It was joyous moment, a wonderful surprise.

But it was also tempered with fear. We'd been through this moment several times before.

And I wasn't sure if we could take the heartache again.

CHAPTER 14

"Dean, I need your help."

It was Rhys. My cell phone had rung the second I sat down in my office to start my week. After the news from Emma last night, I had a smile on my face, and a spring in my step. I didn't even need a morning coffee—I was buzzing on life. I didn't think anything could bring me down. That was, until I answered Rhys's call.

"What's it about, Rhys?"

"Um, listen. I did something I shouldn't have done." He paused for a long moment, and I could sense the nerves in his voice. "I received a temporary restraining order issued by a magistrate and it says I need to go to court next week."

My tone was firm. "Rhys, that means the police believe you've engaged in first- or second-degree harassment or stalking."

"Yeah. That's what they said when they gave me the notice. They were very clear on what I can and can't do over the coming days. I wasn't even at the hearing. Can they do that?"

"I'll check," I grunted and typed on my laptop, finding the relevant law. "Under Section 16-3-1760 of the South Carolina Code of Laws, the Magistrate Court may issue a temporary restraining order without notice to the defendant as long the request meets the requirements under Section 16-3-1750." I continued to read over the laws until I found the information I needed. "And they'll hold a hearing to show cause within the coming weeks to determine if the order should stay in place."

"That doesn't sound good."

"It's not. What did you do?"

"I bumped someone, that's all. Just a shoulder to his chest. I didn't punch them, and I didn't kick them. The person I bumped might've fallen over, but I didn't hurt them. It was just a little tap."

"Who did you bump?"

"Who do you think?"

"Paul Freeman," I stated. "Where were you?"

"In the supermarket."

"And did you follow him there?"

Another long pause. "I was driving that way and Paul Freeman was driving that way as well. He walked into the supermarket as I parked, and then when he was coming out, I was walking in. It was probably just a coincidence that we ran into each other."

"I don't believe you, Rhys."

There was no response on the other end of the line for a few moments. "I've got to go to court next Monday. Can you please be there with me?"

"Yes, Rhys. Send me the details. I'll be there." I sighed and ended the call.

I leaned back in my chair and stared out the window. My happy buzz had been wiped out by Rhys's stupidity. As I sat there, contemplating life, the stress crept back into my head.

Emma and I had lost two late-term pregnancies before. We knew what we were getting ourselves into, we knew the potential pain that lay ahead, but it was hard not to be excited by the possibility of becoming a parent.

I spent the rest of the morning in the office, reviewing information and drafting motions. I wavered between giddy excitement and tempered nervousness. Emma called and we chatted for a while, and it was clear she was feeling the same.

Bruce was out of the office, playing another round of golf, and Kayla was at her son's school, helping with the class. I admired the flexibility of work life in Beaufort. People worked hard here, but it didn't define who they were. They had lives outside of the office.

When the time ticked past midday, I received a notice on my phone for my next appointment. I sighed when I saw the name on my calendar.

Getting in my car, I knew that my healthy buzz was going to be destroyed even further by talking to Stephen Freeman.

Freeman's home was on Morgan River Drive in the Ashdale neighborhood, ten minutes from Beaufort. The sprawling waterfront estate was valued in the millions, and the grandeur of the property was apparent upon arrival, with manicured green lawns situated behind a red-brick fence and tall, cast-iron gates.

While the entrance was stunning, the driveway was not.

The driveway had been smashed by the compact excavator, leaving pieces of rubble sticking out of the ground. Despite the weeks that had passed since the incident, Freeman was yet to have it fixed.

I parked on the side of the road, stepped through his fence, and studied the damage.

"Ah, the city lawyer," Stephen Freeman called out to me as he appeared at the front door of his stately two-story home. He came down the steps from the porch and across the yard. "It's so good to have such a talented man around these parts."

I could sense the sarcasm emanating from his words.

"I'd like to say it's a pleasure to see you," I said as he approached. "But that wouldn't be the truth."

Freeman was dressed in a tight-fitting white polo shirt tucked into black chino shorts. His boat shoes were new, and his Breitling watch looked shiny and expensive.

"It's going to be a big storm season, Dean," Freeman said as he came closer. He looked out to the horizon and squinted. "They're predicting we might even get a hurricane. We don't get many through here, but it all goes on a cycle. We're due for a big one soon. The winds are okay, but you've got to be ready for the storm surge. The flooding is bad enough on a rainy day, but if we hit a major storm surge, then we'll suffer a lot of damage. Who knows what the problem is?"

"You're going to tell me, aren't you?"

"It's the local council. We have a few real estate developers on the council, and they're approving everything at the moment. Their planning isn't even taking into consideration the possibility of storm surges."

"You should do something about it," I said. "You're the most influential man around these parts."

"Oh, I will." Freeman looked over the fence. "I've already set that plan in motion."

"The big one's coming, Dad," Paul Freeman called out as he exited his new pickup truck. He had parked on the street behind my SUV and bounded through the gate. "You can feel it in the air. Everyone's talking about it."

Paul Freeman, dressed in a polo shirt tucked into his blue shorts with flip-flops, looked about as egotistical as one could be. His thick brown hair was full of bounce, and his skinny arms were flung wide as he walked, trying to appear tough despite his short stature and thin build.

I glared at him. The last time I had seen him, I had thrown him across the bar floor and told him to avoid me at all costs.

"And it's going to get even more humid before it arrives," Paul Freeman continued, oblivious to my presence. "I'm just happy to be seeing a few more bikinis around town. Yes, sir. I love it when it gets humid."

"Paul Freeman." I fixed a cold stare on the man who had driven the car that took my sister's life. I stepped forward, towering over him. "You'd better keep walking."

"Oh. It's you." He stopped in his tracks the second he saw me. Sweat appeared on his brow. He bit his lip. He tucked his head down. "Um . . . I've . . . Um . . . I've got to grab something from inside," he said to his father, avoiding eye contact with me.

With his head still down, Paul Freeman hurried inside, scampering away like a scared little boy.

"Weak little wimp," Freeman whispered under his breath, shaking his head. When the front door closed behind Paul, Freeman turned back to me. "What do you want, city lawyer?"

"You know why I'm here."

He thought for a moment and then sneered. "Of course." He looked at the driveway to his impressive home. "Yes. You're representing Luke Sanford." He pointed to the damaged driveway. "Look at it, Dean. Take as many photos as you want. He made a real mess of it. Cracked it all up and smashed all the remaining parts. I haven't been able to use it for weeks now. He'll have to compensate me for the inconvenience, you know?"

"You didn't pay him for the work he did, and you've been using the upgraded driveway for a year."

"I paid his company for the quote he provided." He looked around. "I'm sure you've read the quote and can see there was no mention of a driveway improvement."

I took out my cell and walked away. I took several pictures of the scene before coming back to Freeman. "I've read the quote, but you had a verbal agreement to pay for the extra for the driveway. You didn't honor that."

"We had no verbal agreement," he scoffed, but couldn't control his smile. "Luke Sanford and I discussed some ideas, but we never agreed on anything. His price was too high, so I said I'd think about the work. And then he did the work because he wanted to scam me out of my cash. There's no way I would've paid five thousand for a driveway upgrade. I never would've agreed to those terms."

"I'm sure."

"You should be," he quipped. "I'm going to have to pay so much extra for this now. I'm in the right on this case, and the law is on my side. As is the media. If your client wants his reputation dragged through the mud, then I'll do it. Luke Sanford has tried to rip off the wrong guy."

Stephen Freeman had a long history of getting everything he wanted. A former circuit solicitor, he ran things in Beaufort. He had business and family connections that linked him to every influential person in town. He was married to the daughter of another former circuit solicitor, and his sister married a former sheriff. There were generations of powerful links and generations of control. If anybody wanted anything approved, sped up, or to skip the system altogether, they went to Stephen Freeman.

I stepped on one of the bits of loose tar. It crumbled under my foot. Luke had done a great job of ripping everything up.

"Now, if Luke Sanford would kindly agree to pay for the repairs to everything he damaged, and then agree to pay me an extra five thousand for the inconvenience, I could make his criminal charges disappear," Freeman said. "But it has to be for the right price."

"And if he says no?"

"Then I have everything prepared to run in the papers about scams by contractors who charge people extra for things they haven't agreed to. There are a lot of dodgy contractors out there,

Dean, and I'll let the media know that I've been the victim of a scam. The public loves a good story about a bad contractor. Once this story gets traction, it'll destroy his reputation, and it'll destroy his company. If he wants to go broke, then he's going the right way about it."

"And that's what you want? To destroy a hard-working individual?"

"No. I want him to pay for the damage he did," Freeman said as he walked back toward his mansion. His tone was laced with arrogance and sarcasm. "Always a pleasure to see you, Mr. Lincoln. Have a lovely day."

Stephen Freeman was corrupt, sly, and untrustworthy. I would've ripped up his driveway as well.

CHAPTER 15

Sean Benning called and asked to meet in the small town of Habersham, a fifteen-minute drive from downtown Beaufort. As I walked into Fools and Tools, a bustling sports bar on the main street, I was met with an energetic atmosphere. The place was alive as people chatted and laughed, some taking up space on the dance floor, and country music played over the speakers. The air was filled with the smells of fresh seafood, and as I walked past one of the tables, I caught a glance of their meals—half a lobster each. It had my mouth salivating.

Sean Benning was at the end of the bar, smiling to himself and tapping his fingers on the table to the rhythm of the music. He had an empty plate in front of him, not a crumb left on it, and a half-full beer glass in his hand.

"Sean." I greeted him with a handshake. "What are you doing out here?"

"Had to come out and see a client," he said. "A woman called me to find out if her husband was cheating on her . . . again. I've worked for her before, a few years ago, and she asked me to do the same thing. Last time I found that he was sleeping with his yoga teacher, and my client kicked him out. Apparently, they got back together last year, but now he's up to his old tricks again."

"And what did you find this time?"

"I found out that he's been sleeping with his assistant. But there's a twist this time." He took a large gulp of beer. "The assistant is a guy."

I whistled in surprise. "What did she say?"

"I haven't told her yet. She almost took my head off last time. When I showed her the photos of him kissing the yoga teacher, she flew off the rails and started hitting things with her frying pan. Luckily, I got out of the way," he said and nodded at his glass. "I'm going over to her after our meeting, but thought I needed a few drinks first."

"Wise choice." I smiled. "And maybe walk in with a football helmet on."

He smiled and reached down into his messenger bag on the floor and pulled out a small folder. "I've been looking into Ken Turner a bit further for you." He placed the folder on the bar. "And I've found some interesting things."

"Go on."

"First, I dug a bit deeper into his past. He's got a history of violence, is known to be unhinged, and has a decades-long drug problem. First it was alcohol, then he was arrested for methamphetamine possession, and now, he's loading up on fentanyl. A psychologist wrote in one of the court reports that he was sexually abused as a child, and he's carried that pain through his life. It's a sad story, and I never judge someone who's been through that." He closed his eyes and shook his head. "Anyone who does that to a child deserves to be castrated and hanged."

"Agreed," I said as I opened the file. "When was the last time Ken Turner was in prison?"

"Two years ago. He was locked up for attacking a cashier at a convenience store. He couldn't afford the cigarettes, he was short by a few cents, and the cashier wouldn't let it slide. Ken went off and started bashing the poor kid. Hit him with a full can of Coke around the head, knocked him down, and then kicked him a few times. He took the packet of cigarettes, and a few other things, and left. He was picked up an hour later after the cops reviewed the video footage of the store."

"Sounds like a loose cannon with money problems," I said as I read the file. "I'm surprised the Sheriff's Office didn't investigate this guy. He was at the scene of the crime. He's the perfect suspect, and they didn't even bother to spend more than fifteen minutes with him."

"My guess is that they only had eyes for Haley, given the rumors that were circulating around town about her husband," Benning said. "A lot of people heard those rumors about Prescott, and the second Sammy went missing, all eyes were on her. Although Sammy's case was a missing persons file for five weeks, the police report indicates they thought it was going to be a homicide investigation."

"We'll use that information in the trial," I noted. "We'll show the jury how the scope of the homicide investigation was very limited, and they missed a potential suspect. We'll talk about how the investigators didn't even consider a very clear suspect. It's compelling enough to create reasonable doubt."

"If that's your angle, then you'll love this next bit of information. It's buried deep in the missing persons file, but the police have had it all along."

"Go on."

"When the missing persons investigators went to talk to Ken Turner about his brother's disappearance, they took photos of the house, because it was owned by Sammy. Sammy was known to stay there on occasion, and the investigators took photos of the dining room, the kitchen, and the bedroom where Sammy stayed when he didn't want to go back to Dataw Island."

"What am I looking for?" I flicked through several large photos in the file. "I'm not seeing anything unusual."

"See what's on the kitchen table?" Benning tapped his hand on the photo. "It's in two of the photos."

I squinted as I looked at the image, and when I understood what I was looking at, my mouth dropped open. "That's a copy of a will."

"That's right," Benning confirmed. "But this is where it gets interesting. I zoomed in on the picture, and you can see that it's not the updated will that leaves the money to Haley. It's the will that Sammy made just after he won the lottery, signed years ago. We can tell because of the lawyer's stamp in the top corner. That logo belongs to the previous lawyer, not the one who updated the will. According to the will on the table, half of his wealth goes to Ken. It's possible Ken didn't know Sammy had updated the will. And that photo was taken by the investigators only a few days after Sammy first went missing."

I patted Benning on the shoulder. This was the break we needed. "We need to know why he had that will printed out."

"And there's one way to do that."

I nodded. "It's time to go straight to the source."

CHAPTER 16

Ken Turner. Violent. Drug-addicted. Mentally unstable.

The fifty-page police report into Sammy Turner's death only mentioned his name five times. The Beaufort County Sheriff's Office didn't even look at the man who'd been in and out of prison most of his life.

Ken Turner lived in a small two-bedroom home in Port Royal, purchased by Sammy after the lottery win. The single-story white clapboard house looked to be in decent shape, but the yard was overgrown, filled with long grass and weeds. Trash was scattered throughout the lawn, on the sidewalk, and in the driveway.

Stepping out of my car, I paused for a moment and looked around. Every other house on the street had a tidy front lawn. Some had white picket fences, others had a basketball hoop above the garage door, and most had the American flag hanging from the front porch. I could only imagine how frustrated the neighbors must have been at the state of Ken's home.

Bruce declined to join me on the trip to question Ken Turner. He felt Ken would react better to being intimidated by my large frame.

"You better watch where you step," a voice called out. I looked up and spotted Ken sitting on the front porch, a can of beer in his right hand. "Lots of needles in the weeds."

I took his advice and watched my step. As I walked up the concrete path, I was hit by his smell. Ken Turner smelled like he hadn't washed in days.

He was a short, skinny man in his forties, although he looked closer to sixty. His skin was dry, and he had scratches and infections on his arms. He was missing his front teeth, and his shifty eyes were sunken into his head. He wore a stained, over-sized red T-shirt and dirty jeans with flip-flops. His toenails were long, dry, and yellow.

"I don't know why you came here," he spat out. "I'm not going to talk to you. I told you that on the phone."

"We can either talk now or you can do it under deposition," I said as I approached the steps to his front porch. "That's where we go into a room, with a camera, other lawyers, and perhaps a detective, and you answer my questions in a sworn testimony. Of course, we'll have to ask questions about your personal life, including your drug habit. Do you want the detective to hear those answers?"

He stared at me for a long moment before he turned to his left and spat on to the porch.

Standing on the top step, one foot on the porch, I stared back at him. "Why were you following me through the park, Ken?"

"Just keeping an eye on you. I needed to know who I was up against. And that wife of yours, she's one fine-looking woman."

"Don't talk about my wife." I stepped forward.

"Hey, settle down, big guy." Ken smiled. "Forget I said anything."

I could feel my pulse quicken, my fists tightening. Ken's sly grin was infuriating, but I held myself back, taking a deep breath. The air between us felt thick and heavy with tension, but Ken didn't flinch. He just kept that smirk plastered on his face, like he enjoyed pushing people to the edge. I glanced away, taking another deep breath. I needed answers, not a fight.

"What was your relationship with Sammy like?"

He turned and spat again.

"If you're not going to answer me, then we'll talk under deposition." I started to walk back toward my car. "The cops will love bringing you in. Of course, we'll pick you up when you're at your local bar so that everyone will know that you talked to the cops."

"Hold up," he said. Nobody wanted to be known as a snitch. "I didn't say I wouldn't talk."

I turned back to him. "Then talk."

"Sammy." He shook his head. "Sammy Turner was my brother."

"And?"

"And what? We got along good sometimes and didn't other times."

"Where were you on July 5th?"

"I went to see Sammy around midday, but he wasn't home, so I left," he lied. "The rest of the day, I was here, at home."

"With anyone?"

"No. I live by myself. My mother called me a few days later to say that Sammy had been reported missing, but I knew nothin' about it. She's got dementia and is in a nursing home, so I thought she was talking crazy."

"Is that right?"

"Sure is."

"Then why were you on Dataw Island that night? You arrived at 5 p.m. and left at 5.15 p.m."

"Got proof of that?"

"It's a gated community. The security checkpoint monitors all cars that come in and out. Your car entered the checkpoint at 5 p.m. and left fifteen minutes later. The police gave us the file that showed your movements that day, so there's no denying it. I'll ask you again—why did you go to Sammy's house on July 5th?"

He had a blank look on his face as the thoughts rolled through his head. "I went to see him."

"And what did he say?"

"He wasn't home."

"Really?"

"Yeah."

"What did you do when you went to his house?"

"I had a key, so I went inside and called out his name. I looked around, and he wasn't there, so I left."

"And that took fifteen minutes?"

"Yep."

"Did you check the fishing dock?"

"Nope."

"Did you ever fight with Sammy?"

Ken shrugged and looked away.

"You need to talk to me, Ken."

"Sure. Sometimes we fought."

"What about?"

"Money."

"Did he tell you he wasn't going to bail you out any more?"

"Yeah. He said that." Ken nodded. I let the silence sit between us, and Ken felt the need to fill it. "He said he'd had enough of me causing trouble and wasn't going to keep paying the dealers any more. But I knew it wasn't him talking. I knew that my brother wouldn't do that to me. It was all Haley's influence. She was trying to steal his money from me. That's all she ever wanted from Sammy. She didn't love him, not like family. Not like I loved my brother. All that little witch wanted was money, and she had Sammy twisted around her little finger."

"Did Sammy tell you that he updated his will?"

He scrunched up his face and shook his head. "Nah. He didn't tell me that."

"When did you find out?"

"When I took the will to the lawyers after they found his body. They told me it was outdated, and it no longer applied. I told them they were wrong, but they called the cops on me. I haven't seen a cent of Sammy's money."

Ken wasn't educated, that much was clear, and I knew he was quick to anger. It was time to poke him to see how easily he would fire up.

"Did you kill your brother for the money?"

"What?" He jumped up from his chair. "I didn't kill him. It was that little girl, Haley. That's what the cops said, and they've got it right. She's a killer. Probably killed her first husband as well."

"Or you killed him because you thought you were going to get all his money. But you were too late. He'd already updated his will."

"Watch your mouth," Ken snarled. He pointed his finger at me, but I didn't find him threatening at all. The top of his head didn't reach my shoulders, and he looked like a strong breeze could blow him over. "You need to watch what you say."

"You killed your brother for money," I continued. "How does it make you feel that you won't get a cent of it?"

"I said watch your mouth." His jaw clenched as he approached me. "Or I'll—"

"Or you'll what?" I stepped forward, towering over him. "You wanted to kill your brother before he could update his will, but you were too late. And now you've lost the chance of ever getting that money."

"She doesn't deserve any of the wealth. She wasn't there when times were hard. She wasn't there for him when he didn't have enough money to eat. I was. I was there. It's my money, and that's why I'm going to see a lawyer."

"Are you disputing the will?"

"You bet I am." He grunted. "I deserve that money, not some young girl who had only known him a year. A lawyer from Charleston called me, after he heard what happened, and he said he could get my money back, free of charge if we didn't win." Ken sniffed and stepped back. "I didn't kill Sammy. He was my brother."

I made a mental note to search for the lawyer, and then eyed Ken. "When you testify on the stand, are you going to admit that you killed him for money?"

"I'm done talking to you." He turned toward the front door of his home, swung open the screen door and charged inside, slamming the front door behind him. I heard the door lock. I waited on the front porch for a long moment before I walked back to my car.

Ken Turner was unpleasant, heated, and his presence at Sammy's home made him look guilty.

All I had to do was convince a jury of his guilt.

CHAPTER 17

"It's heating up," Bruce said as he flapped his shirt. "It's going to be scorcher this week. Every day is going to be eighty-five or over."

As I drove, I reached across and turned up the air-conditioning in my car, blasting him with cool air.

"Thanks," he said. "The older I get, the more I need air-conditioning."

"Or the softer you get, the more you need it."

Bruce waved my comment away as I drove through the back streets of downtown Beaufort, under the canopies of live oaks. Many of the tranquil streets in Beaufort were shaded by large mature trees, the splendor of Spanish moss hanging from them and gently swaying in the breeze.

"I called a contact in Florida, and she put me in touch with a psychologist who specializes in age-gap relationships." Bruce wiped his brow with the back of his hand and flapped his shirt again. "Dr. Gemma Richardson. I called her yesterday and we had a long discussion about what we need from her in court. She spoke very well and is clearly very intelligent. She's happy to testify, for a fee, of course."

"What did she say?"

"She talked all that psycho-babble stuff about childhood trauma and how things in our formative years determine what we do in our older years."

"Did you talk about Haley with her?"

"We talked about Haley's past. Haley's father died when she was five years old, and Gemma seemed to think that this is the subconscious reason that Haley seeks the approval of older men. She's looking to mend that trauma and find someone to fill that painful void that she has deep inside. Gemma talked about money, and how it wasn't wealth that Haley was seeking out, but security."

"And you're confident in her ability to convince a jury of that?"

"Dr. Richardson has an impressive past. She studied at Harvard, got her PhD a few years ago, has testified in more than twenty-five trials, and she looks knowledgeable. She's the perfect expert witness to explain age-gap relationships. If she testifies, then any jury member on the fence about why Haley was attracted to Sammy will be convinced that it's a natural process for a very beautiful thirty-year-old to fall in love with an average overweight fifty-year-old." Bruce leaned closer to the air vent, trying to catch all the cool air. "How was Ken Turner?"

"Perfect." I tapped my hand on the steering wheel. "He's quick to anger, he's violent, and he lies so many times that he forgets what the truth is. If we put him on the stand for ten minutes, he'll have told ten lies. With the evidence that links him to the scene after Haley left, the jury will buy into the theory that he killed his brother for money."

"It's a risk if we call him to the stand. We have no idea what the prosecution will ask him under cross-examination, and he won't work with us to prepare him."

I nodded. "He's motivated by money, he lies through his teeth, and he was the last person to go to Sammy's house. It's a risk, but if we're losing the trial, we need to call him."

I parked on the side of the road near Haley's house. Looking across the road, I saw a beat-up white pickup. It was the same one that had been following me around after our visit to Paint's Biker Bar.

Bruce looked at me. He shook his head. I ignored him and stepped out of the car, heading straight toward the white pickup. I heard the car door close behind me. Bruce was following a few steps behind.

As we got closer to the pickup, the face of Jasper Rawlings became clearer. I stopped and studied the truck from a distance.

"Is that Rawlings?" Bruce asked as he stood next to me.

"It is."

Rawlings had his eyes focused on the front of Haley's house. That wasn't a good sign.

"What's he doing here?"

"I have no idea," I said as I stepped toward the truck.

"Dean," Bruce said, "be careful."

I didn't stop, striding across the street to confront him.

Rawlings caught sight of me as I walked toward him. He kept his eyes on me for a few long moments, then wound up his window.

The engine of the truck roared, and Rawlings pulled out of his parking space, rolling down the street away from me. I stood in the middle of the road and watched him disappear into the distance.

Trouble was brewing.

CHAPTER 18

Haley was standing on the front porch as Bruce and I approached. Wearing a white dress and a cream-colored cardigan, her arms were folded and her brow was furrowed.

"Did you know the person driving that truck?" she questioned as we stepped up to the front porch. Haley still looked healthy, her skin had a natural glow to it, but the stress was starting to show on her face. She had bags under her eyes and wrinkles that weren't there before. While her movements were still graceful, her hands were shaky.

"We did," I replied. "How long has he been parked there?"

"I noticed that truck there yesterday. I called the police and they said they'd send someone out to look at it, but no officers came. I called them again today, but they still haven't sent anyone out here. They don't want to help me."

"The police department are very busy, and they do a wonderful job for the community of Beaufort," Bruce explained. "They can't make it out to every call. They need to triage the calls that come in."

"That doesn't help me when I'm in trouble. Who was it?"

"Someone you shouldn't talk to."

She nodded and rubbed her arms for a few moments. "He's not the only one who's been parking there. I've noticed Ken Turner has been parked there a few times over the past week. I went out to talk to him, but he drove away as soon as I stepped on to the street."

"Do you know why Ken is parking out there?" Bruce questioned.

"He's looking for a way into the house. He thinks I have a video of something, but I have no idea what he's talking about."

"What's on the video?"

"I don't know, but Ken came here asking about it before they found Sammy's body. I told him I had no idea what he was talking about." She shook her head. "Sammy was a computer guy. He had lots of things stored on hard drives and flash drives and up in the cloud. It would take me years to go through it all, and the things I've looked at are really boring stuff. Videos of planes taking off and landing, cars driving past in the street, and there are even videos of him just going for a walk and nothing happens. He kept it all. Most of the hard drives were stored at his house on Dataw Island, but he asked to leave some of the videos here. I'd go through it, but there are literally thousands of hours."

"We'd like to review the footage, with your permission," Bruce said.

"Fine by me, but it would be weeks of work," she said. "But what do I do about these cars parked outside my house?"

"If you see them park there again, call the police, and then call me," I stated. "I won't be far away."

Haley nodded and led us inside the impressive house. There was a long marble staircase off the main entrance. The floors were original heart pine. Large windows let in natural light. The fireplaces had the original mantles, with black marble from Italy. Tall ceilings created a sense of light and space. According to the real estate profile, the home had five bedrooms, a library, two family rooms, a massive kitchen, a butler's pantry, and a den. Full of history, elegance, and space, it was a home worth fighting for.

We sat at the long dining room table, and Haley served us sweet tea.

"Currently, we're building a strategy for your defense," Bruce explained as he sipped on the sweet tea. "There are several ways for us to approach this. Our main strategy will be to highlight to the jury all the places where the Sheriff's Office went wrong with their investigation. They decided you had motive, and then that was it. They were so focused on you that they missed so many other pieces of evidence. If we make it into the courtroom, we'll make that clear to the jury."

"There's so much hatred out there." She rubbed her eyes several times. "Why do they hate me so much? I haven't done anything wrong."

"Our justice system is designed to be adversarial," I explained. "At its core, the system is Team A versus Team B. And the moment the police arrest you, you become Team B. The decision of who the bad guy is has already been made, the alleged 'truth' has already been found, and the focus is on winning, not on finding new evidence. That's our justice system, and that's why people on Team B need defense lawyers to represent them."

"Surely there's another way to do this?"

"Some countries have an inquisitional approach," I said. "In that approach, the court leads the investigation into the case, but that process is open to deceit and exploitation, because it's the duty of the court to scrutinize the evidence. If you can buy the court, you can buy the result. In an adversarial approach, it's less open to corruption as the two sides go head-to-head, with the court acting as the adjudicator. It's a contest, a fight, and that's why the process is so hostile."

"So, the prosecutors don't want the truth? They just want to win?"

"They trust that the law enforcement agencies have given them the correct information," Bruce said. "And circuit solicitors are elected officials. They need results, or they get voted out. That's not the individual's fault—that's just the system. If a circuit solicitor is 'soft' on crime, there would be outrage in the community. Even if crime statistics fell, if the media reports them as soft, they won't be re-elected. There are good people, great people even, in the Circuit Solicitor's Office, but they need results."

"They all think I did it," Haley whispered, before she turned and made unflinching eye contact with me. "I need to testify and explain to the jury what happened. I'll explain that Sammy was alive when I left, and I'll tell them that I would never hurt my Sammy."

"It's never a good idea for a defendant to testify," I explained. "If a defendant takes the stand, the jurors will forget about everything else, and they'll only ask themselves one question—do I believe what the person is saying? They'll forget about all the evidence, or lack of it, and they'll focus on your words only. And the prosecutors are very skilled lawyers, and they'll try to make you slip up. If you say one word out of place, if you make one tiny mistake, they'll focus on that and make you look like a liar. It's your choice to testify, but it's not recommended."

"What am I supposed to do then?"

"Let us fight for you," I said. "We're building a solid case to dispute their evidence, and we're adding to our witness list. Their strategy is focused on the motive, and an essential part of their argument is the age gap in your relationship with Sammy."

"Which leads us to our next point. We've contacted a psychologist who specializes in age-gap relationships named Dr. Gemma Richardson," Bruce added. "She'll testify to the jury that it's very normal behavior to be in an age-gap relationship. But before she commits to testifying in the case, she would like to speak with you. She's based in Florida and would be happy to chat for an hour over a video call. Ideally, she'd like to have multiple meetings with you, maybe five or so. Would you be willing to do that?"

"Is she on Team B?"

"She is," Bruce confirmed. "The prosecution is going to argue that the age gap in your relationship proves their theory that you were only after Sammy's money. However, Dr. Richardson will convince the jury that the age gap does not prove any such motive."

"Okay, I'll talk to her." There was a natural pause in the conversation, as Haley stared at her garden. "I can't go to prison," she said. "Who will look after my garden?"

I looked out the window and was about to make a joke about the dying sugar maples in her yard, but decided against it. "As we get closer to the trial date, we're also looking at other options to defend you. One of those options is to present a third party to the court as the guilty party. If we build our defense around this, then we need to be certain that the person is guilty. When—"

"Ken." The name snapped out of her mouth without hesitation. "It's his brother, Ken."

Bruce and I looked at each other and nodded.

"Ken was always trouble," Haley continued. "Rude, nasty, been to prison several times, and was always violent toward his older brother. Sammy was so sweet, but Ken was unbearable. It was strange to think they were brothers because their personalities were so different. I know drugs can do horrible things to a person, but Ken was so revolting. I hated being around him."

"And why do you think he killed Sammy?" Bruce leaned in. "What makes you so certain that he was involved?"

"A week before Sammy went missing, Ken came to Dataw Island to ask Sammy for money. Sammy wasn't home, so he asked me instead. He wanted ten thousand dollars. I asked him what it was for, and he said fishing equipment. Of course, he was lying. He was going to spend it on drugs. That's all he ever bought. I told him that we weren't going to give him any more money, and that he was on his own. He grabbed one of the knives in the kitchen and held

103

it in front of my face. He said to me that if Sammy wasn't around, I wouldn't get a cent of his inheritance."

"Did anyone else hear that?"

"No, but when I told Sammy what Ken did, Sammy was angry. It's what motivated him to change his will. He was so mad at Ken. Sammy had such high hopes for him, but Ken continually let him down. Threatening me with a knife was the last straw. He'd had enough." She shook her head. "Sammy had paid for Ken to go to rehab five times in the last year, but every time Ken went, he'd be back within a few days. He just couldn't hack it. He didn't want to get better."

"When you went to update the will, did Sammy tell the estate lawyer why he wanted to change it?"

"He did. I was there in the office with him, and Sammy told the lawyer that he thought the money was ruining Ken. He said Ken had to learn to stand on his own two feet, and until then, Ken would just keep going back to drugs."

"That's good," I explained. "If we can show that Sammy changed the will of his own desire, it weakens the motive even further for the prosecution. We'll talk to the estate planning lawyer that he used, David York, and we'll ask him if he'll testify about what Sammy said. There'll be attorney-client privileges that we need to consider; however, there will be notes about the will that Sammy wished to make public. Mr. York can testify about those notes."

"Thank you," she said. "I'll send him a message and tell him that you'll call."

Bruce looked at me and nodded.

I leaned forward. "Haley, while the judge has ruled that the prosecution can't make any reference to Prescott's disappearance, they will allow for the witnesses to talk about Prescott, and the prosecution has indicated that it will form part of their trial strategy. We need to be prepared for any surprises in court. Is there any place you can think Prescott would be? If we could talk to him, that might strengthen your case."

"The last time I heard from him was an email earlier this year, wishing me a happy birthday. The email came from a new address. When Maria reported Prescott missing again, I showed the police the email, and they tracked the IP address to Brazil."

"Is there anyone else who might know where Prescott is?"

"Maybe."

"Who?"

She drew a long breath. "Jessica."

"And who is Jessica?"

"Jessica Finch, Bronson's wife." She shook her head. "Jessica was Prescott's best friend growing up. They were so close, and then Jessica married his brother, Bronson. Jessica and Prescott were still close, even after his divorce from his first wife. Maria and I talked about Jessica once, but Maria assured me there was nothing going on between them. They had known each other since elementary school and were just friends, nothing more."

"Why would Jessica hide Prescott's location?"

"I'm not saying she'd hide it. I'm saying that Bronson is a brute, and he doesn't listen to her. Maybe she knows something, but nobody has been able to ask her. You might be able to draw out more information from her."

"I'm not sure she'll talk to us," Bruce noted. "Bronson hasn't been exactly friendly."

"Jessica was always lovely to me. If she can convince Bronson to talk to you, then he might be able to help."

"Then please send her a message," Bruce said. "Anything can help."

"I will, but she won't talk to you unless Bronson is around." She picked up her cell phone. "And a word of warning—Bronson Finch has a very short fuse."

CHAPTER 19

The humidity was drenching.

As Bruce and I drove to Bronson Finch's estate, the air conditioner was pumping in the car, but it was making little difference. A tropical storm was looming in the Atlantic Ocean, waiting to surge through the heat. The clouds that hovered over Beaufort were menacing, covering the city with a gray threatening presence, and there were weather warnings on every news channel.

The fifty-acre hunting estate off the Old House Road, thirty-five minutes from Beaufort, was an impressive property. At the end of a long driveway, there was a modern two-story brick home, and while the building looked imposing, it was the surrounding grounds that took my breath away. Spacious lawns, green enough to be a fairway on a golf course, led to the waterways. Out the front of the house, there were motorbikes, golf clubs, and an inground trampoline. At the side of the house was a basketball hoop, football uprights, and a soccer goal. It would be a child's dream to grow up in a place like this.

Haley had come through for us. She had messaged Jessica Finch, Bronson's wife, and she had said she was willing to answer some questions. We were cautious, but we also didn't want to miss the opportunity to get some information about Prescott. I was sure there would be surprises in the prosecution's case, and we needed to be ready for anything.

As Bruce and I approached the large home, I spotted Bronson standing on the front porch.

"Be nice," Bruce said as we parked. "We're here for information, that's all. This family will have talked to the Solicitor's Office many times since Haley was arrested. If we're nice, we might get a sneak peek at what they told Charlotte Sinclair."

I agreed and we stepped out into the thick humidity.

"Bronson, I know this place well," Bruce called out as he approached the house. "When I was younger, I visited the previous owners on this estate." It was always a good social tactic in the South to talk about family bonds. "I went hunting here a few times, out the western side of the estate, which runs along the river. I'm so glad you and Jessica are looking after it. It's even more beautiful now than I remember."

"What's he doing here?" Bronson glared at me as I took off my tie and flapped my shirt, trying to stop it sticking to my skin.

"He's part of the team," Bruce said. "He's a good man and I can vouch for him."

"He's a city boy." Bronson remained at the top of the stairs, staring at me. "He doesn't understand how things are done around here."

"I grew up here," I said as I approached. "I know how this place works."

Bronson grunted and turned back to the house. He led us inside, where Jessica was waiting. She greeted Bruce with a small hug and kiss on the cheek and offered me a handshake. She walked us through the kitchen and into the dining room, inviting us to sit around the large wooden table. The inside of the house looked like it was prepared for a spot in a country living magazine—there wasn't a thing out of place, not a speck of dust to find, and the furniture looked new and spotless. I could smell a hint of lemon in the air.

"How many kids do you have?" Bruce asked as he looked at the family photos hanging on the walls.

"Five boys." Jessica sighed wearily as she sat down at the dining table. "Our eldest is fifteen and we have two sets of twins—eight and five. They certainly keep us going, and I'm glad we've got all this space on the estate. It gives the boys a chance to run off the energy."

"How long have you lived here?" Bruce looked at Bronson. "The people I knew who lived out here sold up maybe fifteen years ago."

"We've been here five years." Bronson sat down. He was wearing a black T-shirt that showed off his numerous tattoos. "I bought the estate when the business was going well, but we're struggling to keep up the payments. We might have to sell it soon."

"We're doing all we can to keep it." Jessica reached out and rested a hand on Bronson's forearm. "It's so lovely having all this space. I couldn't imagine keeping all the boys locked up in a small house near the city." Jessica drew a long breath. "But you want to know about Prescott."

"We do."

"I don't even know why we're talking to you," Bronson grunted, and looked at his wife. "Jessica's too nice. She's always helping people. If it were up to me, I would've pulled the rifle on you the second you started coming up our driveway."

"We don't know if Haley did anything wrong," Jessica whispered, but there was pain in her voice. "We need to give her the benefit of the doubt. Innocent until proven guilty, right?"

"Facts don't change, even if there's no evidence." Bronson's fist slammed on the table. The table jumped under the pressure. "Of course she did, she killed Prescott. And now she's killed again."

The tension lingered as Bronson stood and walked to the side of the room.

"Jessica, we're hoping you could tell us when the last time you heard from Prescott might have been," I said, trying to not let the friction linger too long.

"It's hard to communicate when you're six feet under." Bronson walked out of the room, unable to control his anger.

"Sorry about that," Jessica said in a soft tone. I could still see Bronson in the kitchen, leaning against the kitchen bench, trying to calm himself down with deep breathing. "Bronson's got a short fuse."

"It's okay," Bruce said. "Jessica, is there anything you can tell us about Prescott's whereabouts?"

"Prescott was a family man until the divorce." Jessica drew a deep breath and leaned forward, keeping her voice low. "The divorce was hard on everyone, but it seemed Prescott was also going through a mid-life crisis. He bought a sports car, a jet-ski, and new golf clubs. He was spending big." She looked over her shoulder at Bronson. "And that frustrated Bronson, because they were business partners and Prescott seemed to be throwing the money away."

"Did they have a falling out?"

"Several." Jessica was almost whispering now. "Bronson wanted to buy Prescott out of the business, but they couldn't agree on the amount. And then Prescott married Haley, despite only knowing her for a few months. It all happened so quickly. Bronson knew it was a mess, so he made sure that Prescott had Haley sign a prenuptial agreement before the marriage. Bronson didn't want to lose everything."

"And then Prescott left?"

"Everything in the business was falling apart. Maria and Prescott weren't really getting along, and I'm not sure how his relationship with Haley was, but he was going off the rails. Bronson saw that he was also drinking heavily, and he was showing up to business meetings hungover. It wasn't a good look."

"And how's the business now?"

"Surviving, just. Thanks to Bronson's hard work." Jessica sighed again. "It would be easier if Bronson had full control of the business. He can't do a lot without Prescott's signature, but nobody has heard from him in years. We've tried to take it to the judge, but without evidence that he's died, the judge won't do anything. Bronson wants to convince the police that Prescott is dead, because then our life becomes a lot easier."

"I've had enough of these people in my home." Bronson entered the room and stood at the doorway. "It's time for them to leave."

I looked at Bruce and he nodded. We thanked Jessica for her hospitality and left with the uneasy feeling that Bronson was connected to everything.

CHAPTER 20

Bruce smashed the ball down the middle of the first fairway.

The sun was shining, the rolling fairways in front of us were luscious green, and a sea breeze had finally eased the humidity. When Bruce insisted on meeting over a round of golf, I was happy to agree.

I had spent the morning in court with Rhys. The magistrate had continued the restraining order and I argued for the conditions to be eased. The judge agreed, and our case was over in fifteen minutes. Rhys didn't say much all morning. He knew he had messed up, and he knew he was struggling to control his anger toward Paul Freeman. There was no justice in letting Paul walk out the doors of the prison after only five months of a ten-year sentence. He had been drunk, well over the legal limit, didn't have a license, and was over the speed limit. He had smashed into the side of Heather's car, leading to her death. Two years later, after lots of stalling tactics from the defense lawyers, Paul was convicted and sentenced to ten years in prison. It was little satisfaction for Rhys, who had lost the love of his life and the mother of his children, but there was at least some sense of justice, some sense that Paul hadn't just gotten away with it. When Paul was released after five months, officially due to overcrowding in the prison, that sense of justice was washed away.

My worry was that Rhys couldn't contain his anger forever.

I kept my head over the golf ball and swung hard. I put all the anger I had into the ball. I connected well, and the sweet, sweet feeling of a perfect drive sang through my body. Bruce scoffed as I outdrove his ball by forty-five yards, and said it was a lucky shot.

While Bruce and I walked through the first few holes, we talked about Haley Finch and her tendency to choose older men. Bruce talked about dating someone ten years younger when he broke up with his first wife, and how hard it had been because they were at different life stages. She wanted to party, and he wanted to settle down. Bruce told me that age wasn't the important aspect, but rather matching life stages, goals, and maturity levels. He talked about his second wife, who had left him to date a man fifteen years her junior. She was constantly called a cougar, and when she was referred to as the man's mother at a function they attended together, Bruce laughed. That relationship lasted a year before she went on to marry someone the same age. Bruce talked about how his third and current wife was at the same life stage as him when they met. I asked if they were the same age, but he skipped over the question. When I asked how old she was, he avoided the answer again. It didn't matter, he said, as long as he bought her flowers and jewelry for her birthday. When I asked when her birthday was, he grinned and said he had an annual reminder on his cell phone for that.

As we walked, I talked about Emma, how we were the same age, and at the same life stage. Bruce smiled and patted me on the shoulder. Some people are born for each other, he said. We spoke about life, loves, and everything in between, passing the time while chasing a little white ball around the green fairways.

"Do you feel like you've settled in?" Bruce asked as he lined up a putt on the fifth hole. "Feeling comfortable here?"

I shrugged.

"Don't tell me you still miss Chicago?" Bruce putted a ten-foot shot. "Help me understand. What do you miss about the city?"

I looked out at the fairway in front of us—long, rolling mounds of greenery lined by tall pine trees and sand bunkers. The sun glistened off the grass, and the blue sky framed the picturesque setting. But still, despite all the natural beauty, despite all the calmness, I missed Chicago.

"There's a feeling in a city that you're at the cutting edge of the world, a feeling that you're part of something bigger than yourself, and the ideas are fresh, they're new, they're life changing. You feel like you're in the beating heart of it all. It's the energy, Bruce. There's a buzz in the city that you just don't get here."

"Didn't you love the Water Festival? There was buzz through the whole county."

"The Water Festival was amazing. Highlight of the year around here." I lined up a fifteen-foot putt but ended up a foot short. "But it's one week, once a year. In the city, you have activities every night of the week. If you want to go to a basketball game, or a theatre show, or an inspirational talk, you've got it. If you want to join some people for discussions about philosophy, you can find it. If your niche is live punk bands that were big in the eighties, you've got it. If you're into the world's best restaurants, you've got it. There's always something to do."

"Tough on family life, though. You're expected to work hard in the city and put in the hours. And on top of that, you've got to put in the hours in the commute. I drive ten minutes from my house, and I'm at work. Ten minutes in one direction and I'm on the golf course, fifteen minutes in the other direction, I'm at the beach. You can't get that in the city," Bruce said. "Beaufort is the perfect place to raise a family. Kids have freedom here they don't get in the city."

"The thought had crossed my mind," I replied as I tapped in the next putt.

Bruce wrote down the scores and we walked to the next hole, and eventually, as always, the conversation turned back to work.

"Do you think Kayla was right?" Bruce asked after he hit a wayward drive. "That I'm blinded by Haley's beauty?"

"You're on your third marriage, Bruce," I quipped. "And by all reports, you were quite the player in your younger years."

"They were good times. Great memories for an old man to have." Bruce laughed. "But what about Haley? She's sweet and innocent, but maybe I've overlooked something? Maybe I've missed something."

"It doesn't matter what we think of her personally. It doesn't matter if we like her, hate her, or adore her. It doesn't matter if we think she did it, or if we think she's as pure and innocent as the driven snow. We've got a job to do, and that's to defend her constitutional right to a fair trial."

"All I hear is that your personal opinion is hiding behind a set of rules." Bruce shook his head. "You've got to open up those feelings one day."

"Not a chance," I said as I swung hard and watched my ball sail into the trees. "What did you think of Bronson?"

"He's strongly pushing for Prescott to be declared deceased." Bruce started walking down the fairway, wheeling his buggy behind him. "Maybe he knows something we don't."

"And Haley keeps stopping him by saying that Prescott is alive."

"Which makes sense because the second she agrees that he's dead, she would lose access to Prescott's bank accounts."

"I'm glad she paid us the retainer then." I followed Bruce down the fairway. "Did we receive the extra pieces of discovery?"

"We did, and it's not good," Bruce said. "They were holding back some of the witness statements from us. One is from a restaurant owner who saw Haley slap Sammy after dinner one night, and there are a few other character witnesses. But the most worrying statement is from a man name Leo McVeigh, a forty-nine-year-old computer technician who looks like he's never done a push-up in his life."

"And how does Leo McVeigh know Haley?"

"The very meek, weak, and bleak-looking man was dating Haley when she first moved from Wisconsin to South Carolina. He says that she drove from Wisconsin in her van with nothing more than a bag of clothes. They met in a nice bar, she seduced him, and they started dating. He offered her a place to stay, and she moved in within days."

I raised my eyebrows.

"It gets worse if you see his photo. Every juror will question why she dated a man like that," Bruce said. "And they'll come to the same conclusion—money."

"That's not good."

"And it gets even worse," Bruce continued. "He says that he remained friends with Haley and when he saw her a few days before Sammy's disappearance, she said, 'Sammy won't be alive much longer, and I'll have all his money soon.'"

"We need to talk to her about Leo's statement."

"We do." Bruce lined up his next shot. "Any updates from your side?"

"I talked to the estate lawyer from Charleston who wants to dispute the will for Ken. He's holding off making any movements until this trial is decided."

"Wise move." Bruce played a nice five-iron shot. He hit the ball up the hill, and watched as it bounced off the edge of the green and rolled next to the hole. He clenched his fist in celebration. "Under the probate code, the Slayer Statute prevents someone involved in the killing of another from benefiting in their estate. I'm not sure how it is in Chicago, but here, you don't even have to be convicted of murder for the Slayer Statute to apply. They base the statute off the preponderance of evidence that someone was involved in the killing, not reasonable doubt. Even if Haley is found not guilty by a criminal court, the Slayer Statute may still apply. The entire will is up for dispute, and it'll be a long process."

"And given that the previous will left a sizable amount to Ken, he has a fair chance of receiving half the money," I noted. "And of course, the estate lawyer will take a nice 20 percent cut."

"He's clever. He got in early, told Ken he wouldn't charge him anything until they won, and he'll get a big payday if Haley is found guilty. It's a good business move on his part," Bruce said as I walked under the trees to line up my next shot. "And the videos?"

"Haley was right—there are literally thousands of hours of footage on each hard drive. It seemed Sammy loved recording everything he did. I watched one sped-up video where he simply sat down and had a cup of coffee and read a book. That was it for over two hours."

"We all have our quirks. I'll contact one of the technology specialists in Charleston and get them to review it all. See if they can find anything."

I took my next shot, skimming past a tree trunk and somehow landing on the green. Bruce looked disappointed when I turned back to him. "How did the meeting with the estate planning lawyer go?"

"David York is an old friend of mine. Our paths have crossed many times before. He was very helpful when I called him." Bruce was shaking his head as we walked up to the green. "David said that Sammy wanted certain things made public after the will was read out. Obviously, Sammy didn't think it'd only be days later, but he said some nice things about Haley in his letter that accompanied the will. David can't disclose everything due to attorney-client privilege, but there's a lot he can."

"Will he testify about what the letter said?"

"David York is a good Southern man. He knows what he can say and what he can't say with attorney-client privilege, and he's willing to testify for us. I talked to him on the phone, but I'll buy him dinner next week, along with a few nice bourbons, and we'll discuss the options. He'll be an invaluable witness for us, especially because he'll confirm that Sammy was not under any undue pressure when he signed the new will."

"A good Southern man speaking with authority on the new will. He sounds like a winner." I walked up to my ball on the edge of the green. Twenty-five feet, sloping left, and a fast green. I took a practice putt, and then hit the ball sweetly. It started right, then rolled left, straight into the hole. "Just like that putt."

"Lucky shot." Bruce lined up his putt. It was closer than mine by ten yards. He putted and the ball rolled too far left. "The breeze picked up. It puts me off when it does that," he complained as he tapped his next shot in.

I smiled. It was nice to be playing golf in the fresh air, but it was more than that.

With David York's testimony, I felt like we had a chance to win.

CHAPTER 21

Thanks to a good short game, or the fact he was the one keeping score, Bruce pipped me by one stroke over nine holes. I favored the second option. He'd done it before, but I didn't care. For me, it wasn't a competition. Our game of golf wasn't a contest of skill. It was a social event, an excuse to spend time in the sun, wandering some of the most beautiful land in the country.

"There's one thing I know," Bruce said as we packed our clubs into the trunks of our cars. He pointed to the horizon. "The big one is blowing in this year."

"Everyone seems to be saying the same thing," I said. "How can everyone be so sure?"

"It's the humidity. It's eased off today, but it's supposed to be humid again later this week. The last time it was like this, we had a hurricane blow through. It destroyed a lot of the infrastructure around the marshes, and some of the docks have never been rebuilt."

And that's how knowledge was passed on in South Carolina. Decades of experience and decades of knowledge. It was the way of life here. People could send through findings from meteorologists, they could send through reports from the weather channels, but unless the locals could feel it in the air, unless they could sense the change in weather, they wouldn't believe it. No whizz-bang report or machine could beat generations of experience.

Driving home from our game, I drove through Lady's Island, a stunning part of the world. The trees were mature, the marshes were full of wildlife, and the sky was drowning in blue. There was a sense of calmness inherent in South Carolina, and it was getting to me. I was missing Chicago less and less each day. I had noticed my shoulders were starting to ease from their height of tension, my headaches were gone, and my overall well-being was at an all-time high.

I felt good. Better than good. I felt great. There was something about the lifestyle here that settled any stress I had.

As I drove, my mind wandered to how happy I felt. My decisions were becoming clearer—this was where I wanted to raise my family. This was where I wanted my son or daughter to learn about life. This was where I wanted to live with Emma and support her to become a mother.

Emma and I could afford great schools in Chicago, we could afford the best classroom education, but there was something about this place that you couldn't teach in a classroom. There was an appreciation for the world here that couldn't be taught in the city. There were great schools in South Carolina, but the outdoor lifestyle was the greatest educator.

With a smile on my face, I pulled into our driveway.

I noticed the front door was wide open. It was unlike Emma to leave it like that.

Confused, I left my golf clubs in the car. I approached the house.

"Emma?" I called out as I walked up the steps. "Emma?"

There was no response. I entered the house. She wasn't in the living room. She wasn't in the dining room.

"Emma?"

Again, there was no answer. It wasn't like her not to respond. My heart rate started increasing.

"Emma!"

Still no answer.

I went from room to room downstairs.

A half-drunk mug of coffee sat on the kitchen table. Her cell phone was on the kitchen island.

My breath caught in my throat. "Emma!"

I ran upstairs.

The bedroom door was open. She wasn't inside.

The door to the bathroom was closed.

I touched the handle. Twisted it.

It opened.

I pushed it open and found Emma on the tiled floor.

"Emma? What's wrong."

She was holding her stomach. She was sobbing.

"Emma, what's wrong?"

She looked at me with tears in her eyes.

"I lost the baby."

CHAPTER 22

A day later, we drove to the beach, barely saying a word to each other.

I parked the car, turned off the engine, and we sat in silence. We listened to the soft rain patter against the windshield, the white noise adding to the ambiance, the windows sweating on the inside as the moisture built up. I didn't know what to say, and Emma didn't speak for five minutes, letting the moment engulf us, drifting between wanting to talk and not wanting to say a word.

Through the rainy window, we stared out at the water, watching the waves rhythmically arrive in sets, break on the shore, and then pull back out into the enormous mass of the ocean.

Emma started sobbing.

I reached across and pulled her into my chest, wrapping my arm around her and holding her tight. The pain in her cries broke my heart. I hated seeing her in pain. I hated seeing her in agony. And I hated that I couldn't do anything about it.

As we sat, and the sounds of Emma's sobbing filled the cabin of the car, we were in a state where time passes but doesn't pass. Where the world continues moving, where the earth keeps spinning, where other people keep living their lives, but our world, the one we had built together, was stuck in an instant, holding on to what could've been, but desperate to move past it. The last day had been much like that, where we were ungrounded, stuck in a snow-like drift where pictures and words and conversations continue, combining to push the clock forward, but we felt left in the past.

We had spent the previous night in the hospital, going through the checks and prods and processes. Emma was strong, and the nurses were supportive. The doctors were emotionless, treating her like nothing more than another piece of work to complete, but they did their job well, they were respectful and they were thorough. After an ultrasound, the doctor defined it as a "complete miscarriage." The name didn't help. Emma went through a full check-up, but from a medical perspective, it was a "complete experience."

Overnight, Emma's eyes had changed. They didn't have the same shine. She had always been the measured one, the sensible one with intelligence beyond mine, the patience of a saint, and the generosity of a monk.

Emma sobbed for ten minutes, wetting my chest with her tears, and then she pulled back. She didn't wipe her tears away, and she didn't say a word as she opened the door and stepped out into the rain. She closed the door, and I stepped out as well. The rain was heavier now. The horizon was a dark gray threatening cloud sitting above the Atlantic, offering an ominous presence in the distance.

Emma started to walk along the beach, and I walked a step behind her. We had our heads bowed to protect us from the downpour of rain. We were getting drenched, but we didn't care. It didn't matter. Nothing mattered.

As the rain fell, the questions were rolling through my head as I was sure they were rolling through hers. Could we ever be parents? Was this in our future? I so desperately wanted to be a father, and I knew Emma was born to be a mother, but nature was taunting us. Persecuting us for some unknown reason. Maybe this wasn't in our future. Maybe we couldn't be parents. Maybe the future had other plans for us.

As we walked along the shoreline, listening to the waves crash against the sand, the rain eased.

I looked at Emma. Her hair was heavy with water, and her black top clung to her body. The rain had hidden her tears.

The sun pushed through a dark cloud, and a small slither of light hit the water in front of us. Emma stopped walking and looked at it. A rainbow appeared on the horizon.

Emma kicked off her shoes and walked into the ocean up to her knees. She folded her arms across her chest and looked at the rainbow. I followed her lead, kicking off my shoes and coming to stand next to her. I didn't say anything, and I didn't hold her. I gave her all the time she needed. The waves broke farther out from shore, and the trough pushed against our shins, before sucking the sand around our feet back into the ocean.

Emma stood still for a while, ignoring the ocean and the rain and the sand, and stared at the rainbow. She opened her arms, kissed her hands, and blew the kiss into the ocean, setting free her love to the future.

When she was ready, Emma turned to me. We hugged and held each other tight. I did my best to remain strong for her.

Without a word, Emma let go of the hug and walked out of the water. She walked back toward our car, leaving her shoes on the beach. I picked them up, then mine, and followed her.

We drove home in silence. We didn't play music and we didn't talk.

I was home when she told her mother the next day. They cried together. I couldn't be in the house when they were crying. It was too much.

Nighttime was the hardest. It was just us in a place where we had dreamed of raising a family. It was just us in a place we had dreamed of filling with children. It was just us in a house that we thought could be a home. We had dared to dream of the patter of feet. We had dared to dream of the giggles of toddlers. We had dared to dream of the joy of youngsters.

What were we being punished for?

I didn't understand how life could be so cruel. It was all we wanted. All we dreamed of. I wanted to throw the football with my son. I wanted to teach my daughter to swim. I wanted to teach my children how to draw. How to write. How to strive to be their best.

But most of all, I wanted to hold them. I wanted to praise them. I wanted to watch them grow, and to laugh, and to love. I wanted to be there for their cute first crush, I wanted to be there for their prom, I wanted to speak at their wedding.

But it had been taken from us.

Again. And again. And again.

"I thought the slower pace of life might have helped," Emma said in the early hours one morning. Neither of us could sleep. "But it's just me. It's all me. It's this stupid body. It won't let me have children. I'm a failure. I'm sorry, Dean. It's my fault. I let you down. I can't do it. I failed."

"It's not your fault," I whispered. "It's not your fault."

Over the next few days, we had many moments like that. First grief, then confusion, but that's where our emotional paths diverged.

For Emma, she felt hopelessness. Like she was a failure and couldn't do anything about it. I repeatedly told her it wasn't her fault, I told her she was strong, and I told her I loved her. None of my words seemed to ease the pain that plagued her.

As for me, I was hiding all my emotions under a veil of anger.

And I wasn't sure how long it would be until that anger exploded.

CHAPTER 23

I sat in the office, staring at the wall.

A week had passed since we had lost the baby, and I couldn't think of anything else. The agony in the pit of my stomach was ever present, and the headaches had returned with force. Not even the strongest medications could take them away.

I stared at the wall for an hour, tapping my finger on the edge of the desk so much that it started to hurt.

I had rolled through so many emotions, as had Emma. I was strong for her, holding her when she needed it, listening when she wanted to talk. As much as it hurt me, as much as it tore me apart, it hurt her more. I didn't cry with her, I didn't express my pain, and I didn't let her know how broken I felt. I had to be strong for her. I couldn't let her down now.

I told her it would be alright. I told her we would try again. I told her not to give up hope. But even my stoicism was taking a hit.

Did I even want to be a parent? Did I want to commit myself to a lifetime of helping a child? I was kidding myself if I thought that was an actual question. I needed a family of my own. I needed children. Could that ever happen? I didn't know the answer to that, and I hated not being in control of that outcome.

I hated myself for having hope. I hated myself for considering that everything was going to be alright. Would it ever be okay?

Or would life continue to throw bombs at us? Was a family even possible for us?

The longer I thought about it, the more the rage burned through me.

Besides the anger, other emotions came in floods—sadness, misery, melancholy. The feeling of the world not being fair stayed with me for a week. I saw families who treated their children like trash, and I felt like yelling at them to appreciate what they had. I saw mothers with strollers and felt a deep pain. I saw cars with car seats in them and felt sick to my stomach. Why couldn't we have that? What was it about us that kept us from having this?

When the emotional floods subsided, all that was left was anger. Over the past week, I had punched so many brick walls that my knuckles were scarred.

The humidity wasn't helping.

Its thickness was driving me insane. Clothes wouldn't dry. I couldn't sleep. I was constantly irritated.

I tried to change my focus, and the only thing that worked was the case files.

I focused much of my thinking on Haley Finch. It didn't matter if she was innocent, it didn't matter if she was guilty, what mattered was that it was my job to defend her in the court system.

Haley Finch was driven by money. That much was clear. She had grown up poor, born to a young mother and an older father. She had lost her father when she was five, and she sought out older men for financial, and perhaps emotional, security. It was outside societal norms, but there was nothing criminal in her actions.

There was a void in her heart, and she needed what she needed. Was she happy? I didn't know the answer to that question. What even was happiness? I didn't know, and I didn't really care. I stopped caring about so many things.

Lightning cracked outside my window, and it brought me back to reality. Another afternoon storm had arrived. With the streets already flooded by weeks of heavy rains, it was going to be a problem for the roads.

I stared out the window and questioned everything in my life. Had I made the right decisions? Had I taken the right path? What would've happened if I had chosen a different city, a different profession, a different focus?

At one point, Bruce entered my office and said that he had asked Haley about Leo McVeigh's comments. She confirmed she had said them, but they had been taken out of context. It wasn't a good look, Bruce explained. He told Haley that we should stall and apply to the court for more time before the trial, but Haley wanted the case finished. She was innocent, she said, and her life had been put on hold long enough. She wanted to go to trial, and she wanted to stop the rumors.

He then explained that the technology specialists from Charleston hadn't been able to find anything on the thousands of hours of videos from Sammy's life. Without knowing what they were looking for, they said it would cost twenty-five thousand dollars for someone to sit down and document each video. Bruce declined to pay that amount and returned the hard drives to Haley.

After a while, Bruce sensed that I was distracted and left my office.

In my state of wallowing self-pity, my cell phone rang. It was Haley.

There was a pickup truck outside her house again. It was a different one, she said. But she knew they were watching the house. Her voice was shaking.

She had called the police, and they told her they couldn't do anything about it for the next hour.

Without a thought running through my head, I walked out of the office, got into my car, and drove to her house. I parked in her driveway, stepped out, and looked across the road.

There, on the other side of the street, was Ken Turner, parked in an old pickup.

I stormed across the road as the rain fell. Ken noticed as I came closer. He stared at me as I approached.

If he wanted to play the intimidation game, then I was willing to play as well.

I gripped his door handle and swung his truck door open.

"What the—" were the only words he could manage as I grabbed him by the collar and dragged him on to the road.

I threw him on to the ground and swung hard. My right fist connected with his cheekbone, once, twice, three times. When the blood began pouring from his nose, I swung again. He was out cold.

Out of breath, I stood over his body, fists clenched.

I stared at his bloodied face for a long moment, then walked away.

CHAPTER 24

"You put him in the hospital?!" Bruce stormed into my office. "We don't need vigilantes in Beaufort, Dean! You're a lawyer. What on earth were you thinking?"

"I wasn't thinking."

"You're right about that." Bruce huffed and paced the back of my office. "Your stupid actions could jeopardize our whole case."

"I was acting in the defense of others, Bruce," I said. "I was within the law."

"Beating a man so he ends up in hospital is not within the law. Ken Turner was legally parked on the side of the road, and you threw him out of his car and hit him multiple times. Nothing is broken, but he arrived at the hospital bloodied and bruised."

"Ken Turner was threatening Haley. She called the police and they responded that they were too busy to help. I had to defend her."

"Defending her is a job for the police." Bruce huffed again and sat down opposite my desk. The chair almost broke under the heavy pressure. "You've become too personally involved in this case, Dean. You're her lawyer. You're not her bodyguard."

I nodded but didn't engage.

"You could be disbarred for this," Bruce continued. "And then where does that leave us?"

"With a lot of headaches."

"Arrgh," he groaned in frustration. "But you're lucky. I've just gotten off the phone with the officer in charge, and Ken Turner has said he doesn't want to press charges. He has a strong dislike for law enforcement and doesn't want to deal with them any more than he needs to. The decision still rests with the police whether the charges go ahead, but the detective has told me that Ken is refusing to provide a complete statement." Bruce looked at me. "Ken Turner told the investigator that he'll deal with it himself."

"Let him come."

"This is not a war. This is a court case. This is us defending a woman in court, not a street brawl." Bruce threw his head back as Kayla walked into the office.

She grimaced as she looked at me. "You okay?"

I nodded. "I'm fine."

"What happened?"

"Dean lost his mind," Bruce explained. "Ken Turner was parked outside Haley's house again. He's parked out the front a few times. He wasn't even breaking the law. He was allowed to park on the side of the road."

"And you thought you'd hit him because of that?" Kayla asked.

"He's been parking there in an attempt to intimidate Haley. That's the only reason. She's called the police several times, and they've done nothing about. I needed to put a stop to it."

"The police said they were convinced Ken was looking for a way to break into her house," Bruce explained. "Haley has a good security system, and they think Ken was studying the house and looking for a weakness in the system, although he didn't admit anything."

"Then I saved Haley from having her house broken into. I was acting in defense of others."

"What you did was assault," Bruce grunted. "If he'd gotten out of the car and tried to push you, then fine. I get it. But you pulled him out of the car and then beat him. It wasn't even a fair fight. The guy is half your size, for crying out loud."

I nodded. "If he wants to continue with the assault charge, then I'll argue it was in defense of others. I'll argue that he was harassing and intimidating Haley, she called the police and then called me. I went to defend her."

Bruce shook his head.

"Do you need anything?" Kayla asked. "Coffee? Sweet tea?"

"He needs a Valium," Bruce said. "Probably the whole bottle."

"Well, I don't have any of those, but if you need anything, I'll be out in the reception area." Kayla had a caring touch. "But please, for my sake, don't go starting any more fights. I don't like it."

"Yes, ma'am," I said. "And thank you, Kayla."

Kayla rested a calming hand on Bruce's shoulder and then left the room.

Bruce huffed and then left the room after her. I stared at my hands for a few moments before Kayla entered the room again.

"I think you need a Coke." She passed a can to me. She knew I wouldn't say no. She always knew when someone needed someone to talk to, or a shoulder to lean on. "Do you want to talk? I'm avoiding going home anyway. My husband is in charge of cooking and cleaning tonight, and it's nice to have a little break from all the house duties."

I cracked the top of the can and took a sip. I could feel the cooling soda run down my throat and into my chest.

"Dean, are you okay?"

Her question wasn't flippant, it wasn't dismissive, and it wasn't just a conversation. Her words were said with sincerity, care, and love. That feeling radiated across the room.

I looked at the Coke can for a few moments and back at her. "We're okay."

"We're?" Kayla could read the room better than most. She sat back, nodding. "If you need me, I'm always happy to talk."

"Thank you, Kayla. I appreciate you."

She held her eyes on me for a long moment, nodded, and then left.

Bruce entered five minutes later. He walked over to my desk, drew a long breath, and exhaled loudly. "Dean, is everything okay?"

I looked away, staring at the wall.

"Dean, I'm your friend first and your colleague second."

"Thanks, Bruce," I acknowledged, but kept my eyes on the wall. "It's personal . . . and I don't know what else to say."

Bruce walked around the desk and rested his hand on my shoulder. "Have a few days off. Spend some time in nature and get your head right."

He held his hand on my shoulder for a long moment, and then patted it twice.

CHAPTER 25

When I arrived home, there were flowers on the bench with a message from Kayla.

Emma asked if I had told her, and I explained that I hadn't, but that Kayla had a sixth sense about these things. Emma understood. She said Kayla was one of the most emotionally intelligent people she'd ever met.

I took Bruce's advice and drove Emma up into the southern Appalachian Mountains for a few days. After a five-hour drive, we rolled into Highlands, a small town on a plateau near the Nantahala National Forest in North Carolina. The quaint town was postcard-perfect, and was a nice, cooler retreat from the heat of the Lowcountry. We stayed in a log cabin on the edge of town, still within walking distance of the nearby restaurants and coffee shops.

Over the next four days, Emma and I walked the trails, admired the waterfalls, and snapped photos of the wildlife. We stopped in craft shops, wandered through clothing stores, and sampled local foods in the diners. There were moments where we smiled, moments where we even laughed a little, but it was all tempered. Mostly, we kept to ourselves and avoided the crowds.

On our fourth night, our last in the cabin, the temperature dropped below fifty, and we set up the log fire. In front of the open fireplace, we rested on a soft rug and appreciated the quiet atmosphere.

Mountain quiet was different to Lowcountry quiet. There was a stillness here, a tranquility that encouraged staying indoors, snuggling away from the world, and forgetting about everything else that existed. With a glass of red wine each, we opened up to each other.

We talked about the memories we had in South Carolina.

We talked about learning to fish in our teenage years, determined to catch the big one as the sun set on the horizon. We talked about the oyster roasts and their overpowering smells. We talked about cooking, and the Southern recipes that told us we were home. We talked about the nights we partied, how we often ended up at Ernest's, a dive bar hidden off Bay Street. We talked about our old friends, and how everyone was so welcoming on our return. We talked about the summers swimming in the rivers and lakes, cooling off as the humidity thickened the air. We snickered at the brief winters, how locals dressed like they were visiting Chicago in January, and how the long, dark nights seemed to disappear as quickly as they arrived. We talked about the smells, the camellias, the pluff mud, the salty seafood.

We remembered the tropical storms that had blown through, pushing massive surges and tearing the marina apart. We remembered a terrifying hurricane from our younger years, how we had both spent nights sheltering in one room with our separate families with no power and no phones. We remembered the anxiety we had felt when the edge of the storm hit our city.

And we talked about us.

We talked about when we met in high school, and how we had fallen in love. We talked about the joy we felt. The nerves. The anxiety. We remembered the moments of apprehension we both felt on our first date to the movies, how new and exciting it had felt to hold hands. We talked about how we had grown with each other, how we became adults side by side.

We talked about our young adult years. How we used to drive to Hilton Head to watch the sun set in autumn and how dazzled we were by the array of stunning colors on the horizon. We talked about our nights out at the local bars, and the nights we were too drunk to remember.

We talked about my proposal and our wedding. We talked about our honeymoon to Australia and being blown away by the relaxed and free nature of the people. We talked about the kangaroos, the open spaces, and the boating-camping-fishing lifestyle that was so similar to that of the Lowcountry. We talked about arriving home to a surprise party organized by my sister. Emma talked about our niece and nephew, and how strong they were.

We talked about my grandparents, about her mother, and about how family was so essential to who we were. We talked about my father and his new wife. We talked about my mother and Emma's father, both long passed. We talked about the memories we had of them, and how those beautiful people had shaped us into who we were.

We talked about the weather, about how Chicago was horrible in winter but alive in summer. And about the Lowcountry, and how everyone was inside during summer, and alive during winter. We talked about the ups and downs we'd faced.

"It hurts, Dean," Emma whispered at one point. "It hurts."

I hugged her and held her tight.

She asked if I was doing okay, and I told her the truth. I was honest. I was open. I told her that it hurt, and that I wasn't doing okay. I was comfortable being vulnerable when times weren't tough, I was comfortable expressing my emotions when it didn't matter, but now, it felt weird to be open and honest.

Emma reacted. She held me tighter and thanked me for being honest. She kissed my cheek and told me she loved me.

It was all I needed to hear.

We spent the evening with a glass of wine in our hands. Our joy was tempered, as were our emotions. We were both doing our best to keep it together, to try and ward off the sadness that was lingering just beyond the door.

We still had hope for the future, we still believed we could be parents, but the journey was beginning to take its toll. I could see it in Emma's eyes. They looked duller, less lively, like a piece of her had been left behind with each miscarriage.

We snuggled together in front of the fire, knowing that the world could throw anything at us, and we would always have each other.

CHAPTER 26

I met Luke Sanford in the parking lot of the Solicitor's Office Headquarters in the unincorporated community of Okatie, twenty-five minutes from Beaufort, on Monday afternoon. Luke walked with a slight limp, coming straight from a hard day of work. His jeans were dirty, his boots were scuffed, and he was wearing a black T-shirt that hid most of the dirt stains.

"Hurt your leg?" I asked as he approached.

He waved my comment away. "I'm always hurting something. It's part of the job. A rock falls here, a tree branch swings the wrong way, a new employee runs over your foot with the compact excavator."

"That must've hurt."

"He tells me it was an accident, but he's buying the beers this weekend." Luke smiled. "Heard a friend of yours fell out of his car and on to the road."

"He fell out of the car and right on to my knuckles."

"I knew I liked you," Luke said. "Now, if you'll let me do the same to Stephen Freeman, we could sort this whole thing out now."

"You can do that to Stephen Freeman if you want to spend the next ten years locked up."

"Why do you get to have all the fun?"

"It's like the old saying, 'Do as I say, and not as I do.'" I patted him on the shoulder. "Are you ready to meet with the prosecution?"

"Only if I have to," he grunted. "I hate these sorts of meetings. It gets under my skin how these guys think all their rules and regulations should override what's morally right and wrong."

"They'd like to meet and discuss the terms of a deal to have this case ended," I explained. "The assistant solicitor asked for you to be there so he could talk with you directly."

"Until I started this process, I never understood how people could plead guilty to something they're innocent of. Now I understand how innocent people are pressured into admitting things they didn't do."

"You're not innocent, Luke. You dug up someone's driveway with a compact excavator."

"Whatever," he said with a chuckle. "Tomato, potato; call it whatever you want. But it reminds me of what my father always used to say, 'You don't get what you deserve, you get what you negotiate.'"

"Wise man," I said as I led him into the building. We greeted the receptionist and were directed to one of the meeting rooms down the wide hallway.

We entered and Luke sat down next to the door, most likely so he could make a quick escape if he needed to.

The beige-colored meeting room looked like it could've been in any government office across the country. The white walls were empty of art or photos, there was a dying potted plant in the corner, and a whiteboard to the left. The white laminate table in the middle of the room had no character, no history, and no feeling, and the smell of pine cleaning products filled the air. It was like any sense of life or expression had been sucked out of the atmosphere.

After fifteen minutes of sitting in the asylum-like room, when Luke looked like he was ready to go insane, Angus Blessington entered and introduced himself. As a figure of bureaucracy, Blessington had an effect on Luke Sanford. He sat up straighter. Pushed his arms out wide. Puffed his chest out. There was no doubt about it, Luke was ready for a fight.

Angus Blessington looked like he had never even seen a person do a hard day's work in his thirty-five years on the planet. His soft white skin looked moisturized, his floppy brown hair looked bouncy, and his smug smile looked incredibly annoying. He was dressed in a black suit with a red tie, not a thing out of place.

Blessington was more than just a person in the room—he was the State, sitting there, rigid and tight, stubborn and relentless, speaking in a dull tone that sucked all emotion out of the situation.

It's hard not to despise strict forms of officialdom. Their rules can reduce life and passion and emotions into a set of overarching instructions, applied to every situation without pretense or consideration.

I will never despise someone for their job—there is honor in all work—but I certainly despised some people employed by government administrations. For a small group of weak-willed people, their work forced them to be a lesser version of themselves, a hollowed-out, scrubbed down, good-boy version of what they truly were. Most workers could throw off the uniform at the end of the day, breathe a sigh of relief, and become who they were meant to be—expressive, creative, and dynamic—but for some workers, stuck in decades of mundanity, they started to forget to make the transition at the end of the day, slowly slipping into the twenty-four-seven version of government rules.

In places like Beaufort, where community had existed and progressed and thrived, the community had figured out how to live with moral decency, people had worked out how to survive as a collective, but the State, with its rules and decrees and orders, wanted to take the autonomy away from the families who had been co-existing for generations, as if the same set of rules applied to the streets of the state capital should be applied to the small town of Beaufort.

Blessington spoke in a monotone, stupefying us for ten minutes as he talked about the case, almost putting us to sleep. While his voice was dull and lifeless, his delivery of information was even worse. I could see Luke was struggling to focus as well.

"What's the best offer?" I said once I thought he had finished his spiel.

Blessington looked at me, confused. Obviously, he hadn't finished his monologue yet, but he settled and tried to answer my question. "The State . . ." He flicked a piece of paper in the file in front of him. "The State will drop the charges if Mr. Sanford agrees to repair the driveway and pay the victim for his inconvenience."

"I won't do that." Luke sat up straight. "Where is he anyway? Why didn't Stephen Freeman come here and confront me like a man?"

"He's very busy," Blessington stated. "And if the offer isn't agreed upon today, then I must warn you that this case will go to court, and you can be sure that the media will cover this story. That won't be good for your business, Mr. Sanford."

Luke's knuckles clenched. I knew why. The way Blessington said, "Sanford," with a slow patronizing drawl, was incredibly annoying.

"We came here in good faith to negotiate these charges," I said. "But all you want to do is threaten my client with destroying his business reputation."

"Not at all. We're willing to negotiate, but our negotiation is set in stone. The case is thrown out if he agrees to fix the driveway and compensate the victim. That's our negotiation. Take it or leave it."

"He'll consider pleading guilty to a misdemeanor, as the value of the driveway is under two thousand dollars, but he won't be fixing the driveway, and nor will he be compensating Stephen Freeman."

Blessington looked at Luke, but Luke didn't respond.

"Then the meeting is done." Blessington closed his file and stood. "Thank you for your time, gentlemen."

Blessington left the room without another word, leaving us feeling that we'd been assaulted by bureaucracy. Blessington had no interest in negotiation, but I also didn't think he had the power to negotiate. He was doing as he was told, and not straying from the company line.

Luke was quiet as I led him out of the offices and into the parking lot. When we reached my car, I could see he was about to explode.

"I'd like to see him talk to me like that out here." Luke's fists were clenched as he spoke. "That smug little prick was hiding behind his set of rules, as if they apply to real life. That's not real life. This is. I'll wait for him here and then we'll talk."

"Settle down, Luke," I said. "The justice system is not the only way to win this case."

"What are you saying?"

I looked around the parking lot and when I couldn't see anyone close by, I continued, "Freeman wants to take this to the media, but what he doesn't understand is that the way media is influenced has changed."

"Meaning?"

"Stephen Freeman comes from a time when powerful people influenced the media by buying advertising space and ensuring the media honored their opinions. That still happens a lot, but things are different now," I explained. "Social media influences mainstream media now. You can have a groundswell of support that becomes too big to ignore, and then the mainstream media has no choice but to report on it."

"What are you suggesting?"

"I'm suggesting that you ask around and see if anyone else is willing to talk about the payment problems they've had with Stephen Freeman. Now, Freeman's influence will ensure those opinions will never make it on to the television, but they'll spread like wildfire through social media."

"What about evidence to back up the claims?"

"You don't need it," I said. "With social media, you don't need facts and you don't need evidence. All you need are good storytellers."

Luke nodded several times and then waved his index finger in the air. "I like the way you think."

CHAPTER 27

Over the following weeks, as we prepared for trial, I went through waves of different emotions. I was focused, I was working hard, doing my best to avoid my feelings, but overall, I felt broken.

The sick feeling in my stomach never left me. I hated the feeling of being out of control. I hated that Emma was hurting. And I hated that I couldn't help her.

We were only days away from Haley's case going to trial, and my head wasn't clear.

I couldn't sleep.

I spent the nights tossing and turning and sweating under the thick humidity. The air conditioner was working its hardest, but still the night air was thick and sticky.

One Saturday morning, two days before the trial began, I'd had enough.

Trying not to disturb Emma, I eased out of bed and went to the kitchen at 3:05 a.m. Knowing there was little chance I would go back to sleep, I opened my laptop, checked my emails, and began to review files for the murder trial. At 5 a.m., I dressed in my running gear and hit the streets.

I stretched, walked a block, and then started my morning jog.

It was quiet, eerie, at that time of the morning. There was no wind, not a breath to move the Spanish moss, and the bugs were quiet. There was no traffic, and no movement from the houses nearby.

I was alone out here, and I felt uneasy. There was something about Lowcountry quiet. There was no background noise, and no constant hum of activity nearby, almost as if the world had stopped moving.

I jogged to the waterfront and as the sun crept over the horizon, the city began to wake.

Gradually, the birds began to make noise, and the traffic started to build. I could smell coffee brewing as I jogged past City Latte on Carteret Street, and I said good morning to the walkers out early. When I jogged past the marsh, I was met by the strong smells of the tangy, oystery, salty goodness of the pluff mud. Farther along, the smell of fresh bread wafted out of a house, and the smells of the blooming perennial flowers tickled my nose.

I returned home, stretched, and showered, and then made Emma breakfast in bed. I made her a coffee and a fresh fruit platter, and she thanked me with a kiss. I didn't expect her to get out of bed until midday. She had never been like that before; she had always been an early riser, but over the past few weeks, she had been staying in bed more and more. I was concerned, but she was doing the best she could. I supported her in every way possible, but more than anything, I knew she needed time.

At 9 a.m., Granddad Lincoln called.

He invited me out for a Saturday morning fish in a new spot, and I jumped at the chance. He had heard about the spot from a friend of friend of a friend. That's how things worked in Beaufort. No need for the internet, and no need for social media. Word of mouth was still the most effective way to communicate.

Granddad Lincoln's friend of a friend of a friend had told him that the flounder were moving along the Coosaw River and were tucked beneath a certain dock, only fifteen minutes from his favorite spot. We were almost guaranteed to catch one, he said; even a city boy like me could do it.

Fishing was one of the great passions of South Carolina, surrounded as it was by waterways. Fishing was an excuse to be on the river, over the river, or next to the river, appreciating the area's stunning beauty.

When we arrived, the rain started to fall, a few drops at first, and I looked to the west. Judging by the clouds and the winds, it would pass quickly. Granddad Lincoln also wasn't fazed. We set up our fishing spot by the marsh and dropped our lines in the water.

"When does the trial start?" he asked.

"Monday morning."

"Think you'll win?"

I shrugged. "It's hard to tell. Everything comes down to the make-up of that jury. If we get the right jury, we win it before the opening statements."

"And do you think Ken Turner will come back at you after what you did to him?"

I stared at the horizon for a long moment before I turned to him and nodded. "I'm certain of it."

We fished for another hour, getting the occasional bite, but mostly, we just enjoyed the calm splendor of the river. After a while, I could tell that Granddad Lincoln was angling to ask a tough question.

"How's Emma?" he asked, and I knew there was more to the question.

"She's okay."

"Dean, I don't know what's going on, but I want you to know, we're here for you. All of us are. This isn't like the city—we're a community here, and that means sharing your ups, but also sharing your downs. We're all here for you."

"Thanks, old man," I quipped. "And I mean, I could tell you anything because you're not far off getting dementia."

He scoffed. "I have many years of solid thinking left." He paused, but I could tell he was about to say something else. I let the silence sit between us until he was ready. "It's okay to be vulnerable, Dean. It's okay to admit that you're hurt."

The comment surprised me. I hadn't expected it from him. I stared at my fishing rod, hoping that a fish would bite and I could avoid the emotional conversation.

"I'll tell you something that took me my entire life to learn." Granddad Lincoln looked out at the water, avoiding eye contact. "Men need to be strong in times of war, and vulnerable in times of peace."

The river shimmered past us. Birds flew through the blue sky. A boat in the distance gently moved down the river.

And I couldn't stop thinking about Granddad Lincoln's statement.

"Most men haven't realized how to switch between the two," Granddad Lincoln continued after several minutes. "That's why the suicide rate is so high in older men. It's five times higher than in women of the same age. And it happens because men haven't learned to switch between being strong and being vulnerable."

"Men aren't supposed to panic," I said without a thought.

"Never panic," he agreed. "But we all need to have moments of vulnerability. Don't go home and cry every night, don't start telling cashiers your emotional problems, but admit the truth of your feelings to yourself. Be strong, be stoic, but be honest. Give yourself a moment to recognize the emotion, to feel it, to deal with it, and then move on. The strongest men I've met have been the ones who can do that. They can be strong, they can be tough, and most importantly, they can be vulnerable."

The quiet sat over us for the next fifteen minutes. When I reeled in a flounder, our conversation turned to fishing. Granddad Lincoln reeled in another, and said it was time to pack. We had enough for dinner. No need to be greedy, he said.

It wasn't the Lowcountry way.

CHAPTER 28

INDICTMENT

STATE OF SOUTH CAROLINA

COUNTY OF BEAUFORT

IN THE COURT OF GENERAL SESSIONS

INDICTMENT NO.: 2025-AB-15-295

STATE OF SOUTH CAROLINA, V. HALEY ROSE FINCH, DEFENDANT

At a Court of General Sessions, convened on 5th of August, the Grand Jurors of Beaufort County present upon their oath:
Murder.

S.C. CODE SECTION 16-3-10. MURDER

That on or about 5th of July, the defendant, HALEY ROSE FINCH, in Beaufort County, did murder with malice aforethought. To wit: HALEY ROSE FINCH did murder SAMUEL "SAMMY"

TURNER per violation of Section 16-3-10 South Carolina Code of Laws (1976) as amended.

Against the peace and dignity of the State, and contrary to the statute in such case made and provided.

———

The Beaufort County Courthouse was the centerpiece of law and order in the county, bringing all the county's felony cases to one central location. Set over expansive landscaped grounds, the two-story red-brick structure was part of the larger Beaufort County Government Center near the center of downtown Beaufort, sitting on the edge of Battery Creek.

As I waited for Haley to arrive in the parking lot, I could see the media vans gathered near the entrance. They were hungry for a story, hungry for a new twist, and desperate for a new headline. The media had dubbed her "The Housewife Killer," and many outlets suggested she had been involved in more than one murder, although no outlet had yet stated she was responsible for Prescott's disappearance. A podcaster had contacted our office, looking for an interview, declaring that she, and only she, could give Haley the chance at a fair interview. We rejected her offer.

Haley rolled into the parking lot in her clean Mercedes sedan and stopped under the shade of a live oak tree. She had dressed in a black business suit, and was doing her best to appear bland, boring, and mundane. That's what we wanted her to look like to the jury.

I greeted her and then explained the process for entering the courthouse. "Haley, the only thing you can say to the media is 'no comment.' They're going to shout at you, they're going to throw questions at you, and they're going to bait you, but you can't respond. Keep your head down and focus on getting into the courthouse. If you give them a death stare or roll your eyes, your face will lead every news outlet in the state. We can't give them that. Keep your face looking close to tears, and do not smile. We don't want the media to portray you as a crazy person."

Haley nodded but didn't respond verbally. She was clearly nervous.

I led her toward the media pack, shielding her behind me as we approached. Once the media saw us, they circled like vultures. I didn't stop walking, using my tall frame to push through the pack, ensuring Haley was right behind me. The reporters shouted questions, pressed Haley for an answer, but she gave them nothing.

We didn't speak again until we were through security and inside the foyer, where Bruce was waiting for us.

"That was good, Haley." I patted her on the shoulder. "You did well."

She nodded, but again didn't respond verbally.

Bruce spoke for a few moments about the heat and humidity, trying to ease Haley's nerves, before I led us toward the courtroom.

The courtroom was stuffy, and we both expressed our surprise as we walked in. Bruce went straight to the bailiff and asked if there was a problem with the air conditioner. The bailiff confirmed there had been an issue overnight, and it was now fixed. He said it would be cooler in fifteen minutes. I hoped he was right or people would start fainting.

Without a jury, a judge, or an audience, the courtroom was quiet, not giving any indication this was a room where lives were destroyed, celebrated, or changed forever. Despite the quiet, there was a lingering anxiety in the room, a tension that hung in the air.

Bruce and I sat at the defense table, and Haley sat next to us. Her leg was bouncing up and down under the table and she was struggling to sit still. She was leaning forward, holding on to her stomach. I asked her to take long, slow, deep breaths, and that helped for a few moments, but the twitching leg started as soon as she stopped the exaggerated breathing.

Charlotte Sinclair, leading the prosecution team, entered fifteen minutes later. She looked confident. Poised. Assertive. She held herself well, shoulders back, chin up. She felt they had the winning case. When I greeted her, she looked at me with professional disdain.

The gallery remained empty for *voir dire*, the jury selection process.

"All rise," the bailiff called out at 10:15 a.m. "The Honorable Judge Dalton presiding."

Judge Dalton entered the room with a confident gait. He looked over his courtroom with the appearance of a man who was in charge. He took his time, sat down, coughed, and then opened his laptop. He spoke to the lawyers for a few moments, welcoming us to the court, and ensuring there were no more pre-trial motions to be submitted. He then instructed the bailiff to bring in the first round of potential jurors.

We spent the day in the jury selection process.

Group by group, the pool of potential jurors was brought in. Prior to the trial, the prosecution had settled on the wording for a questionnaire, with the questions agreed upon by Bruce. The questionnaire eliminated all those who were related to the victims, had dealings with the accused, or had strong biases about the case.

Examining the jurors' belief systems was an essential step in the process. Understanding their values and opinions helped the lawyers predict how they might react to evidence, how they would react to certain witnesses, and how they would react to the defendant. While understanding how the individual jurors viewed authority, how they viewed social issues, and how they viewed the justice system helped the lawyers anticipate how a juror might vote, the jurors' personal experiences could also determine an outcome.

As the jury pool was brought in groups of twenty-five people at a time, Sinclair and Bruce rattled off questions to understand their subtle biases. While the potential jurors were answering questions, all the lawyers were studying not only the language of their responses, but also their behavior. The person with their arms folded appeared defensive, the person with their head down seemed timid, and the person chomping down on their chewing gum seemed like a rule breaker.

To drill further into their biases, Bruce asked the potential jurors about whether they enjoyed their job. Sinclair asked if they liked their neighbors. Bruce asked if they voted in elections. Sinclair questioned what they thought of law enforcement. Did they like to join social groups? Were they happy with the younger generations? What was their opinion on hard work? Did they drive a nice car? Did they donate to charity?

Bruce was looking for jurors who were intelligent enough to understand the legal standard of reasonable doubt, and Sinclair was looking for jurors who would be swayed by emotional decisions. Bruce needed people of strong character who felt they would need to protect someone like Haley, and Sinclair needed people who would be jealous of Haley's history of dating rich men.

After almost a full day of questioning, after hours upon hours of questions and quizzes and answers, the jury was finally selected.

It wasn't perfect, it wasn't an outright win, but with the members selected, we had a chance.

Five jurors were under forty, five were middle-aged, and two were past retirement age. There was the owner of a trucking company, a hairdresser, and a janitor. One was a freelance animator, another an IT technician. One man worked with printers; another was an art teacher. Two worked for the government, there was a retired Air Force veteran, and a carpenter. One was a student, and several worked part-time. Seven men, five women.

While the jury was made up of twelve individuals, they were acting as a collective. A strong leader in the jury deliberation room was as important as any witness. It was easy to identify the strong leaders in the jury box.

For the prosecution, it was juror ten. A blonde, religious mother of two with impeccable dress sense, she looked like she was poised to ask the judge for his manager if he stepped out of line.

For us, it was juror five—a tall, square-jawed civil engineer proud to be performing his duty to the court. He carried himself with an easy sense of authority, and most people would fall behind his opinion. He was a protector, a father of five daughters, someone who wanted to save a pretty woman like Haley from a terrible mistake. He was our target. He was the man that we had to convince there wasn't enough evidence to convict Haley. If he believed our story, if he believed our version of the truth, Haley would be walking out of the courtroom a free woman in a few weeks.

When jury selection finished at 4:55 p.m., Judge Dalton called an end to the day.

Opening statements would wait until morning.

CHAPTER 29

The morning of the first day of a murder trial was always intense. There was a buzz around the city, an electricity, a pulsing energy threatening to explode. The seats of the gallery were filled. Journalists, concerned onlookers, and law students arrived, and there was a constant murmur throughout the crowd.

Haley was struggling to keep it together. Over the coming days and weeks, her future would be decided, and her nerves were destroying her.

Members of the large Finch family sat behind the prosecution desk. They were angry. They stared at Haley like she was evil. Ken Turner arrived by himself, sitting in the chair closest to the door. He was always looking for a quick escape. Bronson Finch entered the courtroom with another cousin and sat in the fifth row. He passed Ken Turner, and I caught both of them glaring at Haley. They were two brothers, connected by grief and a love of money.

"Five minutes," the bailiff called out, alerting everyone that Judge Dalton would soon arrive.

Haley crossed her arms over her chest and swallowed hard. Her moment of judgment was approaching.

The crowd rose when instructed, silent as Judge Dalton took his seat. The gallery sat back down and remained quiet.

Judge Dalton called for the jury members, and when they entered, he spoke to them about their roles and responsibilities, and once they acknowledged they understood, he invited Charlotte Sinclair to begin.

———

"Your Honor, ladies and gentlemen of the jury, my name is Charlotte Sinclair, and these are my colleagues, Thomas Western and Jackie Hill.

"As assistant solicitors, we represent the great state of South Carolina. And as the representatives of South Carolina, we're here to present the charge of murder against the defendant, Mrs. Haley Finch.

"My opening statement will provide a roadmap of what will be presented in this trial, as nothing I say now can be taken as evidence.

"Mrs. Haley Finch is charged with the murder of her boyfriend, Mr. Samuel Turner, or Sammy as he was more commonly known.

"During this trial, you will hear from many witnesses, and their statements will form the evidence for you to consider in your deliberations. These details, and only these details, are what you must use to form your decision on Mrs. Finch's guilt.

"Now, an important point. Mr. Turner was not Mrs. Finch's husband. Mrs. Finch is still married to Mr. Prescott Finch; however, they have been separated for two years. You will hear from witnesses who will explain that Mrs. Finch and Mr. Turner had been dating for a year before his death.

"During this trial, you'll hear from witnesses who will talk about Mrs. Finch's motive to murder her boyfriend. These witnesses will tell you that Mr. Turner was in his early fifties and had been poor most of his life. They will tell you that Mr. Turner had a lifetime of bad luck with women, until he turned fifty.

"What happened when he turned fifty to change his luck with women? He won the lottery.

"Five million dollars, in fact.

"And guess what? Women started dating him. One of the women to show interest in the out-of-shape Mr. Turner was the young and beautiful Mrs. Haley Finch. At only thirty, she was twenty years younger than her rich boyfriend.

"You will hear from an estate lawyer specialist who will tell you that Mr. Turner updated his will only five days before his death. *Five days before his death*. This witness will testify that Mrs. Finch was not listed on Mr. Turner's previous will; however, his updated will left all his considerable wealth to her.

"You will hear from the investigating deputies from the Beaufort County Sheriff's Office, and they will take you through the investigation they conducted into Mr. Turner's death. They will testify that on July 5th of this year, Mr. Turner went fishing at his usual spot at the back of his home in the gated community of Dataw Island. That evening, Mrs. Finch arrived.

"Then, for the next five weeks, nobody knew where Mr. Turner was.

"You will hear from the Beaufort County Sheriff's Office deputies who searched for Mr. Turner when he was reported as a missing person. These deputies will explain the investigation they conducted into Mr. Turner's disappearance, and how they interviewed Mrs. Finch as part of that investigation.

"Eventually, Mr. Turner was found.

"His body washed up in a tidal marsh on the Harbor River, bloated and swollen after spending five weeks at the bottom of the river. During this trial, you will hear from the medical examiner, who will explain how Mr. Turner died. The medical examiner will testify that Mr. Turner died after receiving five stab wounds to the area at the back of his neck.

"You will hear from witnesses who will testify that Mrs. Finch was the last person to see Mr. Turner alive at the dock behind his home on Dataw Island. Her car was seen driving toward his fishing spot on the afternoon he went missing.

"During this trial, you will also hear testimony from the deputies who found the murder weapon in the marshes near Mr. Turner's home. They will testify that Mrs. Finch admitted the knife came from her home collection.

"You will hear from law enforcement officials who will testify that a lot of Mr. Turner's blood was found underneath the dock where he was last seen alive. It's important to note that the blood was only found underneath the dock and not on top. Why? Because the top of the dock had been cleaned with bleach, breaking down any blood samples. A forensic specialist will testify that there were traces of bleach found on top of the dock, indicating that someone had gone to the trouble of cleaning the area to remove any traces of blood.

"You will hear from her ex-boyfriend, Mr. Leo McVeigh, who will tell you that only days before Mr. Turner disappeared, Mrs. Finch told him that Mr. Turner wouldn't be alive much longer, and she would receive all his money.

"You will hear from witnesses who will state they saw Mrs. Finch physically abuse Mr. Turner. They will tell you she slapped him numerous times in the week before he went missing.

"The evidence in this case is overwhelming. This is the case of an angry woman who was desperate for Mr. Turner's wealth.

"Mrs. Finch had the motive. She owned the murder weapon. She was at the place where he died on the day he died. She was the last person to see him alive. She was the only person to benefit from the updated will.

"Do not be fooled by her pretty looks—Mrs. Finch is a killer.

"At the end of this trial, I will stand before you again and highlight all the evidence against Mrs. Finch. At that point you will be asked to conclude beyond a reasonable doubt that Mrs. Haley Finch is guilty of murder.

"Thank you for your service to the court."

———

Most people, jurors included, had a confirmation bias. This bias was based on a person's subconscious tendency to search for and remember information that confirmed their already held beliefs.

In the context of a trial, confirmation bias meant that jurors focused on evidence that reinforced their first impression of the defendant. If they thought the defendant was guilty because of their race, wealth, or personal preferences, they looked for evidence to confirm that belief. If they thought she was as innocent as an angel, they listened for testimony that established that. And when presented with ambiguous evidence, jurors interpreted it in a way that supported their original belief.

Judging by the reactions of some of the jurors after seeing Haley—the shaking heads, the "tsk, tsk" noises—I assumed they already thought she was guilty. We would have to work hard to change that.

Sinclair finished her opening statement, and I stood. I walked to the lectern at the side of the room and looked at the jury, making eye contact with juror five. I nodded. He nodded back, and I began.

———

"Ladies and gentlemen of the jury, Your Honor, my name is Mr. Dean Lincoln and, along with my colleague, Mr. Bruce Hawthorn, we represent the defendant, Mrs. Haley Finch.

"Mrs. Finch is innocent.

"That's where we stand right now. That's the starting point of this case, and I'll repeat it so it's clear—Mrs. Finch is innocent.

"What needs to happen during this trial for that fact to change?

"The prosecution must present evidence that convinces you beyond a reasonable doubt that she isn't.

"They won't be able to, because there's no evidence, none at all, to prove Mrs. Finch murdered Mr. Turner. None. They won't present an eyewitness to the event, they won't present a murder weapon with her fingerprints or DNA on it, and they won't present a video of the murder.

"What do they have? They have a theory, a wild idea, just a thought, about Mrs. Finch. But is that enough? No. The evidence they present will not be enough to convict Mrs. Finch beyond a reasonable doubt. We need evidence, real evidence, to convict someone of a crime. You cannot convict someone on a thought.

"During the state's presentation of their case, you will see gaps in their theory. It will become clear to you that the investigators did not conduct a thorough investigation, and it will become clear to you that they did not look at the broader picture. They missed evidence during their missing persons investigation. They didn't interview prime suspects during their murder investigation. They mishandled the search during the entire investigation.

"In this fact-finding mission, you will hear from witnesses who were near Mr. Turner's home at the time he was last seen alive.

"You will hear from forensic experts who will tell you that Mrs. Finch could've cut herself on the dock anytime in the past year. Other forensic experts will testify that there is nothing to link Mrs. Finch to the use of bleach on the dock. You will hear from a psychologist, who will testify that Mrs. Finch was not motivated by money.

"And you will hear from the estate planning lawyer, Mr. David York, who prepared the second will of Mr. Turner. Mr. York will testify that Mr. Turner created that will of his own accord, without any undue influence.

"As we go through this journey together, we will highlight all the ways the State has failed to present enough evidence to convict Mrs. Finch.

"There are so many holes in this case, so many holes in this investigation, you will have doubts at the end of this trial.

"Those doubts will be reasonable.

"At the end of this trial, when all the evidence has been presented, your decision must be not guilty.

"Thank you for your service to our great justice system."

CHAPTER 30

"The State calls Corporal Investigator Andrew Teague."

As soon as he entered the doors, Teague eyed the defendant. The muscles in his jaw tightened as he walked past her to the witness stand. He had known Sammy personally and, during the deposition, it was clear he had taken a personal dislike to Haley. Teague was dressed in a brown suit, but it was one size too small. His stomach hung over his belt, and the jacket looked like it could rip at any moment.

"Thank you for coming to court and testifying today, Corporal Teague. Can you please begin by telling the court your name and profession?"

"My name is Corporal Andrew Teague, and I've been a member of the Beaufort County Sheriff's Office for over a decade. My current role is as an investigator, and before that I worked with the Charleston Police Department as a detective for fifteen years. I've served and lived in the great state of South Carolina my whole life, and I serve my community with honor and great pride."

"And were you the lead investigator in the homicide investigation of Sammy Turner?"

"I was. Mr. Turner had been missing for five weeks, and the missing persons case was being handled by another investigator, Corporal Kate Pallone. When Mr. Turner's body was found washed up in the tidal marsh, it became a homicide investigation, and it was assigned to me."

"Did you know Mr. Turner on a personal level?"

"Sammy Turner and I went to high school together many, many years ago. It's more than three decades since we were classmates. The years have gone by so fast." He smiled at the jury. Several members smiled back. "We were in the same grade at school and kept in touch over the years. We saw each other at some of the reunions, but we weren't close. Sammy was a nice guy, but we weren't friends."

"Did you declare that potential conflict of interest to your superiors?"

"I did, and they decided I was still the best person to lead the investigation into his death."

"And can you please tell the court the first stage of your investigation into this homicide?"

"The first step was to identify the body that was found. The body was swollen and disfigured after a long time in the waterways. Luckily, there was still a wallet in the back pocket of his jeans. We identified this as possibly Mr. Turner's and proceeded to do forensic identification."

Sinclair looked at her notes, read over a line, and continued. "Who found the body of Mr. Turner?"

"Mr. Len Harrison found the body in the marsh of Harbor River, off St. Helena Island. He's a local fisherman. He's been fishing those waters for over fifty years. He was boating past the area, fishing for flounder, when he went deeper into the marsh. It was after some heavy rains, and he thought it was the best time to come out to fish, but he spotted something unusual. He got closer and could see it was a body. He called it in to the Sheriff's Office non-emergency line and then stayed in the area until we arrived."

"Was he a suspect?"

"No. Although we were trying to understand what had happened, at no point did we consider him a suspect."

"Was it a homicide investigation straight away?"

"The official decision to make this a homicide investigation was made later by the deputy coroner; however, it was clear to all present that it was going to be a homicide investigation. We had already started the investigation when the deputy coroner confirmed it."

"And why was it clear this was going to be a homicide investigation?"

"Because the deceased had five clear stab wounds to the back of his neck and upper shoulder. Mr. Turner's shirt had washed off in the river, and the wounds were clear. And, given the location of the stab wounds, it would be almost impossible for the victim to have stabbed himself. He also had a diving belt attached to his waist, to weigh his body down."

Sinclair nodded and turned a page in her file. "Did anyone take photos of the scene?"

"Yes. Our police photographer arrived about an hour after I did and proceeded to take photos of the body."

"And are these the photos here?"

Sinclair pointed to the screen at the side of the room. A picture of the deceased's body, topless and lying face down in the marsh, appeared on the screen. One jury member gasped at the photo, several looked away, and another leaned forward to get a better look.

"These are the photos of the scene, yes."

Sinclair's assistant scrolled through several photos of the deceased's body and the surrounding marsh. Sammy's body, already overweight, was bloated and swollen. The blue jeans clung to his legs, and a thin gold chain remained around his neck. The diving belt, a yellow strap with weights placed around it, was tied around his stomach. There were chunks of skin taken out of his back, presumably by an animal, and he had one shoe on.

"Was anything else found at the scene?"

"No." He shook his head. "After an extensive search involving ten deputies, we found nothing more at the scene where the body was found."

"Did you conduct a search elsewhere?"

"We did. Once we established the deceased's name, we found that he had been reported as a missing person five weeks earlier. We contacted the lead investigator and reviewed that file. This file had a lot of information that was going to help us, including where he was last seen alive. That was the private fishing dock at the rear of his home on Dataw Island. We conducted an extensive search in the marsh and trees near where he was last seen, and we found a boning knife in the marsh, only a few yards from the dock."

"Interesting," Sinclair said. "And who was the last person to see him alive?"

"That would be Mrs. Haley Finch."

"Did you interview Mrs. Finch?"

"Yes. Mrs. Finch was listed as his next of kin, as she'd been dating Mr. Turner for over a year before he disappeared. She was also the one who reported him missing five weeks earlier. A few hours after we found the body and identified the deceased, we went to Mrs. Finch's house to ask her some questions and then inform her of what we found."

"And how did she seem when you told her that you had found the body of Mr. Turner?"

"Objection to the word 'seem,'" I said. "It asks the witness to speculate."

"Sustained," Judge Dalton agreed. "Please choose your words more carefully, Mrs. Sinclair."

"Yes, Your Honor," Sinclair stated. "Corporal Teague, what do you think she was—"

"Objection to the word 'think.' Again, it asks for the witness to speculate."

"And again, the objection is sustained."

Sinclair drew a breath. "How did she feel—"

"Objection to the word 'feel.' It calls for the witness to characterize the events around the interview."

"Sustained," Judge Dalton agreed. "Mrs. Sinclair, the witness is allowed to talk about what happened during the investigation but is not to assume how someone felt."

Frustrated, Sinclair exhaled loudly. She turned another page in her file and continued. "Did you ask any questions of Mrs. Finch before you told her Mr. Turner was deceased?"

"We asked her if the knife we found near the fishing dock belonged to her. She confirmed that it did, and then we informed her we had found Mr. Turner's body in the marsh in Harbor River, off St. Helena Island. We informed her that he was found with stab wounds to the back of his neck."

"What did Mrs. Finch say when you told her the body had been found?"

"She cried a lot, and we didn't really get a lot of words out of her."

"Was she a suspect?"

"Not exactly, but we were still establishing what had happened to the body."

"At what point did she become a suspect?"

"Mrs. Finch started to be on our radar as a suspect when we looked further into the missing persons file, and the next day, she became our main suspect when it became evident that Mr. Turner had updated his will to leave all his money to Mrs. Finch only five days before his death."

"How much money was left to Mrs. Finch in the newly updated will?"

"Mr. Turner had a little over four million in cash, shares, and assets."

"And was she the only benefactor of the will?"

"Of the new will, yes. Mr. Turner's previous will did not leave any money to Mrs. Finch."

"At what point did you arrest her?"

"The same day we found out about the updated will, which was two days after the body was found."

"Was there any blood found at the scene where Mr. Turner was last seen alive?"

"Not at first; however, when we conducted a more thorough search, we found traces of blood that were tested and found to belong to Mr. Turner and Mrs. Finch."

For the next three hours and fifty-five minutes, Sinclair hurled question after question at the detective, going into fine detail about the murder and subsequent investigation. She used the detective as a tool to introduce evidence into the court, including satellite photos of the currents in Harbor River to show how the body had traveled from the fishing dock to where it was found. He testified about Sammy's home, and how nothing had been stolen from it. He testified that while there was no evidence of blood on top of the fishing dock, they had found dried blood stuck to the wood under it.

I objected where I could, but the testimony was based in fact. Apart from her earlier questions, Sinclair stayed on point. She presented well. Her questions were fast and focused, and the jury was engaged with her interactions with the witness.

When Sinclair turned the witness over, I stood and began questioning.

"Corporal Teague." I walked to the lectern at the side of the room, placed a file down, and looked up at the witness. "Thank you for taking the time to testify and thank you for your service to our great community. Your testimony is very important for this case, and I'm going to ask you some questions to establish the details of the event. Is that okay?"

"It is," he stated, shifting in the chair.

"Thank you." I reviewed my notes before continuing, running my eyes over the questions I had planned. "Corporal Teague, would you call the investigation complete and extensive?"

"Yes, I would."

Perfect. He had stepped into my trap. "And in this complete and extensive investigation do you believe this incident could've been the result of a robbery gone wrong?"

"No, it doesn't appear that way."

"And why would you say that?"

"Because nothing was reported as stolen from his house."

"Can you be certain nothing was stolen from his home?"

"Not certain, but there were no signs of forced entry."

"Was Mr. Turner's home dusted for fingerprints?"

"It was."

"And what was found?"

"Several sets of prints, including Mrs. Finch's."

"Anyone else's?"

"Mr. Turner's."

"Go on."

"We also found prints belonging to several other people."

"Was one of those people Mr. Ken Turner?"

"That's correct."

"And who is Mr. Ken Turner?"

"He's Mr. Sammy Turner's brother."

"Did you interview him about the murder?"

167

"We talked to him as part of the missing persons investigation, but decided he wasn't a suspect."

I nodded. "Despite his fingerprints being found near the alleged scene of the crime?"

"That's correct."

I paused. "Did Mr. Ken Turner have a history of violence?"

"Objection to this line of questioning, Your Honor." Sinclair stood. "The defense is trying to establish third-party culpability; however, the rules of this court state third-party culpability must be established through evidence. The defense has done no such thing."

Judge Dalton looked at me. "Mr. Lincoln, are you attempting to establish third-party guilt?"

"Not at this point, Your Honor. We are merely questioning the witness on the extensive investigation they conducted."

"Overruled for now, but stick to the line of questioning." Judge Dalton turned to the witness. "You may answer the questions."

I kept the questions coming. "And in this extensive and thorough investigation, did you look at the security logs from the gated community?"

"We did."

"And are these the logs here?"

"I believe so, yes."

"Can you please tell the court in this complete and extensive investigation, did you find that Mr. Ken Turner visited Mr. Turner's home after Mrs. Finch had left?"

Teague drew a long breath.

"Corporal Teague?" I pressed. "Can you please answer the question?"

"Yes. He did."

"And what time was that?"

"Mrs. Finch left at 4:45 p.m., and Mr. Ken Turner arrived at 5 p.m., and left at 5:15 p.m."

"After Mrs. Finch?"

"Yes, but Mr. Ken Turner was interviewed as part of the missing persons report, and he stated that Mr. Sammy Turner wasn't home during that time he was there."

"Were you aware, when he told you that, that he was a convicted felon?"

"I didn't speak to him."

"I'm sorry?" I expressed surprise, but in truth, I had rehearsed this moment many times. It was going exactly as I planned. "You have just told this court that you conducted an extensive investigation into the death of Mr. Sammy Turner, and you have evidence that Mr. Ken Turner was the last person at his home, which is connected to the fishing dock where Mr. Turner was murdered, and you didn't even interview him?"

"We had his interview from the missing persons report. We reviewed that statement, and my colleague spoke to him twice on the phone. We found the information to be sufficient."

"Were you aware that Mr. Ken Turner was the recipient of 50 percent of the first will, which was superseded just days before Mr. Sammy Turner's death?"

"Yes, we were aware of that."

"And did you ask Mr. Ken Turner if he knew the will had been updated?"

"No."

I squinted, exaggerating my confusion for the jury. When I saw the look of confusion on the face of juror five, I continued. "Is it true that there was a convicted felon, someone who was violent and had spent time in prison, someone who was set to benefit from the previous will of Mr. Sammy Turner, someone who had been to the home next to the fishing dock *after* Mrs. Finch, and you didn't even interview them?"

He nodded.

"Corporal Teague, you will need to answer the question verbally."

"What we had was—"

"Corporal Teague," I interrupted. "Please, answer the question directly. Is it true that you had a convicted felon, someone who was violent and had spent time in prison, someone who was set to benefit from the previous will of Mr. Sammy Turner, someone who had been to the home next to the fishing dock *after* Mrs. Finch, and you didn't even interview them?"

He looked away. "Yes, that's true."

I closed the file, shaking my head, happy with the first cross-examination, happy with the first witness, but we were still a long way from the finish line. "No further questions."

CHAPTER 31

Sinclair moved to the lectern and called the next witness. "The State calls Dr. Joan Goulds."

Haley's nerves were getting worse. She was biting her nails as she waited. I wrote a note on my legal pad and showed it to her. "*Slow breaths*," I wrote. She nodded and tried to slow down her breathing.

Beaufort County Deputy Coroner Dr. Joan Goulds entered the courtroom with an unsympathetic look. She didn't smile, and she didn't show a hint of emotion. She was dressed in a black pant suit, with black shoes, and black-rimmed glasses. Her black hair, graying at the sides, was tied back tightly.

"Dr. Goulds," Sinclair began, "can you please begin by telling the court your name and occupation?"

"My name is Dr. Joan Goulds. For the last five years, I've been employed as a deputy coroner with the Beaufort County Coroner's Office. I'm a member of the South Carolina Coroner's Association, and I've previously served as a military medical doctor."

"Does the Beaufort County Coroner's Office investigate all deaths within Beaufort County?"

"No. We conduct investigations into deaths where the cause is unnatural, sudden, or unexpected, deaths that involve suspicion, or any deaths that occur in custody. And while we don't usually investigate natural deaths, we will if it involves suspicious or unexplained circumstances."

"Thank you, Doctor." After Sinclair established the witness's professional qualifications, she submitted the autopsy report into evidence. "Can you please tell the court if you performed the autopsy of Mr. Sammy Turner?"

"That's correct."

"And what did you find?"

"The deceased had multiple stab wounds to the nuchal region of the body, otherwise known as the posterior region of the neck. This is the area around the trapezius muscle, and contains the spinal cord, cervical vertebrae, and associated muscles. Mr. Turner had five deep wounds in this area, and this led to a fatal hemorrhage, or loss of blood. The official cause of death is penetrating trauma caused by stab wounds to the nuchal region."

"Sorry, Dr. Goulds. Can you please repeat where these stab wounds occurred?"

"To the nuchal region. One of the stabs wounds severed the vertebral artery, and it was likely there would've been a lot of blood loss in a short period of time."

"To the back of the neck called the nuchal region . . ." Sinclair paused, trying to focus the jury's attention on the location of the cut. "Sorry, Doctor, which artery did it sever?"

"Objection," Bruce said. "Asked and answered."

"Sustained," Judge Dalton said. "Move on, Mrs. Sinclair."

One of Sinclair's tactics had become clear—she was going to highlight the brutality of the crime as much as she could.

The more savage the crime, the more likely it was to be punished. While there wasn't always a direct correlation between the brutality of the crime and a guaranteed guilty verdict, violent crimes often led to emotional decisions from jurors. A touch of doubt was brushed aside when the crime was vicious. Jurors, driven by fear and anger, were prone to look for evidence that would ensure the violent offender was removed from society.

"To the back of the neck," Sinclair repeated. "Did you determine what Mr. Turner was stabbed with?"

"On first inspection, the impact was consistent with a sharp boning knife. A knife was later found in a search near the marshes where he was last seen alive. We matched that boning knife to the stab wounds and found that it was consistent. The length and depth of the knife fit exactly to the wounds the deceased suffered."

"In your autopsy, could you determine where the attacker would've been standing when she stabbed—"

"Objection!" I shouted. "Prejudicial. Characterizing the attacker as female is a clear attempt to influence the jury's opinion."

"Sustained," Judge Dalton agreed. "Mrs. Sinclair, unless there's direct evidence, please don't gender the attacker."

"Yes, Your Honor." Sinclair looked down at her notes, sucked in a breath through her nose, and nodded. "Dr. Goulds, in your autopsy, could you determine where the attacker would've been standing when they stabbed Mr. Turner?"

"Considering the angle of the strike and areas where the deceased was stabbed, it's reasonable to determine that the attacker was standing behind him."

"And could you determine if the attacker was shorter or taller than the deceased?"

"Considering the angles of the stab wounds, and where they were located on the body, it's reasonable to determine that this was the stabbing motion." Dr. Gould showed the court the angle that was likely used in the stabbing, reaching her arm up and stabbing in a downward motion. "And given the flat angle in which the knife entered the area at the back of the neck, it's reasonable to say that the attacker was shorter than the deceased."

"Did the victim have any other injuries?"

"No."

"Dr. Goulds, can you please tell the court if you conducted a toxicology report on the deceased?"

"Yes. The toxicology report was provided by the South Carolina State Law Enforcement Division Forensic Services Laboratory. However, no substances were found in the blood report."

"So, he wasn't drinking or taking drugs?"

"That's correct."

"And were you able to determine a time of death from the autopsy?"

"Unfortunately, no. Considering the state of the body, it was likely that it was submerged in water for several weeks. There was a major rain event upstream in the days before the body was found, which suggests that the rising river levels pushed the body out of the depths of the river and into the marsh."

For the following fifty-five minutes, Dr. Goulds testified about the autopsy and her report, adding small facts to the case. Sinclair presented her questions well, guiding the jury toward looking for an attacker who was shorter than the victim and had attacked him from behind. She highlighted the brutality of the event as much as she could, so much so that one member of the jury closed her eyes when Dr. Goulds went into detail about the stab wounds.

When Sinclair finished questioning, Judge Dalton looked at the clock on the wall. It was 4:25 p.m., heading toward the end of the first day. "Your witness, Mr. Hawthorn," Judge Dalton said.

"Thank you, Your Honor." Bruce stood. He questioned the doctor from behind his desk. "Dr. Goulds, could you determine if the attacker was male or female?"

"No. There was no evidence to suggest the gender of the attacker."

"From the autopsy, could you determine who attacked Mr. Sammy Turner?"

"No, there was no evidence in the autopsy report to suggest who may have attacked him."

"Could you determine the time he was attacked?"

"As I said earlier, no. Due to the state of the body, we could not make that determination."

"Do we know if he was attacked in the afternoon, or say, 5:15 p.m.?"

"No. If the body had been found the day of the attack, yes, we could determine the time of death using standardized techniques, but given that the body was submerged in water for such an extended period of time, it was impossible for us to give an accurate time of death."

"And could you determine where he was attacked?"

"Based on the autopsy alone, no, we couldn't be certain where he was attacked."

"Is it true, then, that all your report says is that a body was found in the tidal marsh?"

"A body that had been stabbed, yes."

Bruce nodded. "Thank you, Dr. Goulds. No further questions."

CHAPTER 32

The courtroom felt like an oven the next morning.

The air conditioner had whirred to life, sputtering loudly, but it would take time to cool the room down. Despite the oppressive conditions, the gallery was full, and the noise of people flapping pieces of paper to cool themselves down echoed through the chambers.

The media had arrived early. With consistent rumors spreading throughout Beaufort, the attention on the case was intense. Finch family members were in attendance. Local politicians were seen to be showing interest. And there, sitting in the row nearest to the door, was Ken Turner. Across the aisle, in the same row, sat Bronson Finch. Both looked angry. Both looked ready to fight.

After Judge Dalton entered the courtroom and everyone had settled, Sinclair wiped her brow and called the next witness. Corporal Kate Pallone was called to the stand to start the second day.

Pallone was a tall woman in her forties who looked like she hadn't smiled in years and would crush anyone who dared to suggest she should. Her blonde hair was cut short, and her callous stare betrayed no warmth. She walked to the stand with a file in her left hand, well prepared for her forthcoming testimony.

"Corporal Kate Pallone, thank you for testifying today," Sinclair began, standing behind the lectern. She had a notepad in front of her. "Can you please tell the court your occupation and your involvement in this case?"

"Certainly. I'm employed by the Beaufort County Sheriff's Office, and part of my role as an investigator is to look into missing persons. I've worked in that section for the past ten years, and while it's a very stressful job, I'm proud of the service we provide to our community of Beaufort County."

"Did you handle the missing persons report on Mr. Sammy Turner?"

"That's correct."

"When did you start this investigation into the missing person?"

"We started the investigation on July 6th. We received a call that day from Mrs. Haley Finch, stating that her boyfriend, Mr. Sammy Turner, hadn't returned home after fishing the day before."

"Did you wait forty-eight hours to begin this investigation?"

"No. When Mrs. Finch called us, there was a sense of urgency in her voice. She told us that this was very unusual behavior from the missing person, and in most cases, the earlier we act, the more likely we are to have a better result."

"Were Mr. Turner and Mrs. Finch living together at the time?"

"They were not living together full time; however, Mrs. Finch stated that every Sunday night, Mr. Turner would stay at her house, and she would cook him a nice Sunday roast. She reported that it was normal that Mr. Turner would fish on Sunday afternoons, while she spent the time in the kitchen preparing the meal. She also said that some nights, she would stay at his house in Dataw Island, and other nights during the week, he would stay at her house."

"And what time did you interview her?"

"We interviewed her at 5 p.m. on Monday, July 6th. She made the call to the office at 4 p.m., and reported him missing, and given the urgency in her phone call, we attended her home as soon as we could."

"During that initial interview, what did Mrs. Finch tell you about the last time she saw Mr. Turner?"

"Can I refer to the notes I made in the missing persons report?" She looked up at Judge Dalton.

"Certainly," Judge Dalton instructed her.

Pallone opened the folder and rested it against the front of the witness box. "She told us that she had begun to prepare her roast on Sunday around midday, and that's when Mr. Turner left to go fishing at his home on Dataw Island. She said she prepared the roast with beef broth, carrots, and new potatoes, and put it in the slow cooker. When we were talking to her, she was very descriptive. We put that behavior down to stress."

"Did she tell you when she last saw Mr. Turner?"

"She said she drove out to his fishing dock that afternoon, and as she noted, she 'hung out' with him. She said that she read a book on the dock while Mr. Turner fished. She advised us that she left before 5 p.m."

"Did she say that she usually does this?"

"She said"—Pallone ran her finger over the notes in her report—"that she sometimes went out there with him to just sit and read and watch the water. She would take a camp chair and sit at the end of the dock while he fished, because, as she noted, it was a beautiful, remote, and very quiet location."

"Beautiful, remote, and very quiet. Would you say it was perfect for a murder?"

"Objection," Bruce called out. "Counsel is testifying."

"I withdraw the question, Your Honor," Sinclair stated, and composed herself. "What else did Mrs. Finch say when you interviewed her?"

"She said she left the dock area after an hour to come home and prepare the dinner. She said Mr. Turner didn't return for dinner, and she thought he might've been angry with her for not staying longer."

"Why would she think that?"

"She didn't know. She said that Mr. Turner sometimes had mood swings, and he couldn't express his emotions clearly. Her exact explanation was that Mr. Turner was 'immature.'"

"She thought he was immature. Interesting." Sinclair highlighted the point for the jury. "And did she attempt to call him?"

"She did, but she noted that the cell phone calls went straight to his voicemail. She explained that once he didn't answer her calls the following morning, she became concerned. She went back to his house and said he wasn't there. She drove down to the security guard at the gate of the community, and he checked the logs. He informed that her that Mr. Turner had not left the previous night. The security guard returned to the house with her, and they both searched the property for Mr. Turner. Mrs. Finch said this is when she became concerned that something had happened to him."

"When did she call the police?"

"When she returned home that afternoon."

"Interesting," Sinclair noted again. She was using the word as a highlighter to ensure the jurors knew it was an important piece of information. "During your missing persons investigation, did you request cell phone records from his telephone provider?"

"That's a normal part of an investigation, and we received a response from the provider the day after the request was lodged and we found that his cell phone last pinged off a cell tower near the fishing dock at 5:25 p.m. on Sunday, July 5th. We can determine that either his cell phone went dead at the point, or it was switched off."

"Did you ever find the cell phone?"

"No. We searched his house, his car, and his yard, and also the marsh near the fishing dock, but we could not find the cell phone."

"Speaking of the house, were there any signs that someone had tried to break into Mr. Turner's house? Perhaps a burglary gone wrong?"

"No. There were no signs of forced entry in his house that were apparent to us in the missing persons investigation."

"And as part of the investigation, did you search the fishing dock where he was last seen?"

"We did. The day after we received a call from Mrs. Finch, we searched the area near the fishing dock. We didn't find any of his fishing equipment there, nor did we find his cell phone, or any of his belongings."

"Did the fishing dock look clean?"

"It did; however, as we noted in the initial missing persons report, there was a strong smell of bleach at the dock, which we noted as unusual."

"Was there any trace of blood on the fishing dock?"

"Not that we could see, but like I said, there was a strong smell of bleach."

"Thank you, Corporal Pallone." Sinclair closed her folder. "No further questions."

When Judge Dalton instructed us to cross-examine the witness, Bruce looked at me and nodded. I collected our file on Pallone's investigation, stood, and moved to the lectern. I rested my left hand on the lectern, standing near the jurors.

"Corporal Pallone, in your testimony, you mentioned that you went straight to Mrs. Finch's home after her phone call because 'there was urgency' in her voice. Is that correct?"

"Objection," Sinclair called out. "The question asks the witness to speculate about Mrs. Finch's state of mind."

"Your Honor," I argued, "this answer formed part of the witness's testimony. We should be allowed to question that statement."

"The objection is overruled," Judge Dalton stated. "You may answer the question, Corporal Pallone."

"Yes, there was urgency in her voice."

"What caused that sense of urgency?"

"The fact that her boyfriend was missing," Pallone scoffed.

"Let me be clearer. When you interviewed her at her home, did she say why she was worried about him?"

"She did."

I waited for her to continue, but she didn't elaborate. "And can you please explain what she said, as noted in your initial missing persons report?"

"Mrs. Finch advised us that her boyfriend's brother, Mr. Ken Turner, had drug debts, and she said these debts were usually paid by Sammy. Sammy had told Mrs. Finch that he wasn't going to pay the debts any more, and she was worried that if he didn't pay then he might've been on the wrong end of violence."

"Worried that if he didn't pay Ken Turner's drug debts, he would be on the wrong end of violence." I paused and looked at the jury. When I saw several heads nodding, I continued. "Did you investigate this line of inquiry?"

"Objection," Sinclair called out. "Again, Mr. Lincoln is trying to introduce evidence into the court about a third-party suspect; however, he hasn't laid out that path in any of the discovery material."

"We're not introducing any evidence, Your Honor," I responded. "We're discussing the missing persons report that has been entered into evidence by the prosecution. This information is in the files that the prosecution has presented to the court."

"The objection is overruled," Judge Dalton agreed. "You entered the information into evidence, Mrs. Sinclair. The defense is allowed the opportunity to question that evidence." He leaned closer to the witness. "You may answer the question."

"We interviewed Mr. Ken Turner; however, he stated that he had been clean for several months. He told us that he had no drug debts."

"And you believed him?"

"We saw no reason to doubt him."

"Did you consider that he was a convicted felon with a long history of drug problems?"

"We did consider that."

"And did you ask Mr. Ken Turner when he last saw his brother?"

"At that time, he said the last time he saw his brother was a few days earlier. He told us he drove out to his brother's house at around midday of July 5th to talk to him, but he wasn't home. He told us he left fifteen minutes after he arrived."

"And did you access the security logs of the gated community?"

"We requested the security logs so we could review the movements of Mr. Sammy Turner's vehicle. Our investigation didn't look into the hundreds of other cars that entered and exited the community that day."

"You didn't review the security log any further than Mr. Sammy Turner's vehicle?"

"That's correct, but I must say, at that point in the investigation, Mr. Sammy Turner was still a missing person. There was nothing to indicate that foul play was involved. We found no blood or any other sign that there had been a crime."

"In reviewing the security logs, did you see that Mrs. Finch left Dataw Island at 4:45 p.m.?"

"We received a large file from the security company that had literally thousands of lines of data, recording each license plate number that entered and exited that day. We only have so many hours in the day."

"Did you see that Mr. Ken Turner arrived at Dataw Island at 5 p.m., and left at 5:15 p.m.?"

"No, we didn't see that, but we also weren't looking for it."

"And when did you say Mr. Sammy Turner's cell phone stopped pinging?"

"At 5:25 p.m."

"After Mr. Ken Turner left the house?"

"That's appears to be correct, yes."

"Mr. Ken Turner told you he went to his brother's house at midday, but the evidence shows he was there between 5 and 5:15 p.m. He deliberately didn't tell you the whole truth, even though his brother was missing."

"That appears to be correct."

I sighed and shook my head. "Did you go to Ken's house to interview him?"

"We did."

"Why did you go to his house and not conduct the interview over the phone?"

"We had been made aware that Mr. Sammy Turner stayed at his brother's house sometimes. Mr. Sammy Turner also owned the house, and we wanted to see if there was any evidence that he had been there or was still there."

"Did you take photos while you were there?"

"We did, and we reviewed them when we returned to the office, but we didn't find any evidence that Mr. Sammy Turner had been there in the last few days. We then called him again the next day to follow up, but Mr. Ken Turner was not able to offer any new information."

"Or the truth." I paused for a few moments, nodding to myself, and then looked to the jury. I had their attention. Now it was time to swing hard. "Corporal Pallone, can you please look at the court monitor and tell us if this is one of the photos you took when you spoke to Mr. Ken Turner about his brother's disappearance?"

183

Bruce clicked several keys on his laptop and a picture displayed on the court monitor.

"Yes," she responded. "That is one of the photos we took."

"And if we zoom in on this picture"—I pointed to the monitor—"can you please tell the court what is on the table?"

Corporal Pallone squinted as she looked at the photo of the dining room table. There were papers spread all over its surface, including unopened letters, bills, and letters stamped with "overdue" in big red letters. But it was the printed document in the bottom left corner that we were focused on. "Well, I didn't see that before."

"Can you please tell the court what it is?"

"It appears to be a will on the dining room table."

"It is," I confirmed. Another photo appeared on the monitor. "And if we zoom in closer, can you please tell the court the name on that will?"

"It says"—she squinted—"'Sammy Turner.'"

"That's correct," I noted. "And can you please look at the lawyer's logo in the top left corner of the will, and tell the court what that says?"

"It says, 'Mr. Les Overton.'"

"Did Mr. Overton write the original will or the updated will?"

"The original will."

I nodded for a few moments before continuing. "Was this before or after the body of Mr. Sammy Turner was found?"

"This was in the first few days of the missing persons investigation and weeks before his body was found."

I let the pause sit in the courtroom. "Can you confirm that the original will of Mr. Sammy Turner was on the dining room table of Mr. Ken Turner only days after he went missing?"

"Oh." She waited for a few moments while the thoughts went through her head. "It appears to be the case, but, like I said, we didn't see that previously."

"Are you aware, according to that will, the one printed out and placed on Mr. Ken Turner's dining room table, that Mr. Ken Turner was set to inherit half of Sammy's wealth in the event of Sammy's death?"

"No, I was not aware of that at the time. That was outside the scope of our missing persons investigation."

"And were you aware that Mr. Ken Turner had not been informed that the will had been updated?"

"No."

"And if you were aware of these things, would this have changed your investigation?"

"I believe so, yes."

"And did you provide these photos to the investigators of the murder case?"

"We did."

"Are you aware if they continued down that line of investigation? Did they consider Mr. Ken Turner, or his associates, as suspects?"

"Not to my knowledge, no."

"Is it true that you had information that convicted felon Mr. Ken Turner was at Mr. Sammy Turner's house at 5:15 p.m. on the day of his disappearance, was set to inherit half his wealth, and neither you nor the homicide investigators even followed that line of inquiry?"

Pallone drew a long breath and looked to the prosecutor's desk. Sinclair avoided eye contact.

"Corporal Pallone?"

"Ah . . . yes. I guess so."

"You guess so." I paused long enough for the jury to pay their complete attention. Again, I saw heads nodding. "No further questions."

CHAPTER 33

"The State calls Dr. Roseanne Rooney-Smith."

Dr. Rooney-Smith was a slender woman with auburn hair and a long face. Although born in California, she had lived most of her adult life in South Carolina, and she held a reputation as being one the most talented singers in the county. She was often found singing karaoke at her local bar, embarrassing her two teenage daughters with a smile on her face.

Sinclair sat behind her desk, laptop open, and began questioning. "Dr. Rooney-Smith, can you please begin by telling the court who you are, and what you do for your occupation?"

"My name is Dr. Roseanne Rooney-Smith, and I work as a forensic chemist for the Beaufort County Sheriff's Office. I've held this role for the past fifteen years, and it's one of the best jobs I've ever had. I'm proud to serve my local community." She sat up straighter. "In my role, I'm responsible for the forensic analysis of samples taken from crime scenes."

"And how does your role connect to this case?"

"Part of my role is forensic serology. Forensic serology involves the identification of biological material, such as blood, urine, and saliva. We collect physical evidence, test the evidence for biological materials, and analyze these results." She adjusted the sleeves on her jacket and continued. "When the investigators found blood underneath the dock, I attended the scene and did a luminol test. Luminol is a chemical that can be sprayed over an area to detect if even the smallest amount of blood is present. This happens because luminol reacts with the hemoglobin found in blood and secretes a blue luminescence. It's important to understand that this test is not conclusive, as other items may create a false positive, and that's why we also take a sample and test it further."

"Did you test the samples any further?"

"We did. After it was determined that there was blood at the scene, we took these samples back to the lab for analysis. In the majority of samples, the tests matched the samples of DNA for Mr. Sammy Turner. We also found a DNA match for Mrs. Haley Finch in the smaller sample, which was taken farther down the fishing dock."

"How long can blood samples be taken, before they're considered unreliable?"

"In certain circumstances, blood samples can be reliable for years; however, given the exposure to the elements in this situation and the relative humidity around the fishing dock, it's likely that the blood would remain testable for up to a year."

"Can you please look at the court monitor and confirm if this is where the samples were taken from?"

Sinclair typed into her laptop and indicated to the court monitor at the side of the room, where a video of the dock appeared. The video showed one of the detectives wading into the water under the dock at low tide, which was chest deep at the end. Once underneath the end of the dock, the video camera looked upward where there were red stains. The video showed another forensic investigator taking a sample of the dock with the stains on it.

"Yes, that's the video that accompanied the samples. The detectives identified that the stains were most likely blood, and as you can see, the blood is stained across an area of around five feet by two feet."

"Would that indicate a lot of blood was spilled on that dock?"

"Yes, it does. By the pattern of the bloodstains, we can see it's most likely that the blood came from the top of the dock and leaked through the wooden slats. As blood is a sticky substance, it ran between the slats, and then clung to the underside of the dock, leaving the red stains."

"You mentioned that it's most likely the blood leaked from the top of the dock. Did you test any blood samples from the top of the dock?"

"The detectives in the homicide case also took samples from the top of the dock; however, these pieces of wood did not have bloodstains on them. When we tested these samples, we found traces of bleach."

"Bleach?"

"That's correct. Bleach is a powerful oxidizing agent that can destroy the molecular make-up of blood. It breaks down the components of the blood sample, including the important hemoglobin, and oxidates the protein strains, breaking them down until they're no longer testable."

"Indicating that someone, at some point, cleaned the dock with bleach?"

"That's correct."

"Is it common practice to clean a dock with bleach?"

"No. I would find it very unusual for someone to clean their dock with bleach."

"You mentioned that you tested the blood samples and found they matched Mr. Sammy Turner. Is that correct?"

"For the majority of blood samples, we found the blood matched the blood sample of Mr. Sammy Turner."

"But not all the samples?"

"We tested a sample of blood that was apart from the others, toward the start of the dock, around fifteen feet away. This sample was also taken from underneath the dock. This blood sample was matched to a sample taken from Mrs. Haley Finch."

"Was there evidence of bleach used on top of the dock above the second sample?"

"Yes. We tested the wood above that sample and found bleach had been used in that area as well. We also tested five random sample areas of the dock. In those samples, there was no blood, nor any traces of bleach found."

"Interesting." Another long pause from Sinclair. "Does the sample of blood indicate what happened?"

"No. However, it's clear that Mr. Turner lost a lot of blood at the end of the dock, most likely a fatal amount, and Mrs. Finch lost a small amount of blood."

"Interesting." Again, a long pause from Sinclair before she continued. "What is the likelihood of samples matching in your DNA testing?"

"We used a type of DNA analysis called Short Tandem Repeat Analysis, or STR for short. This involves analyzing specific regions of DNA and comparing these regions between samples. This type of analysis is accurate to one in one billion, to the exclusion of all others. That's referred to as the probability of accuracy."

For the next fifteen minutes, Sinclair found every way she could to ask the same questions, drilling the evidence into the minds of the jury. Bruce and I objected where we could, but the facts were simple—there was blood found on the underside of the dock, and the two separate samples belonged to Sammy Turner and Haley Finch.

When asked, Bruce began the cross, sitting behind his desk.

"Thank you for talking with us today, Dr. Rooney-Smith," he began. "Do the samples of blood tell you when a person was on the fishing dock?"

"No."

"So, Mrs. Finch's blood could've been there long before that blood sample matched to Mr. Turner?"

"That's possible."

"Given that Mrs. Finch was there every week for over a year, could it be possible her blood sample was from a different time than Mr. Turner's sample?"

"Yes." She shrugged. "That's possible."

"Given the samples were in separate areas, does this also indicate the events could've taken place at two different times?"

"We weren't able to determine the time the dock was stained by blood for either sample."

"Thank you, Dr. Rooney-Smith," Bruce finished. "No further questions."

CHAPTER 34

Another Beaufort County Sheriff's Office investigator testified to start day three.

Their testimony was straightforward. Yes, they searched the marsh near Mr. Sammy Turner's home for evidence. Yes, they found the knife in the marsh only twenty-five yards away from the fishing dock. Yes, they used gloves to pick up the knife. Yes, the knife had a bloodstain on it. No, there were no fingerprints on the knife.

Another forensic expert came next. Their testimony was equally bland. Yes, they tested the knife found in the marsh. Yes, they tested the blood sample but found no detectable amounts of DNA. Yes, it was normal for DNA to break down to undetectable levels after exposure to UV light and humid conditions.

A criminologist, specializing in the study of intimate partner abuse by females, testified to close day three. No, it wasn't uncommon behavior for women to be violent toward male partners. Yes, there had been murderous girlfriends in the past. Yes, there was evidence to suggest intimate partner violence by women could be motivated by money issues.

It was a solid day for the prosecution, but nothing game changing.

The fourth day of the murder trial opened with estate lawyer Mr. Les Overton.

"Thank you for attending today, Mr. Overton," Sinclair began behind the lectern. "Can you please tell the court your name, your expertise, and your relationship to this case?"

"My name is Mr. Les Overton and I'm a law professor at the University of South Carolina Law School. I practice, teach, and have specialized in estate planning and probate law. I've spent over twenty-five years writing wills and lecturing the next generation of lawyers on the value of correct estate planning."

"And you're an expert in teaching and reviewing wills?"

"I believe so, yes."

"Have you testified in previous court cases as an expert in wills?"

"I have. I've testified in over fifty cases as an expert on the issues."

Sinclair leaned against the lectern, standing close to the jurors. "Mr. Overton, as an expert, can you please tell the court some common reasons why a person would update their will?"

"There are several reasons why people choose to update their wills and they are most commonly motivated by a change to personal circumstance, a change to assets, or a change to law or tax planning. But the most common reason a person updates their will is to adjust the allocation of their assets to their loved ones."

"Adjust the allocation of their assets . . ." Sinclair paused. "The intention of the will is to distribute money or assets when someone dies?"

"That's correct."

"And, as an estate planning lawyer, do you have a relationship to this case?"

"I was the estate planning lawyer who witnessed the first will written by Mr. Sammy Turner after he won the lottery. Sammy came to me after the win because he'd never written a will before, and he didn't want his wealth to be disputed after his death. He told me he'd searched the internet for 'the best estate planning lawyer in South Carolina,' and found my name."

"Was there a reason why Mr. Sammy Turner hadn't written a will before?"

"Because he had next to no assets. Apart from his car, which was worth a few thousand dollars, he didn't own anything else. He didn't own a house, or investments, or even any family heirlooms."

"In your years of experience, have you ever seen undue pressure applied to anyone updating a will?"

"Objection, assuming facts not in evidence," I stated. "There's no evidence, at any point or at any time, that there was undue pressure on Mr. Turner."

"He's an expert in the field, Your Honor, and his expertise has been established," Sinclair argued. "He should be allowed to answer, given his expertise."

"Your Honor, the line between expert witness and eyewitness has been significantly blurred by the prosecution's questions. This testimony started as establishing his expertise, but Mrs. Sinclair has asked eyewitness questions. The jury cannot be expected to know the difference."

"The objection is sustained," Judge Dalton agreed. "I agree the line between being an expert witness and an eyewitness is blurred in this instance, and answering expert questions relating to this scenario may confuse the jurors as to what is an expert answer and what is an answer by the eyewitness."

"Certainly, Your Honor," Sinclair said, but her voice portrayed her disappointment. "Mr. Overton, on what date did you witness Mr. Sammy Turner write his will?"

"On June 15th two years ago, only two weeks after the lottery win."

"Was anyone else there with him when he wrote that will?"

"No, he was by himself. My assistant and another lawyer witnessed his signature."

"Can you please tell the court the intention of Mr. Sammy Turner when he wrote his will two years ago?"

"Absolutely. He made notes that he wanted to be publicly available after his death, and I can testify about those public notes without compromising on attorney-client privilege. According to common law principles, and Rule 501 of the South Carolina Rules of Evidence, attorney-client privilege stills exists after death, so I am unable to disclose all of our communications, but I am happy to discuss the information he wished to make public."

"And what were those notes?"

"Mr. Sammy Turner noted that his intention was for half his wealth to go to his brother, and half to various charities throughout the state. As stated in his notes, the intention of the will was to leave part of his wealth to his family, and part of his wealth to help others less fortunate than him."

"And did the first will reflect that intention?"

"It did."

"Did Mr. Turner come to you to discuss updating the will?"

"Yes. A week before he went missing, Mr. Turner arrived for a meeting in my office to discuss changes to the will. He arrived with Mrs. Finch, which I had not been expecting. Still, I was happy to continue the meeting, and we discussed updating the beneficiaries of the will."

"Was the will updated during that session?"

"No."

"Why not?"

"My advice to Mr. Turner was to wait before making any changes. I told him to consider them over the following two weeks, and if he still felt the same after that period of time, we should proceed with updating the details."

"How did Mrs. Finch react to that advice?"

"She didn't like it at all. She shouted at me and said I was unprofessional. She told Mr. Turner that 'they' should find a new estate planner to update the will. Mr. Turner appeared reluctant but agreed with Mrs. Finch."

"When Mrs. Finch said 'they,' did you get the impression that she thought the money was hers?"

"Objection. Speculation."

"Sustained."

Sinclair nodded and continued. "After he left your office, did you hear from Mr. Turner again?"

"No."

"Interesting." Sinclair paused and read over her notes, allowing time for the jurors to focus on that interaction. When she was sure it had settled in their minds, she continued. "And have you reviewed the second will, the one written only five days before his death?"

"Before this court case, yes, I did. I didn't witness the second will at the time it was written, but I have since reviewed it."

Sinclair paused again. "Can you please tell the court how much Mr. Turner left to charity in his second will?"

"None."

"None? Not a single cent was left to people less fortunate than him, even though the intention of his first will was to leave half of his wealth to charity?"

"That's correct. The updated will lists only one beneficiary—Mrs. Haley Finch."

"Just two years earlier, his intention was to split his wealth between his family and charity organizations, and after just two years, he changed his mind to leave the money to one sole beneficiary and not help charity at all? Is that correct?"

"Objection," Bruce stated. "Leading question."

"Withdrawn," Sinclair was quick to answer. "Let me rephrase. Did Mr. Sammy Turner's updated will leave any money to anyone other than Mrs. Finch?"

"No."

"Interesting. That really is an interesting piece of information."

"Objection." I stood. "The assistant solicitor is testifying with the repeated use of the word 'interesting.' She's attempting to influence the jury with opinion, not fact."

"Agreed. The objection is sustained," Judge Dalton stated. "I'll only warn you once, Mrs. Sinclair. You're not to provide commentary on the statements by the witnesses, and if this behavior continues, you will be held in contempt of court."

"Yes, Your Honor." She glanced at the jury and raised her eyes, as if she was the good student being told off by the principal. Two jurors nodded. It was well played by Sinclair. "We have no further questions for the witness, Your Honor."

Bruce stood immediately. "Mr. Overton, is it common for a will to be updated after a new relationship has become serious?"

"That's a common reason to update a will."

"And was Mr. Turner in a relationship when he wrote the first will?"

"Not to my knowledge, no."

"Had he been in any significant relationship prior to his first will?"

"Again, no, not to my knowledge."

"And was he in a relationship when he updated the will?"

"I believe so, yes."

Bruce tapped his finger on a file in front of him, and then picked it up and walked to the lectern. The delay worked—all the eyes of the jurors were on him. "Mr. Overton, who was the sole personal beneficiary of the first will?"

"Mr. Ken Turner was named as the only personal beneficiary of the first will, and he was set to receive half of the estate. The other half was due to go to charity, and those twenty-five charities were listed on the will."

"And do you know if the beneficiary of the first will, Mr. Ken Turner, was told the will had been updated?"

"I don't believe so."

"After Mr. Sammy Turner's body was found, did Mr. Ken Turner visit you?"

"He did."

"And what was the intention of that visit?"

"He wanted to claim the money from the will."

"And what date was that?"

"August 7th."

"Two days after Mr. Sammy Turner's body was found?"

"That's correct."

Bruce looked to the jurors. "When Mr. Sammy Turner died on July 5th, was Mr. Ken Turner still under the assumption he would receive half the estate?"

"It appears so," Mr. Overton said.

"Hmmm." Bruce raised his eyebrows and tapped his finger on the file again. He had planted the seed of doubt, and the jurors were hooked. "No further questions."

CHAPTER 35

Christopher Rossi was in his early thirties, born in the town of Anzio, Italy, to an Italian mother and an American father. Despite moving to South Carolina when he was five years old, Rossi spoke with a thick Italian accent, made exaggerated gestures when he spoke, and dressed like he was from the fashionable streets of Milan. Over the years, he had made his Italian heritage his entire identity.

"Mr. Rossi," Sinclair began, "can you please tell the court your profession?"

"I'm a chef and owner of Rossi's Pasta Ristorante." Rossi's accent had a high-pitched tone, and his hands moved with every sentence. "I love my restaurant, and I've been blessed to have owned it for the past five years to serve my customers. It's my life's work to make great pasta."

"Did Mr. Sammy Turner ever visit your restaurant?"

"Sammy Turner ate at my pasta restaurant every week since the day it opened. He was a loyal customer, and he was coming there long before his lottery win. Back then, he'd order the spaghetti Bolognese and tap water. Nothing more. But he was there every week, and every week he'd leave a great tip. I knew he didn't have a lot of money, so I appreciated his patronage. He wasn't the biggest talker, but he was a kind soul. The only thing he really talked about was his videos. He was always recording something, and it was his real passion. He told me he had so many videos of his daily life that he needed multiple hard drives to store them on. He recorded his dinner on his cell phone a few times."

"He must've had a lot of videos."

"He told me he had many, many hard drives filled with the videos he'd been recording his whole life. It was his passion."

"And did he still visit your restaurant after his win on the lottery?"

"Oh, yes. After his lottery win, he still came every week, but he could afford the more expensive items on the menu, and the tips were so much bigger. Sometimes, his tips were outrageous. He was a good man, that Sammy. We were heartbroken when we heard he'd been killed."

"Did he ever attend the restaurant with anyone else?"

"For the first four years, no, no. It always was just Sammy. Every Tuesday, our specials night, he'd come in at 5 p.m. and sit by himself in the corner. After his lottery win, he only ever came with one other person, his very beautiful girlfriend, Haley Finch."

"Was he alone on the last time he attended your restaurant?"

"No. He was with Haley Finch on Tuesday, June 30th, and he left me an extra big tip. I know that because it was my birthday. When he didn't come in the next two Tuesdays, I was worried, so I called a few people, who called a few people, and they called me and told me he was missing. I was heartbroken."

"And you remember his patronage on June 30th?"

"I do. We also have a video camera at the door to see who comes and goes. I reviewed it after I was told Sammy went missing."

"Why did you review the footage?"

"Because I was worried about the way Haley treated Sammy that night. I wanted to see if their interaction was caught on camera, but it wasn't."

"And how did Mrs. Finch treat Mr. Sammy Turner that night?"

"They had dinner as usual, but they weren't talking. I could tell something had upset Sammy. They left the restaurant and I felt sad for him. I could see he was upset, and I only wanted the best for him. And when I stepped out of the back door of the kitchen to throw the trash in the dumpster, I could see them arguing in the parking lot. She was yelling at him, and she slapped him across the face. Not once, but twice."

"Can you confirm that you witnessed Mrs. Haley Finch slap Mr. Sammy Turner in the face only days before he went missing?"

"Yes. That's what I saw."

For the next twenty minutes, Rossi went through the finer details of that night. He was an expressive talker and the jury enjoyed listening to him. I stared at the paper in front of me, barely acknowledging that Rossi was on the stand. I didn't need to listen; I'd already read his statement fifteen times.

"Mr. Hawthorn." Judge Dalton's loud voice interrupted my thoughts. "Do you have any questions for the witness?"

"Yes. Of course." Bruce moved a piece of paper on the table, reviewed the first lines of the file and turned his attention to the man on the stand. "Mr. Rossi, how long did you know the deceased, Mr. Sammy Turner?"

"For five years, since he first started coming to my restaurant."

"And you considered him a friend?"

"Of course."

"Would you do anything to help your friend?"

"Yes."

"Did you help him when he was slapped?"

"No, no." He shook his head several times. "When a man slaps a woman, I step in. When a woman slaps a man, well, that's on him to defend himself."

Bruce nodded. "Mr. Rossi, do you usually wear glasses?"

"Sometimes."

"When you cook?"

"No. I'm nearsighted, which means I can't see things in the distance. I don't need them when I cook."

"And were you wearing your glasses as you took out the trash?"

"No." He shook his head, confused by the question. "I was coming from the kitchen, and I don't need glasses in the kitchen."

"And how far away were these people who you claim to have seen slapping each other?"

"The end of the parking lot, maybe fifty yards."

"And you didn't have your glasses?"

"No, but I knew it was them. I knew Sammy."

"You knew them," Bruce repeated. "Mr. Rossi, was there much lighting in that parking lot?"

"There aren't many lights there."

"That's interesting, Mr. Rossi. You claim to have seen someone in the dark, more than fifty yards away, without your glasses?"

"I knew Sammy."

"And Mrs. Finch?"

He shrugged. "Not so well."

"Mr. Rossi, do you claim to have seen someone fifty yards away, someone you don't know well, in the dark, with little light, when you weren't wearing your glasses?"

"I know it was Sammy."

"And the other person?"

"Ah." He shrugged. "Maybe I wasn't certain."

"Maybe you weren't certain?" Bruce's voice rose. "Mr. Rossi, this is a court of law where facts, and only facts, are entered into evidence, not assumptions."

"Listen," he interrupted. "I saw someone slap Sammy. Who it was, I can't be certain, but I saw them together earlier that night."

Bruce shook his head, and when he saw several members of the jury do the same, he sighed. "No further questions for this witness."

After Judge Dalton called for a lunch recess, our defense team spent twenty-five minutes reviewing the morning. When I was sure we had everything covered, I left the courthouse for a mental break, walking out into the humid heat. I walked to my car, parked under the shade of a tree at the end of the courthouse parking lot.

An old white pickup drove toward me as I crossed the lot, and stopped right in front of me.

Jasper Rawlings stepped out.

He stood with his arms out wide, and his chest puffed out. I ignored his immature attempt at confrontation and kept on walking.

"I heard Sammy's videos were talked about in court today," he snarled as I passed him. "Are you going to present them to the court?"

"That's none of your business."

"I'm here to give you a warning—don't even think about presenting any of those videos."

I turned. Confronted him. "What's on them?"

"Personal information. And if you present them, then I'll take it as a personal attack on me. And if you make it personal, then I'll make it personal. I'd hate for something to happen to your family."

I stepped closer. "If you come near my family, I'll tear you limb from limb."

He grinned. "I'm glad we understand each other."

I turned and walked away. I had no idea what was on those videos, but it was clear whatever it was incriminated the fentanyl operations.

And as bad as that was, as terrible as the illegal drug operation was, that couldn't be my focus.

I had to focus on winning a murder trial.

CHAPTER 36

On Friday afternoon, Sinclair called several inconsequential witnesses who had little overall effect on the case but added tiny pieces of the puzzle. More forensic witnesses, more experts, more specialists. I could see some of the jury members were becoming convinced by the mountain of small facts, but we were still a long way from the finish.

After Judge Dalton called an end to the week's proceedings, Bruce and I met in a courthouse conference room and considered the videos. We reviewed them again, but without knowing what we were looking for, we were at sea. There were thousands of hours taken over the past twenty-five years. And they weren't stored in any logical fashion. They weren't organized by date or location, and none had file names. We didn't have the time, or the money, to scroll through them all.

On Friday evening after court, I called Luke and provided an update on his case. The prosecution had sent a revised offer. They wanted him to plead guilty to the misdemeanor but still pay for the damages. I knew what his answer would be, but I called him anyway. After the usual pleasantries of talking about the weather, our families, and the impending storm season, the conversation turned to his case. As I expected, he rejected the offer; however, I wouldn't relay to the assistant solicitor which part of his anatomy Luke said he could put it in.

"Luke," I tried to reason with him over the phone, "it's a good offer, given the situation."

"Dean, I've been looking up my sleeve, and I've found an ace to play." The excitement in his voice was palpable. "And I'm almost ready to play it. Give me another five days, and I'll be ready."

"What is it?"

"It's something I found out last week." He sounded almost giddy. "I did a lot of digging around, a lot of talking to people who have been ripped off by the Freeman family, and I found some gold."

"That's good, Luke. Now that you've found something, my advice is to step carefully, and don't do anything stupid."

"If that's your advice, you're speaking to the wrong guy." Luke laughed. "I won't be bullied, Dean. Not by some rich family that thinks they can get away with anything."

"Luke, what are you going to do?"

"I took your advice and found some people who are willing to talk on social media about the Freemans. They're just waiting for my call. And once I did a little more digging, I found there was a whole group ripped off by them. So many people are angry at that family, but they can't do anything about it. They've all tried to take them to court, or to get their money back, but nobody has had any luck. Well, it's time to stop wishing, and it's time to create our own luck. Dean, I'm a fighter and I don't back down for anyone." His voice was filled with pride. "And as my father always said, it's better to die on your feet than to live on your knees."

"Okay." I rubbed my eyes several times. "You do what you've got to do."

"That's the best advice you've given me in this whole drama." Luke laughed again and then ended the call.

I sighed, but I had a smile on my face. I would've done exactly what Luke was doing. The Freemans had a long history of power in the area, and a long history of exerting that power.

On Saturday, in an attempt to forget the stress of the week, I spent the morning at my grandmother's house, preparing for her eighty-eighth birthday party.

Life in the Lowcountry was all about family, friends, and community. People had time for each other. People had time for community. People had time to bond. Even under the stress of a murder trial, I found time to spend a Saturday morning with family. That never would've happened in Chicago.

Rhys arrived and we helped set up the tables and chairs, and Emma helped in the kitchen with one of my cousins. Her mother, Jane, fighting her cancer battle, arrived and supervised a lot of the activity inside. While Rhys was setting up the chairs, his children ran up to him, in the middle of a sibling fight.

"Zoe and Ollie, it's time to break it up," Rhys said. "Zoe, you're the big sister, why don't you tell me what's going on?"

"He's annoying me," Zoe complained. "And everything that comes out of his mouth is stupid."

"Zoe." Ollie blurted out. "Zoe, Zoe, Zoe."

"I'm not stupid!" Zoe complained louder. "Take that back."

I had to hide my smile. The kid was quick.

Rhys took them over to the backyard, distracting them with a game on the old trampoline. The kids looked reluctant to jump on one without netting around the outside, but Rhys convinced them it was the way we used to do things. He forgot to mention the number of broken legs, elbows, and shoulders that came from that time as well, but that wasn't the point.

Over the sunny morning, the porch at my grandparents' house filled with people. There were two rockers, my grandmother sitting in one, and her friend in another, and two lazy dogs at their feet. Friends, relatives, and friends of relatives filled the porch, all greeting my grandmother with a kiss on the cheek. She was loving all the attention. There was a parade of first cousins, second cousins, second cousins once removed, and people I was sure I was related to but had no idea how. I greeted them all and remembered very few of their names.

As the sun reached its highest point in the sky, the noise of children giggling filled the air, interspersed with the occasional cry, and an adult telling someone off. The screen door seemed to be constantly opening and shutting. Glasses of sweet tea were sweating on the front porch. The smell of lunch wafted from the kitchen, made with love and care.

One of my cousins oversaw the cooking in the kitchen, and another one was in charge of the grill. Lunch was served on a trestle table in the front yard, plates spread across the white plastic tablecloth. There were sausages, burgers, a pot roast, dumplings, fried chicken, a sliced leg of ham, and one of the cousins had bought brisket from his smoker. The second table had the sides— lots of mashed potato, various salads, and collard greens. It looked and smelled divine.

However, lunch had to wait. Everyone came into the front yard, and Grandma Lincoln led the prayer of thanks. After the minute-long prayer, as a collective we sang her "Happy Birthday To You," and then cheered several times for her age. Her smile was huge.

They'd come far and wide to celebrate her birthday. She was well loved and adored. The stress of the murder trial seemed a million miles away.

Once lunch was had, the pies came out. Little people charged at the table, and their mothers had to hold them back. Pecan pie, peach pie, chess pie and coconut pie—all the favorites.

As an extended family group, with multiple generations and so many layers of love, we spent the day talking, eating, and laughing. There were hollers of laughter when bad jokes were told, and whispers when rumors needed to be spread. The kids ran free around the yard, kicking balls, throwing rocks at tin cans, and pretend fighting with sticks. Some kids wandered out in the street but were told off by the teenagers near the fence. The teenagers were on their cell phones, their social connection devices, but they were sharing videos and links and pages with each other. The older men talked about how hard it was getting old, and the younger men talked about sports. The women talked about the reality television shows that were filmed nearby, and the new hot male yoga teacher that had arrived in town. Sweet tea was drunk, beers were shared, and wine glasses were knocked over by toddlers. The buzz of the South radiated through the house, a place and time to forget all the other stressors, forget all the pains and worries and dramas, and just live in the moment.

Emma and I stayed to clean up, as did several of the other cousins. Talking to family members, surrounded by so much love, I saw Emma smile. That made my heart sing.

It was the first sign I'd seen that we were going to get through it.

CHAPTER 37

The hardest part of a murder trial is the nights.

Trying to switch off, trying to stop the thoughts cascading through my head, trying to close my eyes and catch some much-needed rest. But it was nights when the doubts were the worst. Every time I tried to drift off, every time I was thought I was going to sleep, the thoughts of losing would crash back through my head.

I tried meditation, I tried whiskey, and I tried sleeping pills. None of it worked. None of it switched off the questions that rolled through my head. Could I have objected to that question? Could I have guided the cross-examination better? Should I have made more eye contact with the jury members? Was an innocent client going to prison because I couldn't save her?

I had Haley's life in my hands. I had her future relying on my questions. I had her hope resting on my behaviors. I rose at 5 a.m. most mornings, surviving on coffee and painkillers. It wasn't the best for my body, it wasn't the best for my mind, but I had to save her.

When I arrived at the office at 8 a.m. on Sunday morning, I noticed the front door of the building was ajar. There was a break in the wood around the handle.

I looked around, gritted my teeth, and stepped inside. Kayla's desk was untouched, but I noticed my office door was wide open.

Stepping forward with my fists clenched, I leaned my head inside.

My office was a mess.

Files had been thrown on the floor, the computer monitor knocked over, and books had been torn off the shelves. The drawers of my desk were pulled out, and my cupboard door was open.

I walked toward Bruce's office. His office was the same.

I called Bruce, then Kayla, then the Beaufort Police Department. All arrived within fifteen minutes.

Detective Terry Wallace interviewed us while other officers scoured the rooms looking for clues. Bruce was annoyed that the alarm hadn't triggered before Kayla suggested we review the security cameras.

Gathered around Kayla's monitor, we reviewed the footage. There was a camera over the front door, and another in the reception area. We watched as a slim man in a face mask, dressed head to toe in black, snuck out of the bushes in front of the office at 2:05 a.m., prized open the front door, and slipped inside. He turned for the alarm system, entered a code, and disabled it.

"How did he know the code?" Bruce shook his head, looking at the control panel.

"When was the last time the code was updated?" Wallace asked him.

"Ah." Bruce rubbed his hand on the back of his neck. "Last year."

"Which means they could've known the code for a year," Wallace said. "Did anyone see you enter it as you came into the office over the last year?"

"Anyone could have," Kayla said. "Bruce is very relaxed about entering it."

Bruce grunted, but he had no comeback. He knew she was right.

We continued to watch the security footage as the intruder ignored Kayla's desk and went straight to my office. They appeared to know what they were looking for. After a minute there, they exited, and entered Bruce's office. Another minute later, and then they were in the boardroom. In under ten minutes, the intruder was in and out. They exited via the front door, not carrying anything with them.

"He didn't find what he was looking for," Wallace said. "He left empty-handed."

The police advised us not to touch anything while they dusted for fingerprints. We spent an hour talking with the detectives before I advised them that I had work to complete ahead of the trial. Bruce suggested that, given the circumstances, we could apply to the court for a recess, but I felt it was unnecessary. I set up my laptop in the boardroom and began reviewing statements ahead of the next day. Bruce handled the law enforcement, helping them as they conducted a forensic analysis of the entire office. I didn't expect them to find anything.

After the officers left at lunchtime, Kayla came into the boardroom and checked if I needed anything.

"No, but thanks," I said. "I'm going to keep reviewing these files."

"You okay?" Kayla looked at me with apprehension. "You look like you haven't slept in weeks."

"I haven't," I responded. "It's the humidity. There's no break from it."

"You get used to it," Kayla said. "It's just because you've spent the last decade in Chicago, and your body has forgotten how to handle the heat. Two summers is what I was always told. If you can survive two summers here, your body will have adapted, and you'll be fine."

"Two summers? Ouch. I'll have melted away by then."

Bruce walked in and sat down in a huff. "Just got off the phone with Wallace. There was also a break-in at Sammy's old house on Dataw Island. It's all locked up, but someone got in there last night. They didn't take anything, but they busted open the front door, just like they did here. It appears they bypassed the security checkpoint on the gated community. Even with the two break-ins, Wallace doesn't have much hope of the finding the culprit. No fingerprints, no chance of identification from any security footage, and no DNA left behind at either scene. It looks clean. What are your thoughts?"

"My first thought was Jasper Rawlings. It appeared like the same body shape on the security footage."

"I thought the same," Bruce agreed. "And I told Wallace that. Someone could've told him the alarm code and paid him to break in here. They'll go out and talk to him, but unless he confesses, I don't have much hope of an arrest."

"It could've been a ploy to disrupt us," Kayla said. "Throw us off our game."

"Could be," Bruce said. "Kayla, we need to figure out how to update the code on the alarm. I don't even know how to do it."

"Already organized," Kayla said. "I just need a new code from you, and I can set it up."

"Thank you." Bruce left with Kayla and they both returned fifteen minutes later. Bruce handed me a piece of paper with the new code on it and turned the focus back to the case. "Sinclair looks nervous."

"She does," I said. "She wasn't prepared for all the questions about Ken Turner, but she opened the door, and we walked straight in."

"Think she'll go for a mistrial and then prepare the case again?"

I sucked in a long, slow breath. "She's going to call Maria Frazer next. That will be her chance to have this declared a mistrial. If Maria talks about Prescott, she could motion for a mistrial."

"Should we object to the motion?" Bruce asked. "We're in front here."

"Slightly in front," I said. "We still haven't convinced the jury, and if Maria introduces evidence that Prescott is missing, the jury will start to look back toward Haley."

"Good point." Bruce turned to Kayla. "Thank you for coming in. You've done more than enough for today. You should go home to your family."

"I will." She nodded. "And you guys?"

"Still work to do," Bruce said. "We need to prepare for tomorrow."

"We need to review the depositions again," I said. "We need to find another hole in their theory. They've put so much faith into that motive, and we're doing a great job of challenging that, but it's close."

Kayla wished us luck and left, while Bruce returned to his private office. He left around five, and I continued to work, ensuring no stone had been left unturned before we walked back into court.

As Sunday night pushed past 8 p.m., I was struggling to keep my eyes open, even though I was fueled by an enormous amount of coffee. As I packed up my laptop, I looked out the window. Night had descended over Beaufort.

My cell rang. I checked the number. It was Emma.

"Dean," she whispered, "I've locked myself in the bedroom, but there's someone trying to break in."

Shock raced through me. "Emma, get your gun."

CHAPTER 38

I raced home. I drove the streets with aggression, slamming the gas, running red lights, and ignoring the speed limits.

I couldn't risk Emma. Not her. She had been through too much. I couldn't live without her. Not my Emma. Not my world.

Pulling up to the house, I screeched the car on to the front lawn. I didn't care about the fence. I didn't care about the grass.

I leaped out of the car and ran toward the house. I didn't close the door.

The front door to the house was closed. There was a light on upstairs.

I bounded up the front steps and burst through the front door. I couldn't see anyone.

"Emma!" I called out. "Emma!"

I raced into the hallway. Still nobody.

Leaping up the stairs two at a time, I tried the bedroom door. There was something pushed against it.

"Emma!" I stepped back and slammed my shoulder into the door. "Emma!"

The door swung open. I found her.

She was sitting on the floor, next to our bed, tucked into the corner. Her eyes were focused on the door. Her hands were shaking.

The Glock, tightly gripped in her hands, was still pointed at the center of the door.

"Emma." I calmed my voice as I approached. "It's okay. I'm here now."

Her eyes remained on the door.

"Emma," I repeated. "It's okay."

"They were here, Dean," she whispered. "They were inside."

I crept along the edge of the bed, out of the aim of the handgun.

"They were here," she repeated, keeping her eyes focused forward. "Someone was inside our house."

"It's okay," I said again. "I'm here now. There's nobody else here. It's just you and me."

Gently, I reached for the weapon. With my open hand on top of the barrel, I lowered it toward the ground. When it was pointed down, I took it from her firm grasp.

"I was ready to shoot them," she whispered, her eyes still looking ahead. Her stare was vacant. "They came to the bedroom door. They tried to get in. They tried to get past the lock. But they ran as soon as you drove in."

I pulled Emma into my chest, and she cried.

I couldn't risk Emma.

Holding her tight as she sobbed, I looked at the gun. I was glad she hadn't needed to use it, but I was glad she had it.

After a few minutes, Emma composed herself. She explained that she had heard someone outside on the porch while she was watching a show on her laptop. The person tried to open the locked front door and then tried the side door. She had called out to them, but there was no response. The house was quiet for a few moments, and then she heard them at the window.

She called out to the intruder, telling them that she had a gun, but again she heard no response. Everything went quiet and she didn't know where they'd gone. A few moments later, she heard someone try the laundry room window. She was terrified and locked herself in the bedroom.

She heard the window in the laundry room break. She heard someone climb inside. She heard them rustling in the kitchen and then the living area. She called out to them again, and the rustling stopped.

Through the quiet of the night, she heard footsteps creeping toward her.

That's when my car drove up on the lawn. The intruder ran.

I told her she did the right thing. I told her I was proud of her. I told her that she was incredibly brave. None of it mattered. She was shaking, terrified that someone had wanted to hurt her.

The police arrived five minutes after me. They came into the house, and I explained what had happened. They investigated the broken window, looked to see if anything appeared out of place, and took Emma's statement. They dusted for fingerprints and asked us for any surveillance footage we had. We had installed security cameras several months ago, but again, it was hard to identify the intruder from the footage.

The police didn't leave the house until after midnight.

Emma went to bed, but she didn't sleep. Neither did I.

This time they had gone too far.

CHAPTER 39

Sitting behind the defense table, I was struggling to control my anger.

As the crowd walked in, as the courtroom filled, I kept my eyes on the doors. When I saw who I was looking for, I stood, almost knocking the chair over behind me. I glared at Jasper Rawlings as I walked toward the back of the courtroom. He sat down, looking up as I approached him. I leaned my tall frame over the top of him, spreading my arms on either side of the row of seats.

I leaned close to his ear. "If you come to my house again, I'll tear your limbs off."

He smiled at me. Behind me, I heard someone chuckle. I turned and saw Bronson Finch grinning. As I stepped toward him, the bailiff called the room to order.

I held my glare on him for a long moment and walked back to the defense table.

"All good?" Bruce whispered as I stood next him.

I nodded my confirmation, but it was far from the truth.

Judge Dalton walked into the room and looked over the crowd. The gallery was packed to start week two. Every space was crowded. Every viewing point was taken. The rumors had spread through Beaufort, the stories had snaked through the streets, and everyone was anxious to see where the case would go next.

Judge Dalton instructed the bailiff to bring in the jury, and he spoke to them for a few moments, confirming that they understood their responsibilities in the second week. He then instructed Sinclair to call her next witness.

"The State calls Ms. Maria Frazer."

Prescott's ex-wife. She was a troublesome witness. Wearing a black skirt, white blouse, and a blazer with wide shoulder pads, she walked to the stand with her shoulders back and her head held high. She looked confident, but she was a problem for the prosecution. They knew it, and we knew it. They had prepared her, they had been through the questions and answers she was allowed to give, but they also knew one wrong answer from her could jeopardize the entire trial. But she had also witnessed violence between Haley Finch and Sammy Turner, and her testimony strengthened their case. It was a risk they had to take.

I stood as soon as she was sworn in. "Objection to this witness. We believe the intention of the prosecution is to lead into territory that has been defined as outside the scope of this trial."

"We've been through this, Mr. Lincoln," Judge Dalton stated. "The objection is overruled; however, I will warn the State not to push her into territory that's been deemed inadmissible."

"Yes, Your Honor." Sinclair stood behind her desk and nodded. One of her assistants passed her a file and Sinclair thanked them. She took the file and placed it on the lectern and then walked to the right of it, stepping closer to the witness. "Ms. Frazer, can you please tell the court how you know the defendant, Mrs. Finch?"

"She married my ex-husband, Prescott Finch. Prescott and I have a wonderful daughter together, and our daughter also spent some time with Haley."

"Has she spent any time with Haley recently?"

"No, my daughter hasn't been to their house in two years."

Sinclair avoided eye contact with Judge Dalton. She knew how close she was to crossing the line. "Can you please tell the court the first time you met Mrs. Finch?"

"The first time I met Haley was a few days after my divorce was official. At the time, Prescott was in his fifties and Haley was still in her twenties. It was clear that she had married him for his money."

"Objection. Prejudicial," I said. "That's a blatant misrepresentation of their marriage and clearly prejudicial against the defendant. There's no evidence to suggest this is the truth."

"Sustained," Judge Dalton agreed. "Ms. Frazer, please stick to answering the questions put to you without commentary about your personal opinion."

Maria nodded her response and looked to Sinclair. Sinclair didn't miss a beat. She continued, "When was the last time you interacted with Mrs. Finch?"

"Earlier this year, in the week before Mr. Turner went missing. I had to go to Haley's house to collect some of Prescott's belongings. She was with her new older, rich boyfriend. She introduced him as Sammy Turner."

"Her boyfriend," Sinclair repeated. "Were you surprised she had a much older, rich boyfriend?"

"No. Haley is pretty, and Haley knows how to get what she wants."

Sinclair let the answer hang in the air for a few moments. She knew what she was doing. She was creating questions for the jury without presenting the whole truth. I could see the looks of confusion on several of the jurors' faces, and I could imagine what internal questions they would be asking—where is Prescott now? Why is she referring to him in the past tense? Why isn't the prosecution asking questions about where Prescott is?

"And did they interact while you were in the house?"

"They did." She sighed and shook her head. "When she spoke to him, she yelled at him like he was a little dog. It made me angry because that's how she used to treat Prescott. It brought back all my feelings about that time, and I tried to get out as quick as possible."

"What did she say to her 'new, older, rich boyfriend'?"

"As soon as I walked in, she barked at him to 'sit down and don't make a sound.' Later, she snapped again, and said, 'I told you to sit down and shut up.' She pushed him back into the chair and then raised her hand like she was going to slap him. He cowered when she did that, but she slapped him anyway."

"Where did she slap him?"

"On the cheek."

"How many times did you see her physically assault Mr. Turner?"

"Twice. She did it when I walked in and then, when I was leaving, Mr. Turner got up off the couch, but she pushed him back down and slapped him again. Mr. Turner didn't seem very physically fit, and he cowered back from Haley every time she approached him."

Sinclair looked at her notes, pursing her lips, displaying her disappointment at Haley's behavior. "And after your divorce, how many times did you interact with Mrs. Finch?"

"Quite a few . . . until we reported Prescott as a missing person to the—"

"Objection!" I jumped to my feet. "This answer assumes facts not in evidence."

"Sustained." Judge Dalton's answer was quick, and his tone was aggressive. "That answer is outside the scope of this trial."

Sinclair looked at the file in front of her, and then to the jury. When she saw several questioning looks, she turned back to Judge Dalton.

"No further questions for this witness." Sinclair was quick to end the testimony on that note.

The jury had heard the statement and it was impossible to un-ring the bell.

I turned to Bruce and nodded. We had prepared for this moment. Bruce stood. "Your Honor, we request a fifteen-minute recess before we continue."

Judge Dalton agreed to our request and we got to work.

CHAPTER 40

"A motion for a mistrial." Judge Dalton looked at his watch, moved a file across his desk, and leaned back in his leather chair. "I should've known it was coming from you, Bruce."

Judge Dalton's dim chambers were to the side of the courtroom, shut off from the heat and humidity behind a pair of thick curtains. The space had a distinguished ambiance. A large bookshelf, filled with legal volumes, lined the left wall, and a black leather couch sat on the right side. The judge's mahogany desk sat at the rear, with two leather seats in front of it, and there was a strong musty smell in the air.

Bruce and I stood on one side of the room, and Sinclair and an assistant stood on the other.

"Your Honor, this case must be declared a mistrial," Bruce began. "The jury could not possibly remain impartial after what they just heard from Ms. Frazer. You set clear guidelines at the start of the trial, and the prosecution purposely called witnesses who blatantly disregarded that. The jury cannot possibly be expected to make an unbiased decision after that statement. How can this trial continue?"

Judge Dalton grunted and turned to the other side of the room. "Mrs. Sinclair, do you have a response?"

"It was a misunderstanding."

"A misunderstanding? I hope you're not serious," I responded. "You called a witness who was directly affected by Prescott's disappearance and then you baited her into disrupting this trial. You knew what you were doing."

"And we know why you did it," Bruce said. "It's because you were losing, and you know the jury was going to return a not guilty verdict."

"We're not losing," Sinclair snapped back. "And if you're so confident about the jury, then this trial should continue."

"Their opinion is changed now," Bruce continued. "They heard that statement, and it's lodged questions in their heads. But the truth is Prescott is not a missing person. He sent an email from South America earlier this year. Any insinuation that he is missing shows a blatant disregard for the rules of this court."

"The witness testified about her experience, nothing more. She said she reported Prescott as a missing person, which she did." Sinclair looked to Judge Dalton. "We prepared the witness as best we could; however, she slipped up in the moment. Her ex-husband, the father of her daughter, has been missing for two years, and we need to cut her some slack. She's under a tremendous amount of pressure."

"Not missing," Bruce said. "Prescott left because he wanted to, and any suggestion of foul play is prejudicial." Bruce turned to Judge Dalton. "Mrs. Finch cannot receive a fair trial after that statement. The jury has been unduly influenced."

Judge Dalton exhaled loudly through his nostrils and read the motion in front of him.

"I understand your position, but I don't believe it was enough to affect this trial. The motion is dismissed."

"Your Honor, you cannot possibly—"

"Bruce, a trial court's decision to deny a motion for a mistrial is reviewed for abuse of discretion, and if I've erred in this judgment, then it'll be reviewed at a later time."

"Your Honor," Bruce pleaded, "the jury has been influenced by that statement."

"My decision is made." Judge Dalton's voice was firm. "I'll interview the jury members about their interpretation of what was said, and if I'm content with their answers, then the trial shall proceed. Once back in the courtroom, we'll put the dismissal of this motion on the court record, and you can make your objection to its refusal official." Judge Dalton indicated to the door. "Now get out of my chambers."

When he returned to the courtroom, Judge Dalton instructed the jury members that they couldn't use Prescott's alleged disappearance to form part of their decision on Haley's guilt. He explained that Prescott was not a missing person and that the Beaufort Police Department had closed the missing persons file. He questioned the jury members about the interpretation of his instructions, and once he was satisfied with their answers, he instructed Sinclair to continue.

Despite Judge Dalton's clear directives, the seed of doubt had been planted in the jurors' minds. They had to question why Maria Frazer thought her ex-husband was missing, and they had to question why the judge wouldn't allow it to be talked about in court. Bruce declined to cross-examine Maria. The damage was done.

As the second week of the trial ended, Haley Finch was looking at life in prison.

CHAPTER 41

The air was humid again.

My clothes clung to my body, wrapping me in a constant wet blanket. I started the SUV and checked my air conditioner. I turned the fan up all the way. Another tropical storm was developing over the Atlantic, and the humidity was getting worse. There was a menacing grayness over the city. Something was brewing in the clouds, something big, and the city had begun to prepare. Shelves were empty at the stores. Homes were being boarded up. People hurried through the streets with an anxious buzz.

Sinclair called. She wanted to talk. And from the sound of her voice, she'd been working twenty-four hours straight. I phoned Bruce and Kayla, and we met in the courthouse meeting room an hour later. Sinclair and her team were waiting for us.

The State put a new offer on the table. It was laughable. Fifteen years minimum security for voluntary manslaughter. We knew the offer was poor and so did they. Sinclair said it was the best she could do. We argued. Voices were raised. Legal precedents were thrown around the room.

No resolution was reached.

We relayed the new deal to Haley at her home on Saturday, but she wasn't enthused. She rejected the offer before Bruce had even finished his sentence.

"It's all so confusing. He said this, she said that. It's so hard to know what's happening," Haley said. "Are we winning?"

"It's fifty-fifty," Bruce lied. With the statement about Prescott lingering in the jurors' minds, we were behind. There was no doubt about it, but it was best not to worry Haley. "The prosecution has presented a good case, but we've raised a lot of doubt about the arrest and the lack of evidence. All they have is a motive, and we're about to destroy that."

"Have you seen anyone around your house again?" I questioned.

"I occasionally see them drive past, but that's it. They're no longer parked out front."

"They're looking for a way in," I stated. "They're scoping out your house, trying to see if there are any cracks in the security system."

"There aren't. There's no way they could get in here without setting off the alarms. And the alarms are connected to the security company, whose headquarters are only around the corner." Haley played with her earrings, twisting and turning them several times to disperse her anxious energy. "You've mentioned Ken a lot in court. He's on some of Sammy's videos. I could check and see if there's anything like Ken taking drugs or that sort of thing?"

"We're not certain if we're going to call Ken yet," Bruce explained. "He's on the State's witness list because he was a witness in Sammy's disappearance. He'll be terrible on the stand, which will look good for us, but he'll also be very hostile toward us. We also don't know what he's going to say, but if we feel like we're losing, we'll call him to testify."

"So you're just going to leave the question hanging?" Haley squinted. "You're not going to fill in the blanks for the jury? We could prove that Ken did it. He'll fall apart if you put him on the stand."

"We don't have to prove anything, Haley," I explained. "That's the prosecution's job. All we need to do is show that there's reasonable doubt that you did it. If we can do that, we can keep you out of prison."

"I can't go to prison. I can't leave my garden." She looked out the window and blinked back a tear. "And I can feel all their eyes on me. I know Bronson is staring at me. Every time I turn around, he's staring at me."

The way she said his name was emphasized differently. I leaned closer. "Haley, how well do you know Bronson?"

"I know him." She brushed her thumb over the tip of her nose. "He was Prescott's brother."

"Haley." My tone was firm as I pressed for a truthful answer. "That's not the full story. And if we're going to win this case, we can't be surprised by anything at the last minute. He's on the prosecution's witness list, and even though they might not call him, we need to be prepared if they do. How well did you know Bronson?"

Haley bit one of her fingernails. "We had . . . a liaison."

"A liaison?" Bruce's voice rose. "You slept with your brother-in-law?"

"Just once."

"Just once." Bruce threw his hands up in the air. "Haley, that's terrible."

"I know," she whispered and continued biting on her fingernail. "It was years ago, and it was a mistake. Prescott and I were married, and he was away on a business trip. Prescott was drinking a lot at that stage, and Bronson came around to talk about supporting him through an intervention. All the emotion got to us, and it just . . . it just happened."

"Who else knows about it?"

"Nobody. Just Bronson."

226

"Does his wife Jessica know?"

"No." Haley avoided eye contact. "And it would break her heart to find out that I did it."

Bruce shook his head several times. He hadn't expected it. I was less surprised.

While Bruce moved the discussion on and talked to Haley about the complications of calling Ken to the stand, I left the room with my cell phone.

I needed to make a call.

CHAPTER 42

Bronson Finch answered on the fifth ring.

When he answered the phone, he waited a few moments, and then said my name with disdain. "*Dean Lincoln.* What do you want?"

"You need to be in my office in one hour."

"Why would I do that?"

"Because if you don't, your wife will learn about your liaison with Haley Finch."

There was silence on the other end of the line.

"Your choice, Bronson."

"I'll be there," he whispered, and ended the call. It sounded like he had expected it to come out at some point.

Bronson arrived at the office fifty minutes later. I opened the front door, and we didn't greet each other. I led him inside to the boardroom, where Bruce was waiting.

I pointed to the seat at the head of the table, and he sat down. I sat at the first seat around the table next to him. He didn't speak and kept his eyes down.

"We know about the affair with Haley," Bruce stated.

"It wasn't an affair. It was a one-off, and that was a mistake." He grunted. "I hate that woman. I despise everything she does."

"But you still slept with her."

"Years ago. Before I knew who she was as a person. I've regretted it every day since. That woman is a witch."

"Did Sammy know about the affair?"

Bronson didn't respond.

"You can answer our questions, or we'll tell Jessica about your liaison with Haley."

"No. Sammy didn't know about it." He didn't move, keeping his eyes on the table. "And Jessica won't believe you."

"If it's mentioned in open court, with a full gallery and the residents of Beaufort listening in, the affair will be hard to deny. Rumors spread fast in Beaufort. Even if it's not true, your wife will have to do something about it. Rumors have weight here."

"What do you want?"

I leaned closer. "Who killed Sammy Turner?"

He kept his eyes down. "Haley killed him. We know that. Everyone knows that. She did it to my brother, and then she did it again. If she's not locked up this time, you can be sure she'll do it again."

"Someone is going to a lot of effort to keep something quiet," Bruce said. "They've broken into our office, they've broken into Sammy's old house, and they've broken into Dean's home."

"It's not what you think," he whispered.

"We know what the truth is—Sammy had information on you that he threatened to expose."

Bronson grunted, put his head in his hands, and then stood. He paced the back of the boardroom for a few moments, trying to work his way through his problem. His fist clenched and he tapped it against the wall. "I don't know who killed Sammy."

"We need answers, not lies."

"I said I don't know," Bronson snapped. "I came here because I thought you were reasonable men, but I can see that you're not.

You're as blind as all of them. Haley did it. She killed Prescott and she killed Sammy. Who knows if there are others?"

I stood. "I'm not convinced by your little act."

"It's not an act. That woman is evil. Sammy didn't like me, but he didn't deserve what happened to him. Not that way. Not being dumped in the marsh."

"We know Sammy had information on your fentanyl operations. And we know he was killed for it."

Bronson didn't respond, folding his arms and leaning against the wall.

"He was going to expose your drug deals with Ken Turner. Sammy wanted Ken out of the drug business, and knew the best way to do it was to take the supplier down. Sammy was going to expose your drug-dealing ring. Sammy wanted Ken to get clean, but you kept pulling him back into the drugs."

Again, Bronson didn't respond.

"You can cooperate with the police for a lenient sentence. If you tell them the truth"—I eyed him carefully, watching for his reaction—"that Jasper Rawlings killed Sammy to stop the operations being exposed."

He didn't flinch. "Don't threaten me with lies. I know you don't have any evidence. You don't have the video."

"You paid Jasper Rawlings to find the video."

"Didn't need to pay him," Bronson scoffed and started to walk toward the door. "You're on the wrong track. Haley killed Sammy. That's all there is to it." He looked at Bruce. "You should be more careful when you enter the security code to your office. You never know who's watching over your shoulder."

He left without another word, and it all fell into place— Sammy had information that would expose Bronson's fentanyl-dealing operations. He'd needed to take away Ken's supply of drugs.

Unfortunately for Sammy, a lot of people would've gone a long way to stop that information being exposed.

Targeting Ken was the best way to win the case in court. It was the best legal tactic.

But the truth appeared to lie somewhere else.

CHAPTER 43

As I drove into my driveway, I noticed the pickup parked across the street.

It was a dirty old white pickup—the same one I had seen outside Haley's house weeks earlier. I didn't go inside. I strode straight toward the pickup. As I crossed the street, the door opened. Rawlings stepped out with his hands raised in surrender.

That didn't stop me. He was near my home, near my wife, and his presence was an act of aggression. I gripped his collar and slammed him against the cabin of his truck, pressing my knuckles into his throat. "Never threaten my wife."

"Hey, pal." His voice was scratchy as my fist pressed against his throat. "I come in peace."

"You don't do anything in peace."

He smiled slightly. "Sure, sure. But let's act like grown-ups. I've come to deliver a message."

"What message?"

"A warning."

I pressed my fist tighter into his throat. His hands gripped my wrist, but he was no match for my strength. I pressed tighter, snarled in his face, and then slammed him against his pickup, letting go as I did. I slammed my right fist into his stomach, connecting solidly. He slumped forward, dropping to one knee, trying to suck in breaths. I was tempted to hit him again, but I restrained myself.

After a few moments, he slowed his breathing and rose to his feet, still hunched over and holding his stomach. "That's a solid punch you've got for an office worker." He stepped back from me before speaking again. "Don't expose us. That's my warning."

"I'll do what I need to do in court."

"And you can win this case by taking down Ken Turner. He deserves to be in prison. I've read about your case; I know that's what your angle is. You're trying to convince the jury that Ken Turner did it."

"You're not as dumb as you look."

"I'll take that as a compliment," Rawlings scoffed. "Take Ken down. I know that's your legal tactic. There's no need to show the video of Bronson dealing to Ken. If you expose that, you cut off a lot of income for a lot of dangerous people. And they won't be happy with you for that." He sniffed, cleared his throat, and then spat on the road. "And if you take down Bronson, you take away my income, and I don't like that. I'll do what I need to do to protect it."

I stepped closer. "Is that why you killed Sammy Turner?"

"I'm not going to answer that," Rawlings said. "Don't expose us, or next time, I won't leave your wife alone."

I went to grab him, but he pulled a handgun from his belt. He didn't point it at me, holding it down. "I told you—I come in peace, but if you want to make this dangerous, I'll defend myself."

"You mention my wife again, and there'll be no peace."

"Then we have a clear understanding." Rawlings reached for the door of his pickup and opened it. He stepped inside, but before he shut the door, he leaned out. "Sammy had it coming. And he deserved every single one of those five stab wounds."

CHAPTER 44

On the third Monday of the trial, the courthouse was packed.

When the courtroom doors opened to the public, there was a controlled rush to the gallery seats. All the available space was filled, and after five minutes, the bailiffs had to turn people away. There was a palpable sense of anticipation surrounding the trial. I could hear constant whispers behind me, and I was sure Haley could as well. This was the theatre of real life, and everyone wanted a front-row seat.

I was conflicted. Using Ken as our third-party culpability target was the best way to convince the jury that Haley was innocent. It was the best way to show that someone else could've committed the murder. But there was so much more at play. There were so many more people with the motive to stop Sammy from exposing Bronson's drug-dealing operations. As Sinclair stood to call the first witness of the day, I had to push those thoughts aside and focus on winning the court case.

"The State calls Leo McVeigh."

Leo McVeigh walked through the court doors with his eyes focused on the ground in front of him. He was a meek man, skinny with a head that seemed too big for his body. He had little muscle tone, and his shoulders were slumped forward. He was dressed in a white polo shirt that was one size too big, and blue jeans one size too tight. He wore glasses and he had little hair left. A strong smell of body odor wafted by as the forty-nine-year-old computer technician sat on the stand.

"Mr. McVeigh, thank you for testifying today." Sinclair remained standing behind her desk. "Can you please start with your name, occupation, and how you know the defendant?"

"My name is Leo Henry McVeigh, I'm employed as an IT specialist, and I dated Mrs. Finch for several months when she first moved from Wisconsin to South Carolina."

I looked at the jury and could see the confusion on their faces. Internally, I was sure they were all asking the same question—how could someone as pretty as Haley date someone like Leo McVeigh?

"Did Mrs. Finch live with you?"

"She did. We met at a fancy bar, and to be honest, I thought she was way out of my league, but she just kept talking to me. I told her what I did for work, and that I owned my house, and that I liked to play online games. And she told me that she was living in a small van that she had driven south in. She moved into the spare room in my house a few days after we met, and we dated for a few months."

"Were you intimate during that time?"

"We kissed, but that was it. We went out to dinner, hung out, and I bought her lots of things, but she avoided sleeping with me."

"Did you always buy dinner?"

"Yes. I thought that was the right thing to do."

"And you paid for other things?"

"Everything. I bought her food, clothes, gas, jewelry. I don't think Haley spent a cent when she was living with me."

Sinclair looked at the jury with one eyebrow raised, showing just what she thought of Haley's behavior. "And why did the relationship end?"

"She told me that I wasn't rich enough to date someone like her."

Again, another long pause to let the information sink into the minds of the jurors. "And did you remain friends after that?"

"We did. We remained close friends."

"Did she continue to live in your spare room?"

"For another month, yes. Even though our relationship ended, I didn't want to kick her out."

"And who did she date after your relationship ended?"

"A week after she broke up with me, she told me that she had gone on a date with a 'rich man' named Prescott Finch. She moved out of my place into his mansion on Bay Street, and they married a few months later. I went to their wedding, and it was a lavish party."

"Did that make you feel used by Mrs. Finch?"

"At the time, yes."

"But you remained friends with her?"

"I did. We spoke every week, either on the phone or over coffee."

"Did you meet Mr. Sammy Turner when she started dating him?"

"Yes."

"And did Mrs. Finch ever talk about her relationship with Mr. Turner?"

"She did. She told me all about their relationship."

"And in the week before the disappearance of Mr. Turner, did Mrs. Finch say anything to you?"

"Yes."

"What did she say?"

Leo McVeigh huffed and kept his eyes down, avoiding eye contact with Haley. "She said, 'Sammy won't be alive much longer, and I'll have all his money soon.'"

One of the jury members gasped. Leo looked at them and was doing his best to blink back his tears.

Sinclair shook her head and then turned to the judge. "No further questions."

When instructed by Judge Dalton, Bruce leaned back in his chair and looked up at the witness. "Mr. McVeigh, context is important in testimonies, would you agree?"

"Yes."

"And in that conversation with Mrs. Finch, were you discussing Mr. Turner's ill health?"

"Earlier in that conversation, yes, Haley and I talked about Sammy's health. He was overweight and struggling to walk up a flight of stairs without huffing and puffing. I think he may have also had diabetes, and some other ailments."

"Context. You were talking about Sammy's ill health when she said those words, weren't you?"

"We were, yes."

"Context." Bruce nodded. "No further questions."

Leo McVeigh left the witness stand, keeping his head down, and not looking in Haley's direction. When he had left the room, Judge Dalton looked at his watch and asked the prosecution if they had any further witnesses.

At 10:55 a.m. on the third Monday of the trial, Assistant Solicitor Charlotte Sinclair stood. "Your Honor, the prosecution rests."

She looked at me and smiled, just a little.

With the suggestion that Prescott was missing, and Haley's history of money-focused relationships, the prosecution was in front, and Sinclair knew it.

CHAPTER 45

After a short court recess, it was our turn to present the defense theory.

This was our chance to show that justice could be served in a small town. We had to show the court that this case wasn't about elaborate narratives. This case wasn't about courtroom tricks. This case, and all its drama, was about the truth.

I rested a hand on Haley's forearm and then stood to call the first witness.

"The defense calls Dr. Gemma Richardson."

Dr. Gemma Richardson walked to the stand with the look of someone who was intelligent, knowledgeable, and just a little smug. A short woman with curly hair, she had an aura that projected confidence and professionalism.

I stood behind the defense table. "Can you please start with your name and occupation?"

"My name is Dr. Gemma Richardson, and I'm a psychologist who specializes in relationships, and my research has been focused on the psychological factors behind age-gap relationships."

"And what is your professional expertise?"

"I have a PhD in psychology, I've studied at Harvard, my work has been published in more than fifteen scientific journals, and I've testified in more than twenty-five trials."

It was necessary to establish an expert witness's credentials early in their testimony. While an eyewitness was only allowed to testify about what they'd directly observed, an expert witness was allowed to present specialized, and general, knowledge to the court, based on their professional expertise.

"And can you please explain what an age-gap relationship is?"

"In the realm of psychology, an age-gap relationship refers to a romantic relationship where there is a significant age difference between the partners. It's important to note that societal expectations determine what these ages are. For instance, in some Asian cultures, men in their thirties have arranged marriages with girls in the early teens, and in some African countries, more than 25 percent of all marriages have an age gap larger than ten years. In western society, a ten-year age gap is huge when one partner is eighteen and the other is twenty-eight but is less so when one partner is fifty and the other is sixty."

"And in the scientific research, what has been found about age-gap relationships?"

"It varies, especially across cultural backgrounds. In general, it was found that younger females find older males more attractive than males of the same age, and older men find younger women more attractive. In large age-gap relationships in western societies, more than ten years, there were many factors at play, including maturity, financial security, and emotional support."

"In your role as a psychologist, did you interview Mrs. Finch?"

"In preparation for this trial, yes, I interviewed Mrs. Finch five times. She also completed several questionnaires about her past relationships and her upbringing."

"And what did you find during those five interviews?"

"That she had a strong need for matching with a partner who was mature and provided her with emotional support. Mrs. Finch stated that she lost her own father at five years old, and while I don't wish to make a psychological assessment after only five meetings, it is something to consider. There are many subconscious reasons why someone seeks out the partner that they do, and one possible reason is that Haley seeks the approval of older men. Haley is looking to mend that trauma she suffered as a child, and she needs to find someone to fill the painful void that she has deep inside."

I tapped my hand on the file in front of me. "Is this normal behavior?"

"It's hard to define what normal behavior is, but this isn't uncommon behavior."

"In your interviews, did you note that Haley was motivated by money?"

"No. In our meetings, Mrs. Finch showed no signs of that."

For the next twenty-five minutes, I asked questions of Dr. Richardson, establishing that while they weren't the norm, large age-gap relationships were not uncommon. Juror five nodded his head a lot during the testimony. He seemed convinced by Dr. Richardson and convinced that the age gap had in no way contributed to Haley's motive.

"Thank you, Dr. Richardson." I sat back down. "No further questions."

Sinclair was quick to start her cross-examination. She was already standing when Judge Dalton asked her to begin. "Dr. Richardson, were you contacted by the defense lawyers to interview Mrs. Finch?"

"That's correct, but my opinion isn't influenced by who contacts me. I was asked by the defense lawyers to provide an unbiased assessment, and that's what I did."

"But you were paid for your time, and you're paid to be here?"

"Objection. That's prejudicial." Bruce stood. "It's normal behavior for an expert witness to be paid by both the prosecution and the defense. It's normal and accepted for them to be compensated for their time and specialized knowledge. The suggestion that the witness's response is anything other than truthful is prejudicial to this case."

"Sustained." Judge Dalton turned to the jury and explained that it was normal for an expert witness to be paid by both sides of the law.

Sinclair shook her head as Judge Dalton provided his explanation, and when he asked her to continue, she scoffed. "No further questions."

CHAPTER 46

Bruce called forensic analyst Mr. Dylan Jones next.

Jones was a forensic expert willing to testify for the right price, and that price was usually high. He presented well—fitted suit, short-cropped black hair, neat and tidy appearance; and he spoke even better—a deep voice echoing with authority on his subject of expertise.

"Mr. Jones, can you please tell the court who you are and why your analysis is important to this case?"

"My name is Dylan Edward Jones, and I work for a specialized forensic company in North Carolina, Deakin Forensics. My specialty is blood-spatter analysis. In general, my role involves studying blood flow, blood-spatter patterns, and bloodstains, to try and understand where the blood came from, what caused the blood to be present, and whose blood it is."

"Did you study the report on what was found on the fishing dock behind Mr. Sammy Turner's home?"

"I did."

"And can you please describe how much blood was on the underside of the dock?"

"Of Mr. Turner's blood, there was a lot. It was clear that he must've lost a lot of blood while standing at the end of the fishing dock."

"And how much was from Mrs. Finch?"

"Just a tiny, tiny amount at the other end of the fishing dock."

"If there was a fight between them, would you have expected more?"

"Given that Mr. Turner was taller, heavier, and generally larger than Mrs. Finch, yes. If there was an altercation, I would've expected more blood from Mrs. Finch."

Bruce nodded. "How long had Mrs. Finch's blood been at the end of the fishing dock?"

"With the exposure to the weather, it's impossible to tell."

"Impossible to tell," Bruce repeated. "Mrs. Finch has been going to that fishing dock for just under a year. Could the bloodstain have been from a year earlier?"

"Of course. Yes, that's entirely possible. It's possible that the bloodstain from Mrs. Finch could've appeared on the dock at any time over the past twelve months. Like I mentioned, it's impossible to tell."

"Is it correct that there's nothing that indicates her blood was spilled on the same day, week, or even month, as Mr. Turner's blood?"

"That's correct."

Bruce found fifteen different ways to ask the same question, and when he was sure it was clear to the jury that the presence of Haley's blood didn't indicate she had killed Sammy, he ended the questioning. It wasn't game-changing evidence, but every little bit helped.

When Sinclair declined to cross-examine, Judge Dalton called an end to the day.

The courtroom emptied behind us with a tense murmur. I could hear some of the conversations, and they weren't favorable to Haley. Haley stayed at the defense table as the crowd emptied behind her, leaning forward, one hand across her stomach, and the other rubbing her cheek.

Once the courtroom gallery had emptied, Sinclair stood and stepped close to our table.

"I really hope we're going to hear from Mrs. Finch," she said as she stared at the defendant. "It would be great to have her on the stand."

"Trying to intimidate people?" I stood, blocking Haley from Sinclair's view. "That seems low, even for someone from your department."

"I'm just looking forward to it, that's all." Sinclair smiled and stepped back. "The way this case is going, it's going to be your only chance to win it."

Sinclair walked out of the courtroom with a spring in her step. Bruce spoke to Haley for a few moments. She had her head down, staring at the table in front of her, and looked close to tears.

CHAPTER 47

Over the coming days, we called witness after witness, and they all delivered as expected.

The forensic experts spoke about the lack of evidence in the case, and how the absence of evidence was not evidence of its absence. The character witnesses all testified that Haley was a nice, charming, and caring person who didn't have a violent bone in her body. The character witnesses all said that people were often jealous of Haley, and that other people often lied about her behavior. Sinclair objected, but the groundwork had been established.

On the third Thursday afternoon of the trial, Bruce stood. "Your Honor, the defense calls Mr. Oman Hossain."

Oman Hossain was a young man in his late twenties. He was dressed in black trousers and a blue shirt, with the top two buttons undone. He had spent his working life as a drug counselor, trying to help those less fortunate; however, judging by his wearied appearance, he was beginning to understand that the fight against drugs was a long, and perhaps impossible, one.

"Thank you for agreeing to testify," Bruce said. "Can you please state your name and occupation for the court?"

"My name is Oman Hossain and I'm employed by the Beaufort County Drug Rehabilitation Center as a drug counselor. I've been the court-appointed drug counselor for Mr. Ken Turner for the past two years."

"Objection to this witness." Sinclair stood. "The defense is trying to muddy the waters with a third-party culpability; however, there's no evidence to support that approach."

"Your Honor," Bruce retorted. "This witness is speaking about the relationship between Mrs. Finch and Mr. Sammy Turner and how the relationship was affected by external influence."

"Overruled," Judge Dalton agreed. "There's been enough to establish that Mr. Ken Turner is connected to Mr. Sammy Turner, and I will allow this witness to answer questions that relate to their relationship."

"Thank you, Your Honor." Bruce acknowledged the judge, and turned his focus to the witness. "Mr. Hossain, how do you know the defendant, Mrs. Finch?"

"I worked with Ken Turner during his drug rehabilitation process. I was the court-appointed counselor, and I often need to communicate with the families of those affected by addiction. Ken Turner's brother was Sammy Turner, and Sammy was dating Mrs. Finch. I had several meetings with Sammy and Haley. They were the people closest to Ken, and we discussed ways to support Ken's recovery from his fentanyl addiction."

"And did he recover?"

"That's a matter for Mr. Ken Turner to discuss."

Bruce nodded. "How did Mr. Sammy Turner and Mrs. Finch interact when you met with them?"

"They were good." He shrugged. "As good as any couple would've been given the pressure they were under with Ken's addiction. Drug addiction affects more than just the addict. There's usually a whole circle of people around the addict who are deeply affected by the addict's behavior."

"You mentioned that family members are affected by the actions of drug addicts. Did Mr. Ken Turner have a nickname for himself?"

"He called himself the 'demolition man.'" Hossain shook his head and sighed. "And he gave himself that nickname because, as he said, he demolishes everything around him, before he demolishes himself. Ken went through periods of his life when all he wanted to do was destroy things. He had a lot of internal conflict, and at times, he was determined to punish himself. As I told the court during one of his appearances a year ago, Ken showed no interest in getting better. All he wanted to do was score his next hit, and when someone is that determined to destroy themselves, there's not a lot anyone else can do."

"Did Mr. Sammy Turner and Mrs. Finch talk to you about Mr. Ken Turner's addiction?"

"They did. Sammy, mostly. He talked about how he didn't want to see his brother go through that pain, and he wanted to help him. Sammy was the sort of guy who always wanted to help everyone."

"Did that include paying off Mr. Ken Turner's drug debts?"

"Yes." He nodded. "Sammy always paid off his brother's debts, even when Ken was dealing drugs. On occasion, Sammy would tell me that he paid between ten and twenty thousand dollars in drug debts for Ken. Ken would take the money and deal drugs to other people, while keeping some for himself."

"Did Mrs. Finch know about this?"

"She did, and she encouraged Sammy to stop paying those debts. And I have to say, as a drug counselor, I agreed with her. In our last meeting, on June 25th, we discussed the best ways to support Ken to get clean, and one of those ways was to stop paying his debts. It was important that Ken took responsibility for his actions, and not have his brother always bail him out."

"And did Sammy agree to this?"

"He did. In that last meeting that we had, Sammy agreed that he would no longer pay off his brother's debts and he would no longer support him."

"Thank you, Mr. Hossain," Bruce said. "No further questions."

Sinclair took her time to begin the cross-examination. She read through several notes, talked to her assistants for a moment, and then stood. "Mr. Hossain, is it correct that Sammy wanted to continue his financial support of Ken?"

"That would be correct."

"And would it be correct that Mrs. Finch wanted Sammy to stop financially supporting him?"

"That's also correct, but I have to highlight that it was under my direction that she made her position known."

"How long had you been telling Sammy that he should stop supporting his brother's drug habit financially?"

"Over a year, at least."

"And what changed his mind?"

"Mrs. Finch was the one who convinced Sammy to stop supporting his brother."

"Would it be true that Mrs. Finch was able to influence Sammy's financial decisions?"

"I guess you could say that."

"And would it be true that Mrs. Finch had influence over Sammy that other people didn't have?"

"Yes." He shrugged. "You could say that."

"Thank you, Mr. Hossain." She sat back down. "No further questions."

CHAPTER 48

David York was a Southern man through and through. He wore black pants held up by suspenders, with a crisp white shirt, complete with a red bowtie. His glasses were red and circular, and his hair was snow white. He was charming and spoke with a distinct Southern accent that seemed to be lost on the younger generations.

"Mr. York, thank you for testifying in court today." Bruce remained seated behind his desk.

"My pleasure." York smiled. "I don't often get the chance to be a witness in a trial, and I'm happy to sit on this side of the well for once."

Bruce smiled back at his old friend and nodded. "Can you tell the court how you know the deceased and the defendant?"

"I've been working as an estate planning and probate lawyer for the past twenty-five years, and I was contacted by Mr. Sammy Turner to update his will. I had an opening in my schedule due to a cancelation of another appointment, and a day after the call, Mr. Turner came to my office. That was on July 1st."

"Did he attend the meeting by himself?"

"No. He attended the meeting with Mrs. Haley Finch."

"And during that meeting, what did you discuss?"

"We discussed updating his will. After a two-hour discussion, we agreed on the wording. The new will was fairly straightforward, and there were no complications about the documentation. Mr. Turner was happy to sign the new will in that meeting."

"Is it unusual to update a will after only one meeting?"

"Not at all." York adjusted his red-rimmed glasses. "Some people want to think about the updates for weeks or months and consider every word of the documentation. Other people wish to update it on the spot. It's common to have a will signed after one meeting."

"And who signed that updated will?"

"Mr. Sammy Turner, and it was witnessed by myself, another attorney who works in my office, and my assistant."

"Was Mr. Turner under any undue influence when he updated the will?"

"No, sir."

"And you asked him that question?"

"Yes, sir."

"Did you discuss why Mr. Turner wished to have his will updated?"

"We discussed the new terms of the will, and in his notes that accompanied the will, he confirmed his intention. May I read off the notes?" He looked up to Judge Dalton for approval. Judge Dalton nodded his approval, and York reached into his top pocket and removed a folded piece of paper. He unfolded it and read off the notes. "Mr. Turner only left brief notes with the will, but he made his intention clear. He stated, 'It is my intention that my entire estate will be left to Mrs. Haley Finch.'"

"Do you think Mrs. Finch unfairly encouraged him to change the will?"

"No, sir."

"Thank you, Mr. York," Bruce said. "Can you confirm that you discussed the previous will with Mr. Sammy Turner?"

"I can confirm that."

"And did he confirm his intention to not list his brother Mr. Ken Turner on the new will?"

"I can't discuss what Mr. Sammy Turner told me, because it's not listed in the notes, and attorney-client privilege exists even after the client is deceased, but I can tell you that Mr. Ken Turner was not listed on the new will."

Bruce tapped his hand on the file. "And did Mr. Ken Turner contact you after Sammy's death?"

"That's correct."

"And what did Mr. Ken Turner say when he contacted you?"

"He visited the office and was quite aggressive toward myself and my staff. To try and settle his anger, I invited him into my office and asked him to sit down. I advised him if he was at all aggressive toward me, I would call the police. He settled down after that. And once he had settled down, he told me that he had been to see Mr. Overton about his brother's will but had been informed it had been updated by my law firm."

"What was Mr. Ken Turner seeking?"

"Mr. Ken Turner was seeking half of his brother's estate."

"And could he access it?"

"No. Mr. Sammy Turner left no money to his brother in his updated will."

"Thank you, Mr. York. It's always a pleasure." Bruce sat back down. "No further questions."

It was a win for us, and Sinclair was about to try her best to disrupt it. She spoke to her assistants for a few moments and then walked to the lectern. She made eye contact with several jurors and then turned to the witness.

"Mr. York, thank you for testifying," Sinclair began. "When drafting the will, do you think Mr. Sammy Turner was under any undue pressure?"

"Objection to the word 'think,'" I called out. "It asks the witness to speculate."

"Sustained." Judge Dalton's tone was firm.

"Mr. York, what do you feel Mr. Sammy Turner's—"

"Objection to the word 'feel.' Again, it calls for speculation."

"Again, the objection is sustained," Judge Dalton agreed. "Mrs. Sinclair, the witness is allowed to talk about what they know but not to make assumptions. Please choose your questions more carefully."

Sinclair drew a long breath and stared at the page in front of her for a few moments, trying to compose herself and figure out a way to ask her question within the rules of the court. "Mr. York, how can you be so sure of what Mr. Sammy Turner's intentions were when he talked to you?"

"Because he told me what his feelings were. Those intentions were listed in the notes."

"Mr. York," Sinclair continued, "did Mr. Turner say anything that might indicate he was under undue influence?"

"No."

She paused, looked at the jury, and then back at the witness. "Have you had any wills disputed in the past?"

"Of course. That's part of the nature of writing wills. It's estimated between 2 and 5 percent of wills are contested in this country. Even the most watertight will can be contested in court if there are family members who don't agree on its interpretation. Some wills are also disputed because the law restricts what a will can do. Take the elective share laws. Under South Carolina laws, even if someone tries to disinherit their spouse, the surviving spouse may still receive up to one-third of the estate, provided they apply to the court within a certain timeframe after the decedent's death."

"Thank you, Mr. York. Were any of the wills that you wrote overturned due to 'undue influence by an external party'?"

He sighed. "Yes."

"How many?"

"I'm not sure."

"I am," Sinclair said. "From what we could see, there have been five wills written by you that were later disputed in court and changed by a judge, due to 'undue influence by a third party.' So, is it true that if there was undue influence by a third party, you wouldn't have recognized those indicators?"

"I've been writing wills for over twenty-five years, and I have written more than five thousand wills. So, you're talking about one in one thousand wills written that have that outcome. That equates to 0.1 percent. And I must say that I directly ask every person who writes a will whether there was undue influence on their decision-making process, and if they indicate there is, I investigate further."

"Undue influence." Sinclair looked at the jury and shook her head. "No further questions."

"Redirect?" Judge Dalton looked at Bruce.

Bruce stood. "In your meeting with Mr. Sammy Turner, did you consider if there was undue influence on his decision-making?"

"I did. Common law principles mean that we consider five things about undue influence. They are: the testator's vulnerability, the influencer's opportunity, the influencer's active participation in procuring the will, the unnatural state of the will's intentions, and the extent of influence or coercion used."

"And what was your decision once you considered those factors?"

"After considering those five factors, I determined there was no undue influence on Mr. Turner."

"And did you ask Mr. Turner directly if there was undue influence on his decision to update the will?"

"I did."

"And what was his answer?"

"He said there was no undue influence on his decision-making."

"Was there anyone else in the room when you asked that question?"

"No. There wasn't." He glared at Sinclair. "Mrs. Finch was not in the room when I asked Mr. Turner that question. It's my policy to do so without anyone else present, if at all possible."

"Thank you, Mr. York. No further questions."

Bruce looked at me and I nodded. It was time.

CHAPTER 49

Haley joined Bruce and me in the smallest meeting room in the courthouse.

It was tight, barely big enough for the three of us and should've been used as a cupboard. All the other rooms were booked, the attendant told us. We didn't believe him. The room smelled of curry, and there were food stains on the white table. The room was most likely used as a secondary lunchroom for the staff. Haley couldn't sit still. She was too nervous. Bruce leaned on the uneven table, and his weight caused it to sway.

Haley was silent, leaning forward and holding her stomach. She was nauseous and asked for a wastepaper basket to be placed next to her. The stress on her face was showing.

"We have to call him," Bruce said. "It's a risk, but we have to call him."

"He's here," I said. "And he's been on the State's list as a witness in the missing persons investigation, so we're justified in calling him."

"But we don't know what he's going to say, do we? Lawyers never ask a question they don't know the answer to, right?" Haley asked as she chewed on her fingernails. "He could get up there and lie about anything. He has no moral compass."

"I agree it's a risk," Bruce said. "But he's the last roll of the dice. I don't like it, but given where the case is right now, we need to do it. The jury needs to see Ken as an unstable, money-hungry liar. If they see that, there'll be reasonable doubt about your guilt. As soon as Ken opens his mouth, the entire jury is going to say, 'Ah, right, they got the wrong person.'" Bruce looked at me. "Even though we haven't questioned him in a deposition, Dean is a very skilled court attorney, and he'll know exactly what to ask."

"What if he's not involved?" Haley leaned forward and rested her elbows on the table.

"We can't think like that right now. We need to focus on clearing your name, and that means creating reasonable doubt in that courtroom. Ken is the right person to create that doubt. Whether or not he's involved is a matter for law enforcement. Our job isn't to find the truth, it isn't to expose someone else, our job is to give you the best defense possible."

"I could testify?"

"No." Bruce shook his head. "Sinclair will tear you apart on the stand, and you'll look like a liar. She's very skilled at tricking people. I've seen her do it before. And if you look like a liar, then the jury will be convinced that you were involved in Sammy's death."

Haley nodded.

Fifteen minutes later, we were back in the courtroom. I looked behind me. Ken Turner was sitting in the back row, with no idea what was about to happen. I had talked to the bailiff, and he stood at the exit, waiting for any movement. "The defense calls Mr. Ken Turner."

"Objection, Your Honor." Sinclair leaped to her feet. "There was no indication in the opening statement that the defense was going to call this witness."

"We did, Your Honor." I looked down at my notes. "We stated, 'In this fact-finding mission, the jury will hear from witnesses who were near the home at the time,' and it's been established that

Mr. Ken Turner was the last person at Mr. Sammy Turner's home before his disappearance."

"Your Honor," Sinclair argued, "there has not been any clear attempt to establish third-party evidence in this case, and the defense wants to end the case by introducing a new theory. That's confusing for the jury and cannot be allowed."

"Your Honor, this witness is on the original State's witness list. He provided a statement to law enforcement about the disappearance of his brother, and we have every right to question him about that statement."

"And this witness is here?"

"He is, Your Honor." I turned around. Ken was standing at the back row with two bailiffs hovering next to him. It was obvious he had already tried to leave but had been prevented from doing so. "He's standing in the back row, ready to go."

Judge Dalton looked to Ken. Ken was shaking his head. "I'm interested in what the witness has to say," Judge Dalton stated. "The objection is overruled. You may call the witness."

I turned around and watched as the bailiffs explained to Ken Turner that he had to go to the stand and present a testimony. He argued with them for a moment and then walked toward the stand reluctantly. He mumbled his oath, and then sat in the witness box looking every bit like the drug addict he was.

I waited until he was settled in the chair before I began. "Can you please state your name?"

"Ken."

"Your full name?"

"Ken Turner."

"And how are you related to the case?"

"Sammy is my brother."

"Can you please tell the court the last time you went to Mr. Sammy Turner's home on Dataw Island?"

"No."

"No?"

"That's what I said. I don't have to answer your questions."

"You do, Mr. Turner." Judge Dalton leaned closer. "If you refuse to answer any questions then you will be held in contempt of court."

"What does that mean?" He looked up at the judge.

"That you'll be spending the night in custody."

"I don't want to do that."

Judge Dalton waved for me to continue, but I didn't look at Ken. I looked down at my notes, and then back up to Judge Dalton. "Permission to treat the witness as hostile, Your Honor."

"Given the answers so far," Judge Dalton grunted, "the request is granted."

"Thank you, Your Honor." I turned back to the witness. "Mr. Turner, when was the last time you went to your brother's home on Dataw Island?"

"July 5th."

"Time?"

Like a petulant child, he refused to answer. "Don't know."

"Mr. Turner, there's a record of your vehicle entering the security gate at Dataw Island at 5 p.m., fifteen minutes after Mrs. Finch left the estate, and then your vehicle left at 5.15 p.m. Is that correct?"

He shrugged. "I guess so."

"You don't have to guess. We have the security log here." I picked a file off the table and handed it to the bailiff. The bailiff took the file to the witness. "Mr. Turner, is that your license plate number highlighted in yellow?"

"Yeah."

"And what time were you recorded as leaving?"

"5:15 p.m."

"And the other vehicle highlighted in that list?"

"I don't know that car."

"It's Mrs. Finch's vehicle. What time does it say she left the security checkpoint?"

"4:45 p.m."

I nodded. "Mr. Turner, what did you do on Dataw Island between 5 p.m. and 5:15 p.m. on July 5th?"

"I was looking for Sammy."

"And what did you do when you found him?"

"I didn't find him."

"I put it to you that you did find him. When—"

"I didn't!"

He was already falling apart on the stand. He was the perfect final witness. "Mr. Turner, have you ever been to prison for violent offenses?"

"Objection. Relevance," Sinclair argued. "The witness is not on trial here."

"Overruled. You many answer the question."

"Yeah. So, what if I have?"

"Have you ever been violent toward your brother, Sammy?"

He looked away. "Maybe."

"Did you ever hit him?"

"Yeah."

"Did you ever kick him?"

"Yeah."

"Did you ever stab him?"

"No! I didn't do it."

I paused for a moment, shaking my head. "Did you know your brother had updated his will?"

"Nah."

"So, on July 5th, when you went to his house, you believed that you would receive half of Sammy's wealth if he passed away?"

"Yeah, and that's what I should've received. That money was mine, not hers. That's my money. I was the one who stuck by

259

Sammy when times were hard. She didn't. She only dated him for the money, and now look at her. She's got all my money."

"Mr. Turner." I paused and shook my head. "Can you please explain to the court why you had a copy of your brother's first will, the one you thought was valid, printed out on your dining room table only days after you were told he was missing?"

"Because I knew he was dead," he snarled. "I knew that little witch killed him."

"Mr. Turner!" Judge Dalton slammed his gavel down. "There will be no accusations on the witness stand. If you continue to behave like that you will be held in contempt, and you will be held in custody for the night."

Ken didn't respond as he slouched in the stand.

I didn't press any further with that line of questioning. I had established that Ken Turner was aggressive. I had established that Ken Turner was unstable. And I had established that he was the last one at his brother's home.

If I pushed any further, then I was pushing into dangerous territory, and any further missteps might cost us the whole case. I decided it was enough for the jury to doubt Haley's guilt.

"No further questions."

Judge Dalton asked Sinclair if she would like to cross-examine. She conferred with her team for a minute, discussing back and forth, and then stood. "We have no questions for this witness, Your Honor."

We had created reasonable doubt, we had done our jobs, and it left Ken looking guilty in the middle of it.

Ken left the stand, sniffing and mumbling as he went. Once he had left the courtroom, Judge Dalton asked Bruce to continue.

Bruce stood, looked at Haley, and then back to the judge. "Your Honor, the defense rests."

CHAPTER 50

"The jury has to see that I'm not guilty." Haley's voice was strained. She held her head in her hands. "There isn't enough evidence. The police made up a story, and they didn't even look at Ken. They need to see that."

Cool air pumped through the conference room vents, a constant hum above our heads. We'd been upgraded, but the room was still small. The tiny round table was at least ten years old and wobbled whenever it was touched. The windowless room felt cramped, almost like the walls were about to fall inward.

"It's close," I agreed. "We've closed our case, presented our witnesses, and now we go back in there and present closing statements. The jury looks to be fifty-fifty on this case."

"But juries can be unpredictable," Bruce noted. "You need to be prepared for whatever happens. If they don't find in our favor, we have grounds for appeal based on the prejudicial statement by Maria. We can argue the judge erred by not declaring a mistrial."

"What happens to Ken if they find me not guilty?"

"Law enforcement will review the case and look at the evidence presented during this trial."

"So they won't arrest him straight away?"

"No," Bruce explained. "And let's not get ahead of ourselves. This isn't over yet."

"But how could they find me guilty?" Haley was blinking back tears. "There isn't enough evidence." She stood and began to pace the room, rubbing her forehead. "I can't go to prison for something I didn't do."

"Our closing statement will be focused on two factors," I explained. "One: there isn't enough evidence to convict you, and two: the investigation didn't even look at Ken." My cell phone pinged with a notification. I looked at it and then nodded to Bruce. "It's time to finish this."

We walked out of the courthouse meeting room and back into the courtroom. The gallery seats were already filled. Nobody wanted to miss the closing statements.

Judge Dalton returned to the courtroom and spoke to the jury. He then called for Sinclair.

———

"Ladies and gentlemen of the jury, you have a case where the facts are clear.

"Mr. Sammy Turner is dead. He was stabbed in the back of the neck with a knife from Mrs. Haley Finch's kitchen.

"That's fact.

"There were bloodstains found on the dock, and those bloodstains belonged to Mr. Turner and Mrs. Finch. She was the last person to see him alive. The top of the dock had been cleaned with bleach in an attempt to wash away the blood.

"That's fact.

"Mrs. Finch was seen slapping Mr. Turner numerous times before his death. You've heard from witnesses who have testified they saw her violently abuse him.

"That's fact.

"Mrs. Finch had motive. She encouraged, almost forced him, to update his will only *days* before his death. She wanted all his money to herself.

"That's fact.

"You've heard from expert witnesses, including eyewitnesses, crime scene experts, and forensic experts. You've heard from Beaufort County Sheriff's Office deputies who attended the scene of the crime. You heard from law enforcement officials who investigated the case.

"They have all said the same thing—Mr. Sammy Turner was stabbed with the boning knife that was taken from Mrs. Haley Finch's house.

"All the facts are clear.

"The defense wants you to believe in some made-up theory that someone else did this. They've put forward the best possible defense for their client, and they've tried hard, but trying hard is not a reason to ignore the facts. Don't be tricked by their story. Don't be tricked by their theories. Don't be tricked by their games.

"Look at the facts. Study them. Understand them. Because if you look at the facts, and only the facts, you'll see there's enough evidence to convict Mrs. Finch of murder.

"A murderer needs to be held criminally responsible for their actions.

"Do not let a murderer walk away without punishment. We must ensure that justice is served and those responsible for such heinous crimes are held accountable.

"The evidence presented clearly establishes Mrs. Finch's guilt beyond a reasonable doubt.

"It is your duty to base your decision on the facts and deliver a just outcome.

"The fact is that Mrs. Haley Finch stabbed Mr. Sammy Turner, and Mr. Turner died as a result of the stabbing.

"The application of the law in this case is simple. There's enough evidence to convict the defendant. There's enough evidence to find her guilty. There's enough evidence to know the truth.

"The decision is yours to make. Thank you for your service to this court."

———

Sinclair walked back to her seat and sat down. Her statement was short, sharp, and to the point.

Several jurors nodded every time Sinclair stated the word "fact." Juror ten, the blonde, religious mother of two with impeccable style, appeared particularly convinced, staring at Haley at one point with a slight snarl on her face. That wasn't good for us.

Juror five, the square-jawed civil engineer, shook his head at the end of the closing statement. That was promising. He appeared unconvinced by her "facts," and he seemed like a man whose opinion wouldn't waiver, even if the entire room was against him.

I made several notes and then stood. I nodded to juror five and then began.

———

"Contrary to what the State wants you to believe, there's not enough evidence to convict Mrs. Haley Finch of murder. To convict anyone of a crime, you need to be convinced beyond a reasonable doubt, but after listening to this case, after listening to all the evidence, the doubt you are feeling is reasonable. That's because there hasn't been enough evidence presented to the court.

"On July 5th, Mr. Sammy Turner was stabbed and killed at the private fishing dock outside his home. We know that. That's a fact.

"We also know that the last person who visited that home was Mr. Ken Turner, not Mrs. Finch.

"You've heard the testimony of Mr. Ken Turner. You've heard the 'facts,' as he saw them. And you've heard him lie and change his story on the stand several times.

"Did the investigators leading the murder case even talk to Mr. Ken Turner? Briefly. In their fifty-page report into Mr. Sammy Turner's death, Ken's name is only mentioned five times. Five times. The investigators in the murder case spoke to him over the phone and didn't even go to his house to interview him.

"That shows you how little investigation went into the crime. The investigators chose their suspect early and missed all the other details. They missed the fact that Mr. Ken Turner had Sammy's original will, the one where he received 50 percent of the wealth, printed out on his dining room table just days after his brother went missing. Despite being a convicted felon, with violent tendencies, despite being the sole personal beneficiary of Sammy's original will, despite being the last person at the scene of the crime, the lead investigators only spoke to Mr. Ken Turner twice on the phone for a total of five minutes. Five minutes! That's all the research they did into this suspect.

"Mrs. Finch is attracted to older men. She has been her whole life, as shown by her dating history. There's no crime in that, and it in no way indicates that she was involved in *this* crime. You've heard from psychologist Gemma Richardson, and her statement that it's very normal for a woman to be attracted to an older male who can provide for her.

"You've heard from estate planning lawyer, Mr. David York, who testified there was no undue pressure on Mr. Sammy Turner to update the will. You've heard from witnesses who have testified that it's normal for a will to be updated after a new relationship.

"You've heard from forensic experts who have stated there is no evidence that indicates Mrs. Finch was involved in this crime. No evidence.

"You've heard from members of the Beaufort County Sheriff's Office who worked on this case. They have testified there was no DNA or fingerprints on the murder weapon. They have explained to you that there was no eyewitness to the murder. The deputies have advised there was no evidence at the scene of the crime that Mrs. Finch was involved.

"There is no evidence, none, that convicts Mrs. Haley Finch of this crime.

"We've shown there isn't enough evidence to convict the defendant of this crime. And we've shown there's another suspect who wasn't investigated by the police.

"Consider the evidence in this case, look at the lack of facts, look at where the holes in the story are, and listen to what the evidence is saying. If you do that, you will find there's reasonable doubt that Mrs. Finch committed this crime.

"And because of the reasonable doubt that you have, you must find the defendant not guilty.

"Thank you for your service to the justice system."

CHAPTER 51

"They haven't got a decision yet?" Kayla said as she approached. "It's been five days."

Kayla and I were in the park off Laurens Street, an acre square of green grass surrounded by mature live oaks. We sat on a wooden bench under the shade of a centuries-old tree, a soda can each. The cans were sweating in the heat, and the grass in front of us looked damp. The Spanish moss hung above us, standing still in the breezeless day.

After closing statements had finished, Judge Dalton spent an hour detailing the instructions on the law that the jurors were to apply to the case. He explained the legal standards and the legal terms, before detailing guidance to the jurors on how they needed to reach their decision. He informed them that they needed to do so based solely on the evidence presented to them in court, and when they understood, he asked them to go into deliberations.

"The storm is coming." Kayla pointed to the horizon. "They think something is brewing in the Atlantic right now."

I nodded. "I'm more worried about the storm that will arrive if they find Haley not guilty."

"Are you referring to Bronson, Jasper, or Ken?"

"All of them," I stated. "They're desperate, slightly unhinged, and dangerous."

"And you think it's in our favor?" Kayla sipped her soda.

"If they've taken five days, it means that someone in that jury room has doubt. We've convinced at least one person that she shouldn't be convicted. The jurors have come back and asked the judge a lot of questions, but they've given no hints to the decision," I said. "Now, all we can do is wait."

"What do you think Ken will do if the decision is not guilty?"

"He'll be angry, and he's likely to lash out when he's angry."

Waiting for the jury decision was the worst—everything seemed to be suspended. Everything was put on hold, waiting for the call.

My cell buzzed in my pocket. I took it out and answered it. "Dean Lincoln."

I listened for a moment and then ended the call.

"The jury has a decision," I said. "Judge Dalton needs everyone back in court this afternoon."

CHAPTER 52

As I walked back into the court, the nerves were flooding through my system.

I led Haley and Bruce through security, through the courthouse foyer, and up the narrow stairs. As we walked toward the courtroom, the conversations stopped. People stepped out of our way. All eyes were on us. All the focus was on Haley.

The questions were steamrolling through my head as we entered the courtroom. Did we do enough? Should we have put Haley on the stand? Which way was the jury leaning? Had we convinced twelve regular people that there wasn't enough evidence to convict her? Had juror five been the leader in the jury room, or had it been juror ten?

Haley rushed back out of the courtroom to use the bathroom. She looked like she was about to vomit. When she left, Bruce nodded to me. "We couldn't have done anything more, Dean. Whatever the jury decides, we did the best we could."

I swallowed hard.

Charlotte Sinclair arrived, followed by members of her team. Two assistant lawyers sat next to her. Two members of her administration team sat behind her. And to the left, with a smug grin on his face, sat Stephen Freeman.

Haley walked back inside, wiping her mouth with a napkin, and the gallery filled behind her.

Ken Turner entered the room and sat in the chair closest to the door. The Finch family entered a moment later. Bronson looked angry. Maria looked angry. And Ken Turner looked furious.

If Haley was found not guilty, Ken would need to be cautious. Law enforcement wanted a result in this case, and if it wasn't Haley, they'd be looking elsewhere. Ken knew that. I was sure he was ready to run the second a verdict was handed back.

At 2.05 p.m., the bailiff stood and called the room to order.

Judge Dalton entered, greeted the court, and then instructed the bailiff to bring in the jury.

One by one they walked out of the side door of the courtroom and along the jury box to their seats. One by one, I studied them for any indication. Not one of them looked at me. Not one of them gave me a wink, or a smile, or a nod.

When they had sat down, not one of them at looked at Haley. I turned to look at Sinclair, and she was smiling.

Judge Dalton welcomed the jury back to the court and thanked them for their service. When he was finished, he let the silence sit in the room for a few moments before he leaned forward.

"Has the jury reached their verdict?" Judge Dalton's voice rose as he asked the question.

"We have, Your Honor." The foreman stood at the edge of the jury box, his chest puffed out. The bailiff approached him, took the slip of paper the man held out, and then walked it to the bench. Judge Dalton read the verdict and folded the piece of paper back up.

He looked at the foreman and nodded.

The court was silent as we waited. Not a sound. Not a breath.

"And what say you?" Judge Dalton asked the foreman to reveal the verdict.

"In the charge of murder, we, the jury, find the defendant not guilty."

CHAPTER 53

We celebrated at Haley's home.

After the paperwork was completed, after the ankle bracelet was removed, after the court drama was signed, sealed, and delivered, we offered to take Haley out to dinner. She declined the offer, saying there was too much tension in the town, and so we went back to her house.

Over the first hour after we arrived, we ate, we laughed, and we drank. We congratulated each other on our success. The joy was tremendous. Haley broke down and cried at one point, the release of stress overwhelming her. When Bruce's favorite country song came on the speakers, Bruce sang terribly, and the smile on his face was huge. Haley and I couldn't help but join in.

Haley Finch lifted her glass of white wine and clinked with Bruce and me.

"To a win," she said.

We all clinked glasses and smiled. It was raining outside, the noise heavy through the rooms, creating a sense of comfort indoors. The winds lashed at the shutters and howled through any open space. The weather department said it was going to be big. Not a hurricane but it was close.

Kayla declined to join us.

"It's going to be a big storm," Haley said, staring out to her backyard, watching as the bare sugar maple trees blew in the wind. "They said it might hit us directly."

"That wind is getting strong," Bruce said. "So, what's next, Haley? Are you going to leave Beaufort?"

"And leave this house?" She shook her head. "No thanks. I love this house, and I love my garden. I'm not leaving them behind, even if the whole town hates me."

"You're a free woman," Bruce said. "You can go about your life any way you like."

"I did have one question," Haley said. "Why was the man in the white pickup targeting me?"

"Because he knows Sammy had evidence about Bronson's drug-dealing operation. I would suggest it was one of the videos that Sammy recorded," Bruce said. "Bronson wanted to find the video and destroy it. Sammy wanted Ken to get clean, and he thought getting Bronson arrested was the only way to give Ken a clean break from his addiction."

"I don't even want to know if they were involved in Sammy's murder. I just need a break from all this."

"Are you going to look for the video?" Bruce pressed.

"I don't want to get involved in any of that. I know it sounds bad, but it's none of my business. It's a dangerous world, and I want to keep well away from it."

"And what about Ken?" Bruce asked. "He's a dangerous man, and he's going to be upset by what happened in the trial. He might even come after you."

"I'll be okay," she said. "Now the charges are dropped, and I'm no longer subject to the bail conditions, I can buy a gun. That'll protect me."

"It will," I said. "But I hope you don't have to use it."

CHAPTER 54

Two days after our victory, I was sitting in the conference room of the Beaufort County Courthouse.

The meeting room was cold. I wasn't complaining. I rested my forearms on the wooden table and looked at Angus Blessington, waiting for him to start the meeting. Blessington was focused on his cell phone, scrolling through his notes before he began.

"The tropical storm is due to hit later today," he said, but he didn't take his eyes off his cell phone. "I've heard that a storm will hit just south of here after midnight. It hasn't formed into a hurricane, but the winds are bad. There'll be some large gusts overnight."

Not wishing to engage in conversation with Blessington, I focused on the work at hand. "Why did you call the meeting?"

"You're going to enjoy this." Blessington looked up from his cell, opened his laptop, and typed a few lines. "There was someone posting on social media about rich people who don't pay their bills in South Carolina, and the post mentioned a few names. Stephen Freeman's name was one of them. Stephen didn't like that."

"Reputation means a lot to him."

"It does. My question is, why did it come out now?" Blessington looked back at his cell as it buzzed. "This person claims that Freeman didn't pay a bill that was ten years old, and it seems a coincidence that they're talking about it now."

"Not my work." I raised my hands in surrender. "I had nothing to do with it."

"Well, you're lucky, because Stephen Freeman has requested that we no longer pursue criminal charges if Luke Sanford pays for the damage."

"There's no chance Luke will accept that change."

Blessington looked up from his laptop at me. He had a confused look on his face, almost like he expected it was a done deal. "Are you sure?"

"Yes."

He sighed, stood, and picked up his cell phone. "I need a minute."

He left the room and shut the door behind him, but I could still hear him loudly talking outside. There was some explaining, and then a lot of, "Yes, sir," "Yes, sir."

Blessington returned a minute later.

"Okay," he huffed and sat down. "As per instruction from my higher-ups, we're not going to pursue the criminal charges. They've been dropped against your client."

"And Mr. Sanford's money?"

"What money?"

"The money he's owed for the work on the driveway."

Blessington looked at me. "You can't be serious."

"You have a volunteer at the Circuit Solicitor's Office who is refusing to pay a legitimate debt. Talk about a bad look for your department. So I'll let my client know that he can still chase Mr. Freeman for the money." I smiled. "And, of course, the unpaid driveway costs would also be circulated widely on social media."

"You don't want to play that game. Stephen Freeman is a ruthless man. Your client doesn't want to test him."

"I'll do what's best for my client." I stood. "And you should advise your 'higher-ups' that Mr. Sanford has more information about unpaid bills to release."

The look of shock on Blessington's face was worth it. With a smile on my face, I stepped out of the meeting room and into the foyer of the courthouse.

Even in the foyer, I could hear the storm outside. The rain was heavy, and the winds were howling.

My cell phone rang.

I took it out of my pocket and looked at the number.

It was Haley. Ken Turner was trying to get into her house. She was in trouble.

CHAPTER 55

The storm was raging as I raced through the streets of Beaufort.

The roads were flooding. The winds were blowing hard. The rain was pelting down in waves. Darkness had descended upon the city.

The streets had emptied. People wanted to stay home. They wanted to be out of the storm. My car skidded across one intersection, aquaplaning across a flooded section of road. I fought with the car for control. I slammed my foot on the gas. The tires skidded and I regained control.

I raced into the driveway of Haley's home.

Ken Turner was on the front porch, banging on the door. He had a pistol in his hand. I reached across to the glove box and grabbed my Glock 19.

"Ken!" I yelled as I stepped out of the car into the rain. "Ken!"

"She took my money!" Ken yelled at me from the edge of the porch. "She's got all my money! That's my money! Not hers!"

"Ken, this isn't the way to settle it." I kept my head low as the rain and wind belted into me. I looked for cover. I was exposed, both to the storm and to Ken's anger. The tree next to the house a few feet away was the closest shelter.

"It's my money! Those millions belong to me!" Ken waved his gun in the air. He was becoming more aggressive. His jerky movements looked like he was on some type of drug. "It's not hers! She needs to give me my money."

"Let's talk about it, Ken," I yelled as another gust of rain and wind blew across. "Let's not do anything stupid."

"Stupid? I'm not stupid!" he screamed. "I'm not stupid." He turned his head to the side and fired the gun into the air. "Don't call me stupid!"

I dove to my right, sheltering behind the tree. "Put down the gun, Ken!"

He fired into the air again and sprinted to the side of the house.

I took aim, but the weather was too wild. The gust of wind blew my aim off balance.

"She killed my brother for the money!" Ken yelled as he ran. "I want my money!"

"Ken!" I called back as I crouched behind the tree. "Put the gun down!"

Another shot fired. A window broke.

He was getting into the house.

Under the cover of the storm, I charged toward the side of the house.

When I turned the corner, Ken was starting to climb through the broken window. I tackled him, slamming my left shoulder into his hip, tearing him away from the shards of glass. We tumbled.

His gun fell free. There was blood pouring from his arm.

"Stop, Ken. It's over." I rolled to my left. "The police are coming."

"I'm not going back to prison!" he yelled as he sprinted away. "They won't catch me!"

Ken didn't stop. Covered in blood, he ran toward his car. I wasn't going to let him go.

I heard sirens in the distance. Ken jumped into his pickup. He didn't close the door as he started to tear down the road, in the opposite direction to the sirens.

I charged back toward my car.

He wasn't going to escape justice. I wasn't going to let him run away. Leaping behind the wheel, I sped out of the driveway in pursuit.

I roared my car, flying down the road, racing through the rain.

Ken's pickup was fifty yards ahead. He ran a red light. I followed.

His car weaved around the tight corners. Running on adrenalin, I didn't slow, determined to catch him.

Ken turned his pickup around another corner. I gripped my handbrake, sliding my SUV across the wet road. I spun the steering wheel, almost losing control, and slammed on the gas. My tires spun, then gripped, and I raced forward.

I floored the SUV, thundering around the next bend. I got close and clipped the back corner of Ken's truck. His vehicle slid on the wet road.

Out of control, he hit a speed bump. His truck careered across the road.

He had lost it.

His front edge clipped a sign, and his truck crashed into a fence. The vehicle stopped.

I slammed on the brakes. Grabbed my gun. I jumped out of my car and sprinted toward the mangled wreck. The rain continued to pelt down.

With my gun pointed down, I watched Ken crawl out of the wreck.

He looked up at me and then rested his head on the ground in defeat.

CHAPTER 56

The police lights swirled in the rain.

When I arrived back at Haley's house, I was soaking wet, run down, and tired. Bruce was already there when I walked inside. Two police officers were asking Haley questions.

Haley gave me a hug and towel. She thanked me for protecting her from Ken, and then turned back to the police officers. They talked for another few minutes, before the officers asked me several questions. I advised them that the officers at the scene of the car crash already had my statement. They understood, and then checked on Haley again. When she confirmed she was okay, the officers left the house, and Haley locked the door behind them.

"You're safe now," I said, watching as the police cruiser pulled out of the driveway. "Ken will be locked up tonight, and maybe even longer."

"What a mess." Haley sat down, shaking her head. "There was so much evidence against Ken. At least the police have him now."

"We're not sure Ken did kill Sammy," I said.

"What do you mean? That's what all the court evidence said, didn't it?"

"There's a man named Jasper Rawlings who could've been involved," Bruce explained. "He was the man parked outside your house several times, and we think he may have killed Sammy because Sammy was going to expose him for dealing drugs. And the not guilty verdict means law enforcement will need to investigate the murder again. They'll investigate Rawlings. And if he's pushed against a wall, there's no telling what he'll do. He may even kill again."

"Kill again?" Haley squinted. "You really think he killed Sammy?"

Bruce sighed and nodded. "It looks that way. All the evidence points to him."

Haley tilted her head. "Are you serious?"

Bruce nodded again. "I'm afraid so."

Haley couldn't hide her grin. I held her gaze as her smile widened.

"What?" she scoffed when she noticed me staring at her. "You didn't actually think I was innocent, did you?"

The air sucked out of the room. Bruce and I stood still with our mouths hanging open.

"Oh, come on." She smiled. "Of course I did it."

"What?" Bruce whispered. "Why?"

"Why? Why does anyone do anything? The answer is always money. Sammy didn't deserve the money. He was an unambitious, lazy, immature, and weak man. He didn't deserve a cent of that money. I deserved it. I've been through a lot in my life, and I deserved that money. Tough people deserve wealth, not someone like Sammy. It's my money."

"Haley." Bruce's mouth hung open as he processed the statement. "You cannot tell anyone else what you've just told us."

"As if I would." She laughed. "And I know that neither of you can tell anyone else. We're still covered by the attorney-client confidentially agreement. Anything I say to you is covered. Now, come on. Let's celebrate my win again."

"Our association with you is finished," I stated. My voice was firm. "As of this moment, we're done representing you."

"Oh, come on. Don't be so silly." She smiled. When I didn't smile back, she turned to look at Bruce. "Babe, you're not that sensitive, are you? You're still on my team. I need a handsome man like you by my side."

She stepped toward Bruce, but Bruce took a step back.

"Dean's right. We're done, Haley." Bruce's tone was also firm. "I'm not representing you any more."

"Bruce . . ." She fluttered her eyelids. "Come on. You and me. We make such a great team."

Bruce shook his head, then turned out the door.

I held my stare on Haley for a few long moments and then followed Bruce.

CHAPTER 57

Bruce and I sat in the office boardroom the next morning.

We didn't say a word to each other. I had my head back, staring at the ceiling, and Bruce was staring at the white wall.

After many minutes of silence, Bruce leaned forward. "The Sheriff's Office did an amazing job. Those deputies, who we tried discredit on the stand, saw what we couldn't see. They deserve a medal. They might not have had the evidence, but they got the arrest right. Sometimes, you've got to trust your gut instinct."

"It was obvious, Bruce." I rested my head on the back of my chair and continued staring at the ceiling. "How didn't we see it?"

"The same way the jury didn't see it," Bruce said. "We bought into her pretty façade and didn't see the narcissistic killer behind the eyes."

"Ah," I exhaled. "It's a part of the job. It was never our job to find her innocent. We defended her constitutional right to a fair trial, and we showed that the State didn't have enough evidence to convict her. That's our job."

"It is," Bruce confirmed. "But we usually know the truth, no matter what the defendant tells us. We know when someone's lying to us, and we know when someone's not telling us the whole truth. Haley convinced us she was innocent. That's why it feels so bad."

Defending criminals was a part of the job of a defense lawyer, it was a part of the world we interacted with, but when I didn't see the truth, when I had the wool pulled over my eyes, I felt betrayed.

"And Prescott?" I asked. "What do you think happened to him?"

Bruce winced at the thought. "We never represented Haley in Prescott's disappearance, and she never sent anything to this office about his disappearance. Attorney-client privilege doesn't apply to whatever happened to him. Attorney-client privilege applies to communications between the attorney and the client, and she's no longer our client. Anything we find out now is outside the scope of that privilege. If we can find something out about Prescott, we might be able to help his daughter get answers."

"That's walking a fine line with legal ethics, Bruce," I said. "But I get it. We have a moral obligation to the constitution, to ethical standards, and to honesty and integrity. I still remember the oath I swore. I memorized it so many times."

"'*I will respect and preserve inviolate the confidences of my client.*'" Bruce stated part of the oath to the South Carolina Bar.

"True," I said. "But we also swore to '*maintain the dignity of the legal system*' and to, '*assist the defenseless or oppressed by ensuring that justice is available to all citizens.*'" I drew a breath. "I couldn't see it at the time, but Sammy Turner was the defenseless."

"And Prescott Finch. We know he's lying in a ditch somewhere. You and I both know that now." Bruce shook his head for a few moments. "And there's nothing we can do about it."

"We don't know that he's dead."

"Are you kidding?" Bruce scoffed. "Of course we know it. She killed him for the money, and when she realized she wasn't going to receive his estate, she went looking for another wealthy man to live off."

I hated to admit it, but Bruce was right. "We need to move on. Defending guilty clients is part of the job."

Kayla came into the room with two coffees. "Good morning, gentlemen. What an interesting night. I'm glad that storm didn't do much damage. A few trees down, lots of flooding, but nobody was hurt. Except for Ken, of course, but by all reports, he'll be fine. Was there much damage near your homes?"

Neither of us responded.

"Oh," said Kayla, studying us. "I know that expression." She looked at Bruce. "What happened?"

Bruce didn't answer.

Kayla turned to me and raised her eyebrows. I didn't answer either.

"Haley admitted she killed Sammy Turner, didn't she?"

"We've ended our association with her," I said. "Anything that happens now, she'll be on her own. We won't defend her again."

Kayla sighed. "I told you from the start—you're blinded by beauty."

"Kayla," Bruce said, "we're defense lawyers. This is what we do. You know that most of our clients are guilty, and we do our best to get the best outcome for them. We don't defend the innocent. We defend the integrity of the system."

"But you didn't think she was guilty, did you?"

Bruce didn't answer for a few moments, then turned to his assistant of many years. "I'm sorry, Kayla," he said. "I'm sorry that I didn't listen to you."

"I know." Kayla rested a hand on his shoulder. "But this one hurts."

CHAPTER 58

For the first time in weeks, Emma asked if I wanted to go out for dinner.

I agreed and moved things around in my schedule to make sure I had the time for her. When I arrived home from work, Emma was ready. She didn't wait. She wanted to branch back out into the world and experience life again. We walked down to Bay Street, Beaufort's main shopping street, and into one of our favorite restaurants, Found Taco.

Even on a Tuesday night, the relaxed setting was busy, with almost every table filled. The atmosphere was lively, joyful, and full of fun. The bartender danced while serving drinks, and she encouraged others to join in her little movements as well. The wait staff were busy, but happy, laughing with each other and giving high fives to locals. The smells of foods filled the air, of fresh lime and cooked meats and Mexican spices, only adding to the upbeat atmosphere.

Our dinner arrived and it was perfect—a selection of tacos for us to sample, from beef barbacoa, carnitas, and a buffalo fried chicken with blue cheese. While we ate, Emma asked about my week, and I told her about the new case files I had on the books. I was taking on more cases, talking to more clients, but at some point, if we were moving back to Chicago, I would have to cut back on work. We knew the decision date was approaching, but it was a discussion for another time. Our plan had always been for a year in Beaufort while Jane went through treatment, but even I was starting to doubt that date now. The Lowcountry life was seeping into my soul, and I wasn't sure I could pull myself away from it.

After dinner, we walked the long way home, watching the river ease past. The tidal marsh had an appearance of calmness in the evening light. The grasses swayed in the breeze, exposed as the tide receded. The mudflats, thick and gooey, glistened in the moonlight, and the air was filled with a salt-tinged odor. There was a sense of history to the marsh, of the river crafting the landscape for thousands of years, bringing life to all that surrounded it.

"What's going on here, mister?" Emma leaned in close and patted my stomach. "It's feeling a little fuller."

I grinned and looked at her. "Too much good Southern cooking."

"Or too many beers," she said. "But hey, I just want you to know that you could be as wide as a house, and I'd still love you."

"That's nice to hear that you're with me for my great personality."

"Personality?" she scoffed. "I'm only here for the money."

She laughed and it was great to see her vibrance returning. Her laughter had a way of easing any growing anxiety that was building between us. We hadn't laughed much over the past few weeks, and it was beginning to show. It was so great to see her broad smile again.

"I need to tell you that I haven't given up hope yet." Emma's smile remained but her tone was serious. "I still want a family."

"So do I." I pulled her in close. "We can do it."

She smiled and embraced me tightly. "Yes, we can."

CHAPTER 59

It took the assistant solicitor Angus Blessington a week to process Luke's case.

I spent much of that week giving statements to the police about Ken. The police charged Ken with several felonies, including discharging a firearm into a dwelling, but the officers involved advised that they'd apply to divert Ken away from prison and into a drug rehabilitation program. There was a new program that might help him, they said. I told them I thought that was a good idea.

Luke Sanford walked into my office, holding a bottle of whiskey in one hand, and a box of cigars in the other.

I greeted him with a solid handshake. "Luke, it's good to see you."

"This is from Stephen Freeman's money," Luke laughed. "I don't know how you did it, but you got my charges dropped, and you got Stephen Freeman to pay my bill. After a year of chasing him around, he finally paid for the work on the driveway."

"It wasn't all my work," I said. "It was also your great work. You're the one who found the rumors and encouraged them to be published on social media."

"Yeah." Luke chuckled. "This social media thing is alright. I might quit my job and become an influencer."

I laughed and, over the next hour, we enjoyed a glass of whiskey, savoring its delicate flavor, and after I had opened a window, we lit up the cigars. Luke shared a few jokes, and I told a few stories of law and order from Chicago. Having now experienced it, he was fascinated with the whole justice system.

"Talking about justice"—he sucked on the cigar, held the smoke for a moment, and then blew out an almost perfect circle of smoke—"I did a lot of digging around Stephen Freeman's name and I found some things that may interest you and Rhys."

"How so?"

"I heard a rumor."

"Any truth to the rumor?"

"I have no idea, that's what you'll need to find out."

"Go on."

Luke looked around. "The rumor is that Stephen Freeman was involved in a murder, and some other poor soul is in prison for it. Freeman pulled some strings, got someone else arrested, and then wiped his hands clean of it."

I squinted. "Name?"

Luke wrote the name down on a piece of paper. He told me he had no idea if there was any truth to it, or even if the name was correct, but he wanted to relay what he'd heard. I thanked him but didn't know how far I could take it. I set it aside on my desk.

After finishing our cigars, Luke and I shook hands again. "It was wild out there last week," he said as he began to exit my office. "I'm glad the weather has cleared now. It's impossible to work when the weather's like that. And if I don't work, I don't get paid."

"It was a big storm with so much humidity," I said. "No wonder sugar maple trees don't survive down here."

"Sugar maples?" he scoffed. "In Beaufort?"

"I know someone who planted them in their yard on Bay Street."

"There's no way sugar maples would grow here. They can grow Upstate near the mountains, but the coastal environment is terrible for them. A red maple can possibly grow in the Lowcountry, but there's no chance a sugar maple would. Any gardener with half a brain knows that."

"Some people love them, I guess."

"Sugar maples have extensive root systems, and they destroy the soil underneath them." Luke shook his head. "No matter how much you love them, they're terrible in this part of the country."

CHAPTER 60

The call from the Sheriff's Office hadn't come in over a week.

I was sitting with Bruce, discussing rumors that had been circulating around Beaufort. Haley was the talk of the town. Everyone had an opinion, everyone had a theory, and everyone had their own version of the truth. She was a serial killer, said some. She was framed, said others. Her case was divisive, spilt down the lines of male and female. Most women didn't believe a word out of her mouth, and most men were convinced she had been framed.

"I've got a new possible case," I said to Bruce. "I haven't talked to him yet, but there's a man in prison who says that Stephen Freeman killed someone and he's in prison for it."

"Really?" Bruce scoffed. "And what evidence does this man have?"

"None. That's why he needs us."

Bruce leaned forward. "Dean, I know how much pain the Freeman family has caused you, and I understand that you're still angry about Heather's death, but you can't go chasing ghosts."

"There's no harm in talking to him." I shrugged and looked at my emails. "I got an interesting email this morning about Prescott Finch."

"What did it say?"

"I requested this information before the trial, but it only just came through. The email that 'Prescott' sent to Haley was from an IP address in Brazil, but with a little further digging, the IP address belonged to an internet routing company. I sent them an email five weeks ago, and they just got back to me. They said they received a call from a distressed woman who needed them to fake an email address for them. She told them it was for a divorce case, and for a small price, they were happy to help."

The silence sat over the room while we both shook our heads.

"I also got a call from Detective Terry Wallace this morning," I said. "Based on the information we gave them about Sammy's videos, they issued a search warrant for Sammy's belongings. They searched through the videos, and they must've found something because they opened an investigation into the pharmacies."

"They must've known what they were looking for."

"And once the investigation was opened, they found there were large discrepancies in the fentanyl amounts ordered and sold by the pharmacies, and it was obvious Bronson was dealing it to the black market. Fentanyl is such a terrible drug that they didn't waste any time on that investigation. Bronson was arrested and charged yesterday, and he's looking at a long stretch in prison. There's a warrant out for the arrest of Jasper Rawlings, but he's gone to ground. I'm not worried. The police will catch up to him."

"It looks like Sammy got his wish—Ken's suppliers have been exposed and charged."

My cell phone rang. I looked at Bruce and nodded to the number on my cell. Bruce smiled.

It was Haley. I answered her call and put it on speakerphone.

"Dean, they're here." Haley's voice was panicked. "I need your help."

"Hello, Haley," I responded. "Who are you talking about?"

"The Sheriff's Office and the police department. There are fifteen people in my house right now."

"What are they doing there, Haley?"

"They're looking for something. They think they have something on me."

"What do they have?"

"I don't know, Dean." Her words were quick, and her voice was huffing. "But I need you to defend me. I need you to come here and tell them that their search warrant is invalid. I need you, Dean. I need you and Bruce to come here. I'll pay you whatever you want. I'll double your rates."

"Haley, Bruce and I don't represent you any more. We ended our association with you. You'll need to contact another defense lawyer."

"Dean, I don't think you understand. They're coming after me because of all these rumors around town. They want to convict me for something I didn't do. The police received an anonymous tip-off that something was buried under my sugar maple trees. They're digging up my sugar maple trees right now."

"And where are you?"

"I'm in my bedroom. I locked myself in here when they started digging up my yard. But I don't know what they're looking for. I'm innocent, Dean, and I'm begging you—I need your help."

I paused for a few long moments and looked at Bruce. Bruce smiled, and then nodded.

"I'm sorry, Haley," I responded. "But I wish you the best of luck when they find Prescott's body buried under the sugar maple trees you planted."

ABOUT THE AUTHOR

Peter O'Mahoney is the author of the best-selling Joe Hennessy, Tex Hunter, and Jack Valentine thrillers. O'Mahoney was raised on a healthy dose of Perry Mason stories, and the pace and style of these books inspired him to write, and he hasn't stopped since. O'Mahoney loves to write fast-paced stories filled with exciting characters, thrilling legal cases, and mind-bending plot twists. His thrillers have entertained hundreds of thousands of readers around the world.

O'Mahoney is a criminologist, with a keen interest in law, and is an active member of the American Society of Criminology. When not writing or spending time with his family, O'Mahoney can be found in the surf, on the hiking trials, in the boxing gym, at home reading, or staring at a beautiful sunset in wonder.

Follow the Author on Amazon

If you enjoyed this book, follow Peter O'Mahoney on Amazon to be notified when the author releases a new book!
To do this, please follow these instructions:

Desktop:

1) Search for the author's name on Amazon or in the Amazon App.
2) Click on the author's name to arrive on their Amazon page.
3) Click the "Follow" button.

Mobile and Tablet:

1) Search for the author's name on Amazon or in the Amazon App.
2) Click on one of the author's books.
3) Click on the author's name to arrive on their Amazon page.
4) Click the "Follow" button.

Kindle eReader and Kindle App:

If you enjoyed this book on a Kindle eReader or in the Kindle App, you will find the author "Follow" button after the last page.